30¢

SKYLINE OF NASHVILLE

THE ST. CLOUD HOTEL

McKENDREE CHURCH

Charlotte T.P.

Capitol Hill

HIGH ST.

CEDAR

GAY ST.

LINE ST.

City Spring

Sulphur Spring

Bath House

Lick Branch

Gas Works

FRONT ST.

RIVER

Suspension Bridge

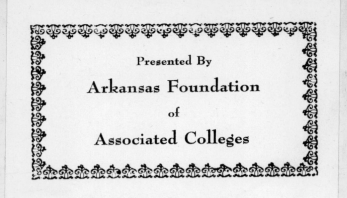

LODGING AT THE SAINT CLOUD

Lodging at the Saint Cloud

A TALE OF OCCUPIED NASHVILLE

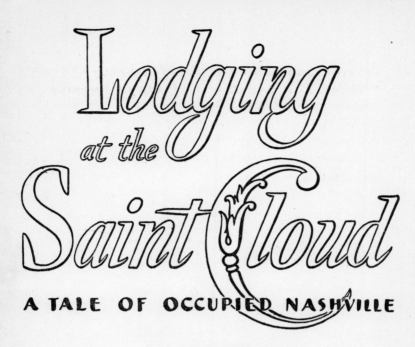

by Alfred Leland Crabb

THE BOBBS-MERRILL COMPANY, INC.

Publishers

INDIANAPOLIS   NEW YORK

To the Ladies

WHO HAVE ALWAYS EASED
THE WRETCHEDNESS OF WAR

TABLE OF CONTENTS

I.

IN WHICH GENERAL FORREST DESIRES INFORMATION

1

THE Ladies Hospital and Clothing Association was meeting in the library at Polk Place. The day was in midsummer, 1862, and Nashville was hot and humid. For a week daily rains had fallen and by all the signs the wet spell was not over. Mrs. Polk had provided a supply of fans but there were not enough to go around, so one lady would wield hers furiously for a minute and then pass it on to her neighbor. It was a technique apparently gratifying to the Ladies, but not unfavorable to the preservation of the heat. The sounds of the afternoon traffic on Vine Street came in through the open windows, but they were casual sounds and the Ladies paid them no heed. The hot winds alternately pushed out the heavy curtains and let them relax in swaying movements. There was an icehouse still a third full at Polk Place, but Mrs. Polk had assigned it to more vital needs than to the alleviation of the discomfort of perfectly healthy Ladies, however worthily engaged. So the Ladies drank water of only the native coolness of the great cistern at Polk Place, and adjusted themselves as best they could to the heat.

Only that morning Mrs. Polk, with the consent of the Union authorities, had sent two large tubs of ice to the Confederate sick and wounded confined in the Maxwell House. Berrien Lindsley had carried it down in his spring wagon, and his report of the pleasure it had given the poor fellows had been very gratifying to Mrs. Polk. She in turn had relayed Berrien's words to the Ladies. There would be no more ice used in the daily routines of Polk Place.

11

There was plenty of need for the help which the Ladies Hospital and Clothing Association could give. The war had lately wrought its fury upon Nashville. Some of the wreckage of those furious days at Fort Henry and Fort Donelson was still in the city. In a small house on McLemore Street three brothers lay, still stricken from wounds in the early fighting at Fort Donelson. Somehow General Forrest had managed to send them home to Nashville. They had become wards of the Ladies. There were others scattered about the city. General Albert Sidney Johnston had left four hundred sick there as he marched southward to his death at Shiloh. Of course most of them had followed the army after a few days of treatment and rest. But many had stayed on, some critically ill, some merely unable to cope with the rigors of active army life. And to some who still remained the Ladies were angels of mercy.

But their main wards were the prisoners being held in Mr. Overton's Maxwell House. What a fall was there! Mr. Overton had planned the building for the grandest of hotels. But not a guest had been received when the Northern troops with measured tread came marching into Nashville. Mr. Overton's pride and joy was promptly metamorphosed into a grim prison for the very ones whom he had envisioned as honored guests. It was a dreary and desolate place, littered with all the dirt and debris of incompletion, and with war's subsequent disorder. The men slept upon the bare, dusty floors and ate the poor food given them. They were not permitted to approach the open windows for a glimpse of the world outside—the immediate world so dear to many of them. Two had found the windows too alluring and rifles had answered their lack of restraint.

The Ladies finished their few items of business and proceeded to the work in hand, namely the making of shirts. Mrs. Francis Fogg had bought a bolt of shirting material at Mr. Thompson's store, and the Ladies were performing, with precision and dispatch, the chore of shaping the goods into shirts for Confederate prisoners.

Mrs. William Cooper held up an unfinished garment. "My goodness!" she exclaimed, smiling. "How big is a Southern soldier anyhow? Surely not this big."

"Don't be worried, my dear," said Mrs. Polk. "Your shirt will be filled."

Sallie Lindsley lifted her face from the shirt which she was sewing and there were tears in her eyes. "I wish I could make a shirt for Randall," she said. Randall McGavock, her brother, captured at Fort Donelson, was also a prisoner, but in far-away Fort Warren in Boston Harbor.

Again Mrs. Polk counseled against worry. "Don't be troubled, Sallie. Randall, if he wished, could charm the shirt off any Boston Yankee's back."

"He won't wish. He'd have no dealings with a Yankee. He'd go without a shirt first."

"I doubt if Randall would bear a shirtless condition with such fortitude, my dear. I can't quite conceive a McGavock going without a shirt or reasonably satisfactory food. He would manage somehow."

"They permitted Berrien Lindsley to go through the building and talk to the prisoners," said Mrs. Hight. "From what he said I'd really rather one of my men would be killed than captured and put in there."

Mrs. Fogg looked up from her work for just a moment and there was tragedy in her eyes. Mrs. Hight saw it and understood. "Oh," she added contritely, "I shouldn't have said that. It wasn't true."

"No," said Mary Fogg. "It wasn't true. If Henry could..." Her grief gripped her for a moment but then she was again under control and her fingers again moved nimbly about the garment she held in her hand.

Said Mrs. Polk, "I think Henry Fogg was the finest and

gentlest boy I ever knew. There was something terrible in his dying so young, but war is made of terrible things. It treats terribly those who deal in it. But I am a Presbyterian and I accept the purpose of terrible things. . . ."

"What purpose, Mrs. Polk?"

"I think that what I should have said was I accept the purposiveness of all things. There are no accidents. I believe devoutly that all things fit together into a unity, but of course only God sees how. It was terrible for Henry to be killed, oh, so terrible, but how much more terrible it would have been for him never to be born. We may say he died too soon, but we know that his life was pure profit."

"Thank you, Sarah," said Mary Fogg quietly, "but Henry was all the child I had."

"Mr. Polk died thirteen years ago this month. He was all I had—except friends. Do you know how much I had planned on life with him again in Nashville? It was one of my dearest dreams. We had so little time together in Washington. There was war then, my dears. It was a long distance away but it seemed to me that he was in the midst of every battle fought. Oh, how I had looked forward to Nashville! And yet he was ill when we got here. He was all I had."

For a while there was no sound except the rustle of fingers against cloth and the gentle flap of the curtains in the hot wind. Water freshly drawn from the cistern was passed to the Ladies. They heard on Vine Street sharply spoken commands and the clatter of passing soldiers.

"The town is full of Yankees," said Adelicia Acklen.

"So many that I do not go on the streets except when I have to," said Sallie Lindsley. "I've heard rumors that most of them will be sent to Kentucky soon."

"Good riddance," said Adelicia.

"I met their General Thomas when he was here recently," said Mrs. Polk. "In fact, he paid me a call. It was very brief and very formal, but I distinctly got the idea the man's a gentleman. I liked him."

"But, Mrs. Polk, he's a Yankee."

"My husband was born in Connecticut," said Mary Fogg.

"Precisely, my dear! And worthy indeed to be your husband and Henry's father. If intellectually he bends to the North is he any less the gentleman? General Lee is a highborn gentleman. If he should capture Chicago or Philadelphia would he be any less one? No, my dears, we might just as well realize that a great many of our enemies are gentlemen. If General Thomas isn't one, my observation is weakening."

"Gentleman or not," said Mrs. Ned Baker, "it will be the happiest day of my life when our troops retake Nashville and General Forrest at the head of his troops comes riding down Church Street. They say . . ."

"Do you expect that to happen?" inquired Mrs. Polk.

"Of course I do. They say we may expect the attack any day now. They say nothing happens in Nashville that General Forrest doesn't know about it before midnight. They say that any number of his men are in Nashville now wearing blue uniforms, and that they find out everything. They say . . ."

"Oh, come, Clara, *they* must stand in line bearing you the choicest morsels of late gossip. Who are *they*, anyhow?"

"Anyhow, General Forrest has spies here. I guess I saw one of them myself today. I've known him since he was a baby. And from what they say I'm not the only one here who knows him. No, he's not from here, but pretty close. A lot of people here know him. I'd been out to see Mrs. Ewing at Mansfield. Well, as I was on my way back on Lafayette Street I saw a Yankee soldier, and when I looked at him closely it wasn't any Yankee at all. It was this boy I've been telling you about. And he's been with General Forrest since Christmas. Now how would you explain that?"

"I'm sure I can't. Did you speak to him?"

"Certainly, but he looked straight ahead. I'd know him anywhere, though. They say the Yankees have some sort of master spy here whose business it is to catch Southern boys. I'd love to poison him. They say he's as common as dirt and as ornery as pig tracks, and that he works in a very prominent place, but I can't find out where. Well, this one's done. I promised to make two, didn't I? They say they hung . . ."

"It's too dreadful to talk about," said Mary Fogg.

"I walked along Church Street today all the way from Cherry to Spruce," said Adelicia, "and I saw a street full of Yankees, but not a one I knew."

"Have they opened the church yet?"

"No, I stopped to see. It's still barricaded. I did see the fiddlin' man and listened to him play for a while. He's really a wizard with the fiddle. I gave him some money and he played several pieces for me."

Mrs. Baker launched on her second shirt. "They say he's a man of mystery."

"Well, it's a mystery the way he can handle a fiddle. He's the best fiddler I ever heard. *They* don't say he's the Yankee master spy, do they?"

"No, but he could be." Mrs. Baker shivered a bit with delight at the prospect. "Though I don't think he's common at all."

"He's extremely uncommon. He's as gaunt as Abe Lincoln is supposed to be and he's even tall sitting down. His face is covered with a heavy black beard, and his eyes almost glitter. I don't believe for a moment that he's ever been anything more than an itinerant fiddler. I don't believe he's any Yankee spy."

"They say the Yankees are mighty fond of him. They give him a vulgar lot of money."

"Well, anyhow, they are fond of his fiddling. A lot of them do come across from the Saint Cloud to hear him. I've heard a great many country fiddlers and he's by far the best."

"They say the Saint Cloud is a regular beehive of Yankees. They've taken over just about everything in town. It's got so we can't go to the theaters any more. They are jammed with them. Chloe Ordway and Elsie Spurlock went to a show at Duffield and Flynns' not long ago and they couldn't stand it. They left at the end of the first act."

"I'd love to know who will wear this shirt," said Caroline Goodlett, holding it up and inspecting it critically. "That'd be a lot more fun than anonymous like this."

"It's not for a man; it's for a cause," affirmed May Alden.

"What kind of cause is there without a man in it?"

"It was my plan to serve you some modest refreshments," said Mrs. Polk. "In fact, I had prepared them, but when I talked with Berrien Lindsley I changed my plan. He's going to take your refreshments to the Maxwell House."

"I don't want any refreshments, not an extra bite till the war is over."

"Well, that one is finished." Mrs. St. Clair Morgan arose, relaxed her cramped body, and folded the shirt neatly and placed it on the stack that was growing on the table. "I'll be glad when one of our men is wearing it."

"When do you suppose the war will be over, Sallie?" asked Mary Cooper, who sat next to Sallie Lindsley.

Sallie smiled wanly. "Not very soon, I'm afraid."

"I think it will be over by Christmas," said Mrs. Baker. "Or maybe before. They say General Forrest is likely to take the city any time."

"There are other cities," answered Sallie Lindsley, "and he might not take this one even if he tried."

"If he does try he'll capture it, and I think it will be soon. I wouldn't be surprised at all if the man I saw on Lafayette Street this morning was sent here to get everything ready for the attack. They say that . . ."

The Ladies never knew what it was "they" said for at that moment Mrs. S. B. Spurlock with a show of pride in her speed announced the completion of her shirt. Then Mrs. Polk answered a knock at the door and admitted Berrien Lindsley. He came into the room mopping his brow.

"Good afternoon, ladies. What a symbol of our invincibility is in this room! I'm in no hurry, ladies. Finish your shirts. Why, how fine they are! Beautiful! Why is it, Sallie, that I can never have one as good?" Mrs. Lindsley looked gently at her husband and smiled faintly but with no interruption of her work. Mrs. Polk inquired of Berrien whether in addition to the shirts he could carry some food to the Maxwell House.

"The Ladies have voted their refreshments to the prisoners," she said whimsically.

"There aren't enough of us Ladies," said Mary Fogg. "Even though Mrs. Polk is generous in the refreshments served us there won't be a taste around for the men at the Maxwell House. I'm going home to see if I can't add something. Can you wait, Berrien?"

"My time has no other uses."

"Dr. Lindsley, you get around among the Yankees a great deal. Are they as bad as people say they are?"

"I don't quite know how bad that is, Mrs. Baker. They're pretty well mixed—good, bad and in-between, precisely as any considerable cross section of mankind. I have met with some who are perfect brutes. . . ."

"Ah," said Mrs. Baker with obvious satisfaction.

"And some who would be creditable to our best traditions. It takes a gentleman of high quality to rise above the brutal spirit of a conquering army. But some have done exactly that. Of course it is a conquering army's prerogative to destroy. They have cut down our trees and demolished our homes that blocked their purposes. They have required for their use some of our best houses. They are rapidly ruining our streets. But that is an inevitable routine of a conquering army. We'd as well accept it. It would make our fate easier to accept it with some grace. Of course we have killed a great many of their comrades and that so enrages the weaker ones of them that they rejoice in destruction and pillage. One should think of war as what it is. It's vandalism, it's robbery, it's murder——"

"Oh, Dr. Lindsley . . ."

"It's a fact, Mrs. Baker, and all our protests won't change it. When decent people go to war they do not necessarily lose their decency, but too often they are forced to hold it in abeyance."

The hot wind drifted into the room with the sound of a deep-drawn sigh and the curtains again swayed languidly. The low rumble of thunder sounded in the southwest.

"In war," continued Berrien after a pause, "there is never time for happiness. It is always marred by something that has been, or is yet to come. Even a victory is shadowed by the prospect of a defeat, an escape by the forecast of recapture. Joy is a prelude to sorrow, and one woe doth tread upon the heels of another." Berrien stopped, smiling. "Excuse me, ladies. I know I oughtn't to talk that way but I've just been reading Shakespeare."

"I love Shakespeare," murmured Mrs. Baker. "When I was in Boston I went to see *Hamlet,* by Shakespeare, you know. It was played by the great actor—what's his name? Why, the same as our great general—Forrest, of course. But he wasn't the main attraction, not in the least. There was a young Southerner from Alabama—I forget his name, but he was magnificent."

"Only this afternoon," said Berrien, holding to his main theme, "the Yankees captured a Southern soldier here in the city. They have, it seems, been visited so often by Confederates that they set a trap and this fellow walked into it. They took him to the jail. I tried to see him but they are holding him incommunicado. I don't know him, but I've heard much about him, and I think a great many here do know him. He is one of General Forrest's most trusted scouts. He is from Franklin. . . ."

There was a sudden movement at the back of the library and an antique chair creaked sharply. The Ladies most tactfully didn't look around, but kept their eyes on Berrien.

"He's the man I saw, the very man," said Mrs. Baker, awe in her eyes. "I spoke to him, but he didn't say a word, just looked straight ahead. I passed right by him. I knew him the minute I saw him."

"The tragic part of it is," said Berrien, "that he was wearing a blue uniform when they caught him. You know what that means. Only Providence can help him now."

"Oh, no," said Mrs. Baker, "we mustn't let anything happen to him. You don't think they'd——"

The Ladies were startled by a low moan from one of their younger members. She sat rigid, clenching a half-finished shirt in her hand, her bosom heaving, her face chalk-white, her eyes staring straight ahead at nothing.

It was Mrs. Polk who spoke in low tones. "Don't let go, child. I think I understand. It will turn out all right. Oh, I am sure it will! Providence is still in charge."

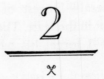

GENERAL NATHAN BEDFORD FORREST had a much greater grievance against the Yankees than that they had merely opposed with military force the withdrawal of the Southern

States from the Union. There was nothing personal in that. But when they captured Hume Crockett and confined him in a filthy prison in Nashville the war was turned into a monstrous insult aimed directly at General Forrest himself. The general's vocabulary could respond adequately to such insults. It did. He damned the Union army in all of its parts and phases. He proclaimed the maximum of vengeance. He vowed that if Hume were not released, and that promptly, he would with his own hand slay at least twenty Yankee major generals.

"And I'd lose at that," he shouted hoarsely. "I'll make it forty. But I'm to blame. A feller that don't know enough not to send his best scout to the place where his best girl is at ain't fit to be a colonel—I mean a general. Here I knew about his girl. He told me about her himself. He described her just like she was an angel with wings. Three days later, like the double-dyed ignoramus I am, I sent him into Nashville to spy out things. After he'd told me about that girl I sent him to Nashville on important business! And they've made a general out of me! I ain't got enough gumption to be a sergeant! I don't know, but I'll bet a couple o' good hosses he saw that girl and then like a mule with the blind staggers and his eyes wide open he just walked right into the Yankees. And I need him back! I need to know what's goin' on in Nashville. I need to know a lot o' things—things Hume could find out for me if he didn't have a girl and could stay in his right mind. I need him back. There are a lot of things I ought to know right now. Well, you got anything to suggest, Sergeant?"

The sergeant acted as if he had expected the question all the time and was prepared for it. Sergeant Mack Goforth usually acted that way. "Yes sir. I'd send Lieutenant Nichol in to get him."

"Oh, you would! And he'd go get him and take him by

the hand and bring him home to me. By himself, I suppose?"

"No sir. I'd send me with him."

"Don't tell me, Sergeant, that you got a girl in Nashville. That might upset me."

The sergeant's hesitation was but momentary. "I just need me some excite-ment."

"Lieutenant Nichol need some excite-ment, too?"

"Yes sir, I expect he does."

"I was afraid of that. It's been worrying me a whole lot. Any time the last three weeks we ain't been chasing the Yankees we been runnin' from them like rabbits. I been afraid things was gettin' too dull for some of you. It's been plumb tedious, I reckon. Send for Nichol."

Lieutenant Beasley Nichol reported to General Forrest.

"Could you find your way about in Nashville, Lieutenant?"

"Yes sir, Colonel—I mean, General. . . ."

"That's all right, Lieutenant. I ain't used to the new one yet myself. But about Nashville. How well do you know the town?"

"I've been there. I don't know it very well but if I started for some place I guess I'd get there."

"The Yankees caught Hume Crockett. They got him in prison there, that is, if they ain't hung him yet."

"They caught Hume? That's bad, Col—I mean, General."

"I know it's bad and I want him back. Reckon you could get him, Lieutenant?"

Lieutenant Nichol sighed a bit sadly. "What is to be will be. But it might be difficult, General."

General Forrest snorted. "Difficult! Don't talk to me about difficult. You gettin' chicken-hearted, Lieutenant?" The general paused a moment, bending an eye suddenly intent upon Lieutenant Nichol. "You got a girl in Nashville, Lieutenant?" There was a touch of accusation in the tone.

"Certainly not, General." Then Lieutenant Beasley Nichol paused, his mind whirling. The lieutenant was remembering Lucy Stratton, whom he had met at Beersheba Springs only two summers before, Lucy Stratton of Nashville. Three golden days at the Springs his eyes had feasted upon that vision of loveliness, and then Time, that ruthless interrupter of human happiness, that blotter-out of visions, that destroyer of well-laid plans, had sent him back to Alabama and Lucy to Nashville. It had then been his firm determination to visit Nashville presently. But things happened. Many things happened. His world went to pieces and here he was taking part in a war, righteous enough, he thought, but no end disconcerting. He had graduated from Princeton the following spring and had fully expected to go back to Beersheba for the summer, but most contrarily his sister had decided to get married then. He never could quite understand why it took so long to get married. It was almost as if she couldn't quite make up her mind to go through with it. It had turned out fine, but it had kept him away from Beersheba Springs. And late in the summer a precious opportunity had developed. For a season he had been employed so happily that he still remembered it breathlessly. Then war had settled down upon the country, and its alarums were upon all the winds that blew. And one didn't follow something, however he loved it, when his country needed him.

A hint of suspicion darkened General Forrest's face. "Set down, Lieutenant, and let's talk a minute. Do I know enough about you to send you on this trip? It's important. I need Crockett mighty bad. But he ain't all I need, Lieutenant. I need to know what I sent him in to find out. If he can't get it for me somebody else's got to. Of course I want Crockett back but I just plain got to find out what's going on. I want to know what Buell's got in his mind and I think Nashville's the

place to find out. If Negley or Nelson is fixin' up any shenanigan I want to know it. I don't want 'em surprisin' me. It's
plain unhealthy for me to be surprised."

"Had Hume found out anything when the Yankees captured him?"

"I don't know. I doubt if he had been there long enough.
How long you been with this outfit?"

"Since February, General. I've been with Crockett most of
that time. I'll do what I can to get the news for you, and I'll
come back with Hume—unless they hang us both. I reckon
you can trust me."

General Forrest regarded him intently. He absently picked
a small stick from the ground and broke it with a sharp crack.
The sound seemed to arouse him. "All right," he said harshly.
"When you get to Nashville—if you do—hunt up the fiddlin'
man. He's been a right smart help."

"Who's the fiddlin' man, General?"

"I never set eyes on him, but he's been a right smart help
to us. He sent me word about Hume. He sets on a chair on
Church Street in front of the Methodist Church and fiddles all
day long and sometimes at night. They say he fiddles so good
the Yankees liable to make a rich man out o' him, though,"
he added grimly, "I expect it'd make 'em powerful stingy if
they knowed what he does with his money. They'd be more
hangings than you and Crockett. You listen to me, Nichol.
When you get to Nashville—if you do—go to the Saint Cloud
Hotel——"

"Hold on a minute, General. How are we to get into
Nashville?"

General Forrest grinned wryly. "Take the sergeant with
you and if the Yankees resist tromp 'em down."

The lieutenant matched the general's grin. "We'll give
them no quarter. But really——"

General Forrest was serious again. "You'll have to get in the best way you can—just like you'll have to find out their plans the best way you can—just like you'll have to get Hume Crockett out o' jail the best way you can. Just like all three o' you will have to get out o' town the best way you can. You're a right able feller and maybe you can do it. Still, I heard the Yankees in Nashville have got in a new batch of hanging rope."

"I'll not help them waste it. Any instructions, General?"

"You watch out for the Yankees. There's a lot of them scattered around. Some places they're thicker'n fleas. Three miles the other side of Lebanon, you go to Les Campbell's. Anybody'll tell you where it is, but be careful who you ask. Better sneak in the back way. You holler hello and when they come ask 'em if they've got any gooseberries for sale. Of course it ain't the gooseberry season, but that's what they understand. They'll fix you up with beautiful blue Yankee uniforms. That'll make first-class spies out o' you both."

"That makes it easy, General."

"I ain't so sure about how easy it'll be. Sometimes the Yankees act plumb contrary, like a Maury County mule. Well, anyhow, when you get into Nashville—if you do—go to the Saint Cloud Hotel. You go in and set down like you was a-goin' to eat a meal. There's two black boys in there to wait on the tables. Anyhow, they ought to be. One o' 'em is as mean-lookin' as New York sin. Don't let him wait on you. The other one grins all over his face. You see the grin before you see him. He's the one. Tell him you want some gooseberry pie. Leave the rest to him. If you can be helped—and I reckon you can—he'll help you. I ought to know. I own that boy."

"Own him?"

"Every kinky hair on his haid. That boy's smart as two

Philadelphy lawyers. I got uneasy about Nashville and sent
him there six weeks before the Yankees moved in. If the
Yankees ever find out about him and the fiddlin' man I reckon
we'll miss 'em a right smart. If anybody can help you get
Hume Crockett out they can."

"All right, General." Lieutenant Nichol smiled broadly.
"It so happens that I am fond of gooseberries."

"You'll have to find out what you want to know from the
boy at the Saint Cloud, or maybe the fiddlin' man."

"Must I ask him about gooseberries, too, General?"

"No, gooseberries ain't in his line. Ask him to play 'Sourwood Mountain.' Then while he's a-tunin' up his fiddle tell
him you'd ruther hear 'Billy in the Low Ground.' He'll
know what you mean. Maybe he can tell you where to snoop.
If you find out what the Yankees are plannin' to do and get
word to me, you've sure made a place for yourself in this
army. If besides that you bring Crockett back with you, me
an' you'll swap places, Lieutenant. Well, I guess you'd better
be on your way. There's a wagon goin' into Lebanon for salt.
You can ride in it. After that I guess you'll have to furnish
your own travelin'. You'll have to be careful. If some of
our boys see you you'll get shot and if the Yankees catch you
you'll get hung."

General Forrest's mind turned back to the malignancy of
the Yankees. "Damn 'em!" he exploded. "The whole ca-
boodle of 'em! You get Crockett out o' that stinkin' jail,
Nichol, or I'll make a Yankee out o' you."

Lieutenant Nichol and Sergeant Goforth left the commissary wagon at Lebanon. They stopped at Les Campbell's and
when they mentioned a desire for gooseberries were promptly
and properly fitted with Yankee uniforms. They were fed and

given a package of food to last them until they reached Nash-ville, and they were given directions as to the safest roads to follow. These directions omitted the turnpikes. Scouting parties of both armies were ranging about the country and they hoped most eagerly to meet neither, so they used the more obscure side roads.

Nichol knew nothing of the country, but Sergeant Goforth had traveled it often in times of peace, and in the rapid ebb and flow of Forrest's facile troops, and so, first and last, had established a fair acquaintance with all the terrain south and east of Nashville.

Spring had gently warmed into summer. The fragile wist-ful beauty of the one had matured into the other's stabler glory. Sometimes the two soldiers skirted fields in which the white field flowers bowed gracefully to the gentle winds that blew from the south. The day was hot and sultry and bore a forecast of rain. Sometimes a stone fence would line their way, and honeysuckle vines yielding still a faint flavor of ver-nal fragrance clung in heavy masses to the stones. White, fleecy clouds lay like rugs of lambs' wool against the blue skies.

Sergeant Goforth broke a long period of silence. "Crops good, ain't they? Ever'thing's mighty purty, Lieutenant."

"It will be prettier coming back, Sergeant. How obvious then will be the beauty to which you refer. It's a bit obscure now."

"Same here. I was just talkin'. I ain't seein' it too well myself."

"You're given a voice to speak with, not to make sounds like eating mush. Listen, Sergeant, if you can't sharpen up that Tennessee speech of yours, better not use it."

"Sharpen it up, Lieutenant? You don't think I'd pass?"

The lieutenant grimaced. "There you go. *Pa-a-a-s!* You'd

pass right into prison when the first Yankee heard you say the word. You say it flatter than we do in Alabama."

"How you want me to say it—*pa-a-a-s,* I mean?"

"It's *poss* from now on, Sergeant, and you'd better start saying it that way. Mend your speech, my lad, if you don't want to mar both of our necks."

"Like this? If we *pawss* a Yankee——"

"No, not that way. It's *poss,* as in possum."

"All right. If we *poss* a Yankee I'll fix him so he cain't——"

"They'd hang us for that one. It's not *cain't,* at least till we get back—if we do. It's *cont,* as in *contract,* only you don't say the *ract.*"

"All right then, *cont.* It's goin' to be right tarsome to say——"

"Watch out! It's *tiresome.* Try the long *i* for a change, Sergeant."

"I reckon I'd better keep my mouth shet, Lieutenant. I'm a-gettin' hungry."

"We'll eat at the next spring we come to, if it isn't too far away. I'm hungry, too."

Not many minutes later they came to a spring. It flowed from the bottom of a high and thickly wooded ridge, upon which oak and cedar grew in profusion, though the area about the spring was clear for a hundred feet back except for a luxuriant maple not ten feet distant. A heavy carpet of bluegrass lay all about, up to the edges of the branch whose rippling and tinkling flow was as music on the soft summer air. There were no near sounds other than those of the brook and the intermittent breeze which gently kissed the maple tree. To these the faraway call of a plowman to his team made a fit and pleasing accompaniment. If a bloody war was being waged but a few miles away there was no hint of it discernible to the two men who sat under the maple tree and ate the food provided them at Les Campbell's.

"You got any notion what we goin' to do, Lieutenant? It ain't fur to Nashville."

"Not a very good notion, Sergeant. I fear that notions do not come to me very rapidly until I've got to have them. Then they arrive in legions."

"I'm that-a-way too," sighed the sergeant, "only sometimes I don't get 'em that quick."

"One time I . . . But let it rest. I fancy it wouldn't interest you, Sergeant."

"It might. I've wondered some about you, sir."

"You have? I feared I had been ignored. What really do you know about me, Sergeant?"

"Nothing, sir, except you spout a lot of poetry. I guess you been to college."

"Princeton, Sergeant, Princeton." He hummed a bar of "Old Nassau." "Class of—but technicalities would bore you, Sergeant."

He paused and became strangely silent. The surprised Sergeant Goforth, watching closely, saw a veritable transformation grow upon his face, in all of his body, saw that he held himself erect, rigid, and that on his face there was the vivid imprint of cold horror. His voice was fringed with the overtones of one who gazes upon the scenes of the damned.

"Angels and ministers of grace defend us!
Be thou a spirit of health or goblin damn'd,
Bring with thee airs from heaven or blasts
from hell . . ."

He relaxed, became normal and broke into a light laugh. "How'd I do it, Sergeant?"

Sergeant Goforth never took his eyes from the other's face.

Clearly Lieutenant Nichol suddenly had gone crazy. "Do what?" he asked hoarsely.

Lieutenant Nichol laughed cheerfully. "Oh, never mind. I graduated *cum laude* at Princeton. What do you suppose I did then, Sergeant?"

The sergeant stared at him, saying nothing.

"I went on the stage, Sergeant, immediately. Oh, I was the button on fortune's cap. With whom, Sergeant, do you suppose I played?"

"How would I know?" The sergeant's voice was still hoarse.

"Forrest, Sergeant, Edwin Forrest! The incomparable in grace, in voice! *In action, how like an angel! in apprehension, how like a god!* Yes, Sergeant, I played with Forrest and when the war is over I shall play with him again. He told me I could. I shall play with him again. But not in *Lear!* That is too terrible! It is worse than the war. Spartacus, yes, and Hamlet and Richard, yes. They are beautiful, most appealing, but not Lear. It is too terrible!" His laugh rippled musically. "I played with Forrest then; I am playing with Forrest now. Edwin and Bedford. How droll! Both good actors, Sergeant, but in different parts. By the way, my dear companion in danger, what did you do formerly?"

"Blacksmithed at Manchester." Sergeant Goforth's voice was still hoarse.

"Why, that's a good role, a first-rate role. How well you could act it! We'll build a play around it sometime, Sergeant. We were talking a while ago about thinking quickly in an emergency. Forrest and I were in Boston one time. We played *Richard II.* Forrest did it grandly, but when I congratulated him, his hand felt hot and his face looked flushed. The next night we were to play *Hamlet.* I don't know what, something moved me, and all that night and all the next

morning I memorized the lines. I was already acquainted
with their sense, but by noon the next day I knew them as
Forrest did.

"That afternoon I went to his room. He was in bed and
his face was burning hot. 'We can't do it, Nichol. I have
had no understudy since Cornette died. We'll have to cancel.'
There had been no definiteness of purpose in my memoriz-
ing the lines until then. But at that moment it came to me
clearly what to say. 'I know the part, Mr. Forrest.' He sat
bolt upright in bed as if shocked. 'No, Nichol, you do not
know it. You could only crawl through it.' 'Try me,' I asked.
He said, 'Say Hamlet's speech, when the ghost enters.' I
said it all as I spoke three of the lines a few moments ago.
Edwin Forrest looked at me, his eyes burning, his hand trembling. 'Say Hamlet's lines in the Fourth Act—*I'll be with
you straight. Go a little before.*' I said it, Sergeant, and
Forrest sat there in bed looking at me. 'It'll be all right,
Nichol, for me to be a little sick now and then. We will not
cancel. You will take the part tonight.' I took it, Sergeant.
Not as Edwin Forrest would have taken it. I am not foolish
enough to think that. But there was no complaint. Indeed
there was praise. Not much later I left the company to join
the Southern army."

Sergeant Goforth knew of nothing to say, so they sat in
silence while a few moments passed. Their food was eaten
and it was time to be going. The quiet had deepened as the
morning passed, and the sultriness was more oppressive. The
call of the plowman seemed eerie and faraway.

"We got to be extry keerful," said Sergeant Goforth, a
little relieved to grasp a more familiar topic. "There might
still be some Rebs about here and we'd look like Yankees to
them. You remember what General Forrest said."

"Quite well indeed. It is also conceivable that we might

experience some difficulty in establishing ourselves as full blood brothers to the Yankees. Well, when the time comes we'll think fast."

The sergeant stood up so quickly that it seemed the act of some curious machine. "Better begin now," he said pointing.

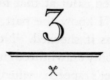

FIFTY yards behind them the road curved sharply. Nothing to cause alarm was in sight, but the sergeant's sharp ears had heard the crunching of metal shoes against the stones of the little road. Then the lieutenant heard it, too. His eyes searched the terrain. They wouldn't have the time to reach concealment. "Up the tree, Sergeant," he commanded.

"My notion, too, Lieutenant," said the sergeant, leaping for the lowest limb. And Nichol was only a split second behind him.

The agitated limbs of the tree had barely quieted when two Union soldiers rode under the tree.

"This is a good place, Sergeant. Get out the food," said a sharp crisp voice. "We'll rest a while. I'm fatigued."

"Very well, sir." The sergeant's voice was stiff and formal. They dismounted from their horses.

Lieutenant Nichol looked up at Sergeant Goforth squatted on a limb above his and winked broadly. It was as if to say, "There's your pattern for speaking."

There were the sounds of unfolding a package of food. Then they heard the two men beneath the tree eating. Some-

thing crunched methodically between their teeth. The sounds
of their horses eating corn were loud in that summer quiet.

"Tired, Captain?"

"I've been tired for—I can't remember when I wasn't
tired." The sharp crisp voice was uneven from fatigue. "I
wish this war was over. I wish I was back in Philadelphia.
I wish . . ." He broke off suddenly. Then he asked, "Have
you any idea how far it is to Nashville, Sergeant?"

"Twenty miles, I guess. Maybe more. We can make it by
night. There are Rebels in this section. We must keep our
eyes open."

"I will need some rest before I report to General Nelson—
and that's at eight o'clock tomorrow."

"General Buell must be in a hurry, Captain."

"Everybody is in a hurry. I suppose in war they always
are."

"This is a long trip to carry a little message. Why couldn't
he have sent it by telegraph wire, Captain?"

"Too many Rebels along that line. They have read too
many of our messages lately. This one is important. What's
the name of that hotel, Sergeant Bowie?"

"The Saint Cloud, Captain. Church and Summer Streets.
The horses'll be through in two or three minutes."

Two or three minutes! That sounded like eternity to
Nichol, in the agony of cramped legs. There wasn't anything to do but stand it. Presently he could hear the sergeant
putting the bits back in the horses' mouths.

"All right, Captain Ford." Nichol knew that unless they
left and that quickly he would somehow have to yield to his
tortured legs. Above him squatted his sergeant, apparently
in some degree of comfort, his legs immune to twist and
strain. The leaves below them were so thick and heavy that
they could see only fragmentary hints of dark blue when the

two men beneath shifted positions. Nichol knew that any-thing short of certain death was preferable to what he was enduring. He raised his eyes to Sergeant Goforth, and meet-ing his, pointed downward, indicating his intention to de-scend. Sergeant Goforth shook his head. Nichol, his face drawn in pain, pointed to his legs. It was better to go down quickly with the element of surprise in his favor than to an-nounce his presence by a change of position. It would have to be one or the other.

He could take his torture no longer. As he moved the crisp voice below cried out, "What's that? What's that?"

There were the sounds of the two Union soldiers spring-ing to their feet, and tugging at pistols in holsters.

Then there came a strange and surprising interruption. From back toward the timbered ridge a drawling voice spoke with unwonted sharpness. "Don't move, you Yanks. Stand still, I say. Get your hands up. Quick!"

The quick sounds of movement and confused voices from beneath the tree suggested that the orders were not being obeyed. There was the scuffing of pistols being drawn from holsters.

And then the sleepy calm of a summer noon was shattered by two rifleshots so close together that only the narrowest margin separated them. Curiously, they seemed to echo and re-echo among the hills.

From beneath the tree a scream started but stopped, dying away into a muffled gasp. There came the sounds of men slowly crumpling to the ground, and then dull vague thuds. Footsteps raced across the cleared space. There was a brief instant of silence, then a drawling voice spoke.

"Deader'n a mackerel—both of 'em."

"Let's search 'em," said a second voice.

"We ain't got time. Bed Forrest might start missin' us."

"Anyways we got hosses now."

"Good-lookin' hosses, too. Let's be ridin' 'em."

"Got to be keerful. Them hosses might git us hung."

They could hear the men mounting the horses and then clattering away along the road to the eastward. They climbed stiffly down from the tree. The two bodies lay sprawled, twisted and ghastly. Nichol turned the officer's face up and on it was an expression of profound surprise. He stood looking at him. Then he dropped on his knees and began systematically to search the pockets. Sergeant Goforth stood watching, but there was a crisp intentness in his body and face.

"We better not stay here much longer, Lieutenant. It's dangerous."

"You heard what he said, Sergeant. He was carrying a dispatch from General Buell, an important dispatch. How meet for our purpose! Delivered into our hands. Sergeant, doesn't this simplify our immediate future a trifle? Now where do you suppose he kept that dispatch?"

"Maybe in saddle pockets, left on the horses. Listen, Lieutenant, if we're goin' to stay here much longer let's tote 'em up in the woods. It ain't safe here."

Beasley Nichol straightened and stood staring at the sergeant and decision grew on his face.

"*A hit, a very palpable hit.* Sergeant, there's sense behind that owlish face." He paused. "But blood on our clothes might bring on results. And our policy, Sergeant, whate'er may betide, is to avoid results." He gathered an armload of thickly leafed weeds and placed them beneath and about the body. Then he bent and without apparent effort lifted the body of the captain, and started across the cleared space. He called back over his shoulder, "Fetch the other one, Goforth."

They deposited their grisly burdens under a cedar tree well

up the hillside. The sergeant was breathing a bit heavily, the lieutenant quite evenly.

"I think I know where that dispatch is." He ripped open the blouse and ran expert fingers around the waist. "I thought it felt bulky." He released the catch and removed the belt. The dispatch was in a buttoned compartment formed by the belt's folding over and buttoning into a sort of sash. It was a long, thin, brown, official-looking envelope folded lengthwise. On it was written:

Immediate
for General William Nelson

Bearer: Captain Enoch Ford
Specially assigned

"That will make interesting reading, but it will have to wait. And here's Captain Ford's pass. 'Through all lines.' Well, I don't know about all, but there are some of them at least that I'll need to get through."

"I got a pass, too," said the sergeant, straightening from the body he was examining. "It says 'Through all lines' too."

"Clear everything out of his pockets. We're going to swap uniforms with them."

"I thought maybe we would. The one you got at Campbell's ain't quite fit for a captain."

"It does leave something to be desired. Our side isn't at its best in the Yankee uniforms it provides for its soldiers, it really isn't. But we'll improve, Sergeant, we'll improve."

A few minutes later the change had been made.

"Much better," said Nichol. "By my troth, I'm a better Yankee captain. There has even been an improvement in you, Sergeant."

"We ought to get 'em buried," said Goforth dryly.

"By all means. Not only decent but it might conceivably divert a crisis. Any ideas where, Sergeant?"

"Yes sir." He pointed a few feet away to two boulders, perhaps three feet apart, standing high above the surface forming in part a natural vault. Nichol nodded. The soil between the stones was loose humus made mainly of rotted cedar twigs. To clear it away to a depth of a foot and a half required comparatively little time of the former Manchester blacksmith. They placed the two bodies in the depression and covered them with dirt and twigs and leaves. Then the two men started toward Nashville, twenty miles away.

It was after dark when they were halted by a blue-coated sentry at Fairfield Street. He read closely their credentials, regarded them speculatively, then waved them on into town. He stood looking after them, his brow puckered in thought. He was wondering what a captain and his attendant bearing passes inscribed plainly with the name of General Buell were doing afoot. Such usually came on horseback. There was something about them. . . . Still, it was none of his affair. Their passes were in perfect order.

At the Saint Cloud the clerk behind the desk smiled as affably as one with his face could. Yes, they were holding a room for Captain Ford and Sergeant Bowie. What was the news up Chattanooga way? Without waiting for a reply he plunged into a recounting of affairs in Nashville. He mentioned that it was a shame for Bed Forrest to be allowed to arouse so much unrest in Nashville.

"He's got our generals buffaloed, that's what it is, plain buffaloed. All they'd have to do would be to shoot a gun close enough for Bed's men to hear the bullet whistle. That's all. Two hours later the Rebs'd be in Alabama if their horses held out. But they don't shoot a gun. Bed's got 'em buffaloed." His protruding eyes revolved nervously in their orbits as if protesting Union inertia.

"We'd like to go to our room."

"All right, Cap'n, but I ain't certain it's been swept up. It's got so you can't get nothin' done. Looks like Bed's got the help buffaloed, too."

"Then could we get something to eat?"

Again the clerk wasn't disposed to commit himself. The dining room was still open. They could go in and try. He doubted if there was a crumb of anything left. It looked to him like the Union army fought a lot harder in the dining room than on the battlefield. Bed didn't have them buffaloed there.

"Aren't you a trifle impudent, sir? I haven't eaten in a dining room in four months."

"No offense, no offense," the clerk said hastily. "But they's some ain't hardly been outside a dinin' room in four months. It's a lot safer'n fightin' battles. I still think Bed Forrest's got 'em buffaloed. You might find a bite to eat. Better go try."

Nichol, gorge rising within him, went into the dining room, followed by the sergeant. The half-light of two uncertain gas jets added visibility to the room but without detail. A dozen Union officers sat at tables and three or four of them were noisy, and a bit unguarded in their speech. One of the noisy men was speaking as the two pseudo Yankees entered the room.

"I'm tired of being cooped up here in this God-forsaken mudhole by a handful of cotton-hoeing Rebels. I'm tired of it, I tell you. I always thought a war was to fight in. But I was wrong. It's to wade mud in."

No one answered him and he relapsed into his chair.

Nichol and Goforth waited at the table. Presently a young Negro came over to their table. Nichol watched him closely. He clearly was not the one General Forrest owned. This was the mean-looking man.

"We are famished," said Nichol. "What do you have in the kitchen?"

The Negro said nothing in reply but went into the kitchen. He returned presently and very surlily placed some bread and cold sliced meat on the table.

The clerk saw them come out of the dining room. "Your room's swept out. It's Number 16. Here's the key."

"What time do you expect General Nelson?"

"I don't waste no time expectin' nobody. If something don't happen he'll be here sometime. It's got so I look for a feller when I see him. At the top of the stairs turn left. Your room's the third door."

Room Number 16 didn't appear much the better off for its late sweeping, and the bed was rumpled from former use. The room was bare except for two chairs, a worn and scarred table, and a washstand. At one end of the room was a closet, a wide-open door revealing its emptiness. The room was hot and the air foul.

"Open that window, Sergeant. I'd smother in here."

Goforth found the window stuck but a powerful jerk loosened it. He raised it as high as he could and propped it with a stick. Then there came into the room the sound of music, wild and sweet, played in a fierce sort of rhythm.

"Why, that's 'The Hunters of Kentucky,' " said the former blacksmith of Manchester who knew the fiddle tunes of the Cumberland Mountains. "I reckon that's the fiddlin' man playin' it. He's the one General Forrest told us about."

They stood at the window looking down on Church Street. The summer night was hot and murky. As they watched, lightning blazed across the sky, revealing in outline the twin towers of the First Presbyterian Church. Then distant thunder rumbled and echoed among the river hills. There was the clatter of traffic upon the street, soldiers walking with military precision along the sidewalks, the echoing clang of the steel shoes on horses' feet striking against the cobblestones.

But above the confusion rang the stirring strains of "The Hunters of Kentucky."

"I'm going out for a while, Sergeant. I'd smother here. Want to go along?"

"Yes sir. I'd like to see the fiddlin' man, too."

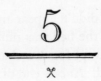

THE popeyed clerk looked at them curiously as they passed the desk but he said nothing. They went outside to Summer Street. A breeze had risen that sighed gently, almost mournfully. To the north and west the lower reaches of the sky were blazoned by lightning that wrote its paths in brilliant zigzags. At intervals the distant thunder rumbled. There were fewer people on the street, for it was close to ten o'clock. At that hour the streets were supposed to be cleared of all except those on urgent business.

The fiddlin' man was still playing "The Hunters of Kentucky." They went to the corner and crossed to the south side of Church. The fiddlin' man sat on a crude chair a few paces east of McKendree Church. One Union officer stood and listened with great intentness. Then he pitched a coin into the open gourd that sat on the sidewalk near the musician's feet and walked out Church Street. The fiddlin' man made preparations to depart.

"Play 'Sourwood Mountain,' " said Nichol.

The man paused, fiddle in mid-air. He looked sharply at the two Union soldiers. Then he jerked a thumb toward the gourd. Nichol understood the gesture and threw in a coin. The fiddlin' man tested his strings.

"No, I believe I'd rather hear 'Billy in the Low Ground.' "

The fiddlin' man plunked a string sharply. For ten seconds he said nothing, waiting, his bow poised. Then it fell upon the strings in an ecstasy of wild merriment, the bow flying, his facile fingers dancing upon the strings with incredible ease and rhythm.

The fiddlin' man was tall and gaunt, the visible parts of his face tanned by countless suns. No trace of emotion, no response to his own music marred the immobility of his expression. His feet tapped a stirring background for the strains that rose from his fiddle. He was chewing tobacco and the rise and fall of his jaws bore a curious unity to the beat of his flying bow. When he asked them the question the music never faltered. Nor did he look at the two men.

"Who sent you here?" His voice was low and grim but it broke through "Billy in the Low Ground" and they heard it distinctly.

"General Forrest."

"What's he want?"

"They captured Captain Crockett. He wants him back. He sent us to get him."

"A spy?"

"I guess you'd call him that. Do you know where they have him?"

"I been lookin' for you. I don't know where he is but I can find out. Early tomorrer, I reckon. You better be a-goin' now—wait a minute. Don't come aroun' effn I'm a-playin' 'The Mournin' Dove.' That's a sign it ain't safe. Do you know it?"

"No. . . ."

"I do," said Goforth.

"Effn you hear it git out o' sight. There's them that ain't so certain about me. I'll play it." He shifted to a piece of a primitive sweetness, distilled of loneliness and bereavement. He played it through and then his voice lifted the words.

> "Did you ever see the mournin' dove
> A-flyin' roun' the vine?
> It's a-mournin' for its lost true love
> Jest like I mourn for mine."

Beasley Nichol nodded. He would know "The Mourning Dove" if he heard it again. Then he and Goforth walked to High Street, crossed Church and returned to the Saint Cloud, walked through the deserted lobby, climbed the stairs, and went to bed. They slept soundly throughout the night. They knew nothing of the storm which broke and raged after midnight, nor were they haunted by dreams of a lonely grave on a hillside among the cedar trees. This was war and graves were a part of it.

THEY ate breakfast early the next morning. The dining room was moderately filled. They sat at a table by a window that looked out on Summer Street. Presently a grinning Negro boy brought them food. The eyes of Nichol and Goforth met, and there was agreement in the glance. This was the boy who had belonged to General Forrest, but it was not the time to use the password. A request for gooseberry pie would draw too much attention. It was their wish to avoid attention without seeming to do so. Presently an officer entered and took a seat at their table. It was the one who the night before had expressed such resentment at being cooped up in a mudhole.

"It rained again last night," he announced loudly. "Good God, what a place! Rains all the time! Everything knee-deep in mud! Get off the main streets and they have to pull you out with an ox team. Worse'n Washington! Worse'n anywhere!" He turned a baleful eye upon Beasley Nichol as if he somehow were responsible. "What outfit you with?"

"Special service, General Buell's headquarters." Nichol's voice was crisp with the accents of the North.

"Couldn't get me attached, could you? Anything to get

away from here! I tell you this town could supply creation with mud."

"I could speak to General Buell about you—when I see him."

"Do. When did you get in?"

"Last night."

"Most interesting. Must be something afoot. God knows it's time!" The outrage on his face deepened. "I live in Trenton—Trenton, New Jersey, sir. One rarely sees mud there. A man could live his whole life there and never get a smear of mud on him. In fact, I had lived a mudless life till I came here. But in Nashville, just go out to Fort Negley and it'll take a year to get it off, maybe forever. Here, I wear mud as a garment. I breathe it, I eat it. . . ."

"It has been a rainy season," said Nichol, looking steadily out the window.

"Well, what if it has? It rains in Trenton, doesn't it? Doubless our rainfall exceeds yours—but not yours, of course. You'd never be from this God-forsaken mud bed. Where, may I inquire, Captain, are you from?"

"Philadelphia," said Nichol, still staring out the window at Summer Street.

"Most interesting," said the other, regarding him with wide-open eyes. "You're my neighbor, sir, my close neighbor. May I ask your name?"

"Ford, Captain Enoch Ford."

The man pushed his chair back with a sudden force. "Enoch Ford! By gad, sir, you're my cousin, my third cousin!"

"Oh," said "Enoch Ford," feebly accepting the outstretched hand. "Oh." It was an emergency and he wasn't thinking quickly. In fact, he wasn't thinking at all.

"Never set eyes on you before, but I've heard aplenty of you. Aunt Elspeth Sidebottom always claimed you were her prize nephew. I'd heard you were in the service. And to think

I'd run across you here! Why, it's almost a miracle! Here, in
creation's original mudhole!"

"I've heard my mother speak of you," said Nichol. His mind
was moving again, though slowly, and with traces of mud in
its processes.

"You've heard your mother speak of me! Your mother,
now. She's not living, is she?"

"No, dead seventeen years."

"No, eighteen. I remember now. It was the year our house
on Brunswick Avenue burned down."

"But you haven't told me your name yet."

"How stupid of me! So I haven't. My dear cousin, I'm
Philip Yorke, Major Philip Yorke of the Tenth New Jersey."

"Yorke! Why, of course, Yorke."

"But I'm kin to you through the Noels. My mother was a
Noel."

"I know, I know," said Beasley Nichol cheerfully. "But
I've always felt just as close to the Yorkes as to the Noels."

"That's not to your credit," said Major Yorke firmly. "The
only thing I ever got from the Yorkes is a name. But I fairly
wallow in virtue from your side of the family. Just fancy
meeting you here. . . ." Again his sense of indignation
crowded in upon him. "Here!" he exploded. "Here in the mud
center of the universe. I enlisted to fight, not to wade. I'd
like a lot less mud and a lot more Rebels."

"I have had considerable experience with the—er, Rebels,"
said Nichol, "and I find that mud is safer."

"Then heaven protect me from the Rebels! I go out with
my men every day and we drill and play at war, ankle-deep—
no, knee-deep in filthy mud. I'd take my chances against the
Rebels."

"I wouldn't, and I know them better perhaps than you do.
The Rebels, dear cousin, are an active people."

"Anyhow, have supper with me tonight. I'll bring some

whisky, which is mud's great anodyne, and we'll toast to solid ground and the smallness of the world."

"It is small. It is delightful to find you here—cousin—but my time is not my own. I may be on my way back to General Buell by evening."

"Of course, of course. Business before kinship. I understand."

"I may see you again before I leave. If not, then someday, and we'll talk further of the Noels—and others."

THE unkempt, sandy-haired, bulging-eyed, voluble clerk who felt so keenly the inaction of those buffaloed by General Forrest was again behind the desk. Nichol paused long enough to ask him if General Nelson had returned.

"No. I reckon General Forrest's captured him. His orderly's there, though. Room Number 20."

The orderly didn't know when General Nelson might be expected. He guessed the general had run into trouble of some sort. Captain Ford would, of course, wait pending the general's return. The orderly hoped it would be soon. A message so forwarded by General Buell was undoubtedly of grave importance.

Back in their room Goforth looked searchingly at the walls on either side of the room and at the door to the hall. His voice when he spoke was low and guarded.

"You goin' to give him that message jest like it is?"

"Why, Sergeant, how you read my mind! But I don't believe we'd better change it any. That might be dangerous.

Still, I think it is my duty to read that message, don't you, Sergeant?"

"Yes sir, and I'd put another one in."

"You couldn't mean an order for the release of Hume Crockett?"

"Yes sir, that's what I mean."

"Why, then, the deed we'll do before the purpose cools. We need the help of an expert forger. That is not among my more shining talents. Now how could we arrange . . . ?"

And as if in answer there came through the open window the rippling notes of a fiddle.

"We can ask him," said the sergeant, jerking his head in the direction of the fiddlin' man.

"So we can." He put on his hat and they went down the stairs and out on Summer Street. They turned west on Church and crossed at High to the south side of the street. Suddenly, as they approached, the fiddlin' man's merry tune sank into silence. Then his bow rose and fell on something plaintive and filled with a terrible loneliness. The eyes of the two men on the street met. The piece was "The Mourning Dove." They walked by the fiddlin' man erect and military, their eyes straight ahead. But from the corner of his, Beasley Nichol saw that the sandy-haired, fish-eyed clerk was looking out a window of the Saint Cloud.

A regiment of soldiers came marching along Church Street from the river. Then came four horses drawing a heavy cannon.

"I fear that traffic like this will provide more mud for Cousin Philip. By the way, I remember that church. I attended services there once. Let's call on the First Presbyterian Church. We might need an excuse for being out."

They climbed the steps but found the church closed, the door securely barricaded.

"I came here for services one Sunday, and it was crowded.

Some were even standing. What an irreverent thing is war!"

They returned to the Saint Cloud. A minute later a knock sounded at their door and there entered the grinning Negro whom they had seen that morning in the dining room.

"Jest thought I'd sweep up," he said, his bright grin abating not a jot.

"Pretty music," said Lieutenant Beasley Nichol, pointing vaguely toward the fiddlin' man.

"He sho can mek a fiddle talk. I hyard him a-playin' 'The Mournin' Dove' while I was a-mekin' up Number 8."

"What about this General Forrest? It seems that he has all of us buffaloed—is that the word, Sergeant?"

"They say he's a powerful fightin' man. You ever see Gin'ral Forrest, Captain?"

"Oh, did I ever see him? How could I know? In my travels I have seen a great many people. He might have been among them." He paused, and while the grinning Negro watched, an odd transformation was wrought upon the lieutenant's features. His face lengthened and narrowed, and his eyebrows seemed to grow strangely bushy. His mouth twisted into a commingling of defiance, impudence and daring, and when he spoke it was the voice of General Nathan Bedford Forrest. "You get Crockett out of that stinking jail or I'll make a Yankee out o' you." His face relaxed, became normal. The grinning Negro watched him as one hypnotized.

"You sho do know Gin'ral Forrest," he said. He paused a moment, pondering something. "It's done too late for gooseberries," he said in low tones.

"But not too late for some help," suggested Nichol.

"The fiddlin' man said they got him in the county jail."

"So? Well, that's fine. But right now we need a good forger, one who can fix up orders that will look all right and then seal them so they would fool Abe Lincoln himself."

"I 'spect they's men who could."

"What says my Lord Hamlet—*folded the writ up . . . sub-scrib'd it, gave't the impression; plac'd it safely, the change-ling never known*. Ah, that's what I need."

"Yassuh," said the grinning Negro.

"Do you know the man who can do it?"

The Negro most surprisingly dropped on his knee, his eyes keenly upon Nichol's left boot. "Ain't it too bad the way yo' boot is rippin'? They's a man on Cherry Street jest three doahs no'th o' the Maxwell House who does fust-rate fixin'. He might fix yo' lettuh, too. Yassuh."

"How will he know me?"

"Jest ast him can he fix it like he done the fiddlin' man's. Reckon I done better be sweepin' out now."

8

✄

THE cobbler sat at his table in the dingy shop on Cherry Street. He looked up inquiringly as Nichol entered. He said nothing, for his lips held a half-dozen tacks, but his searching eyes peered out from under dense bushy eyebrows. Nichol pointed to the ripped place in his boot.

"Could you fix that like you did the fiddlin' man's?"

He looked at Nichol with eyes that probed. "I reckon. They's a place back here you can pull it off."

He led the way back into a hot little room and carefully closed the door. Then he asked, "What is it you want?"

"I have a dispatch from General Buell to General Nelson. I expect to deliver it, but I want to read it first. I have excellent reasons for wanting to know what the message is. Also, I should like to enclose a second dispatch."

"I reckon you'd better tell me about it." The man listened alertly to Nichol's story. "I don't do the writing. The man that does will be here directly. You wait in here."

He returned to his work. Nichol sat impatiently fidgeting about. Ten minutes later a man came into the room. He was thin and stooped and a chalklike pallor was on his face. Obviously the cobbler had told him what was expected. He didn't bother about introductions.

"Let's see that dispatch," he said in tones distinct but not much louder than a whisper. He looked at the envelope, then turned it over and sat there studying it. He arose abruptly but silently and disappeared through a door which Nichol had not noticed before. A minute later he returned with a large box which when he opened it displayed many small compartments. He then slit the envelope containing the dispatch and removed very deftly a folded sheet of paper. He handed it to Ford. "I reckon you want to read this," he said in low tones.

There were a few lines only, but Nichol's eyes brightened as he read them. This would be news to General Forrest.

> *To Major General William Nelson:*
> *Have your troops prepared to march on brief notice into Kentucky to turn back the invasion now being prepared by the enemy. You will be advised officially when to move as soon as the enemy's plans are more fully revealed.*
> *D. C. Buell*
> *Major General Commanding*
> *Stevenson, Ala.*

Nichol read and reread the lines, imprinting them indelibly upon his memory. Then the thin man took the paper and studied the lines intently. "That handwriting isn't hard to copy. What was the message you wanted written?"

He handed Nichol a piece of paper and a pencil and he,

after pondering a moment, wrote a brief command addressed to General Nelson requiring him to deliver to the bearer one Rebel officer named Hume Crockett, held as a spy. The bearer in turn and in all dispatch would bring him to General Buell's headquarters for questioning.

The thin man searched in his compartment and found a sheet of paper identical with that of General Buell's message. He set out an array of ink bottles and matched the color of the ink with which it was written. Then with eyes shifting from the original dispatch to the page before him he wrote, and when he had finished Beasley Nichol could not tell the slightest difference in the handwriting of the two pages. The thin man searched and found an envelope like the one he had destroyed. He addressed it with great care. Then he set out some little bars of sealing wax and lighted a candle. A minute later he handed Nichol the completed dispatch. It was in perfect order.

The thin man bowed him out of the hot little room.

The cobbler had finished his boot. With great care he fitted the boot to Nichol's foot. Then he said, "When you get out on the street stop and look at the place I have sewed. Look as if deciding whether you ought to accept it. Somebody might be looking."

BEASLEY NICHOL walked north on Cherry Street, then west on Church. He stopped, examined the repaired place, ran his finger over it, and nodded his head as if satisfied. As he approached Summer Street he heard the music of the fiddlin'

man. He was not playing "The Mourning Dove" then. Menace was no longer abroad.

The clerk with the fisheyes was not at the desk. The lobby was almost deserted. A man rose from a chair and approached Nichol.

"Have you come for the sick officer upstairs?" He stopped suddenly, evidently in some confusion, his eyes resting upon Nichol's insignia. "Excuse me. I didn't——"

"Certainly," Nichol said. "I didn't know there was a sick man here."

"Captain Joynes. They are sending an ambulance from the hospital. It ought to be here by now."

Nichol climbed the steps and walked down the hall to his room. It was unlocked, but that meant that Sergeant Goforth was awaiting him within. He pushed the door open and entered the room.

But it wasn't Sergeant Goforth who waited. It was the fish-eyed clerk. Nichol didn't see him at first. The man stood close to the wall by the door. In his hand he held a most venomous pistol and it was aimed unwaveringly at Nichol's heart.

While a clock might perhaps have ticked off ten there was silence in the room. It was Nichol who spoke, very evenly and in clipped Northern accents.

"Be careful, sir. What sort of foolery is this?"

"No foolery, Captain Ford, no foolery at all. I'm really better at other things than clerking in a silly hotel—as you likely will discover presently. I don't know what your game is—yet—and I don't know who you are—yet. But I will soon. It might even help if you talked a bit freely about several things."

Nichol noticed that there was a malicious glint in the man's eyes and that the hand that held the pistol was steady. Where was Goforth anyhow? The clerk in part read his thoughts.

"If your sergeant comes in say nothing, and make no move. I will surely shoot you if you do. I have another pistol in my pocket and I shoot quite well with either hand. Where is he?"

"I do not know. I expected to find him here. I haven't been gone half an hour. Please tell me in heaven's name what this means."

The man ignored the question. "Where have you been? Tell me the truth."

Nichol glanced involuntarily at his stitched boot, but checked himself. "On the streets for a breath of air. Will you leave the room immediately?"

"So you won't tell. Well, it doesn't matter. It gave me a chance to get in here. I would have had my search completed in a few more minutes. It doesn't matter, though. I think I know enough about you to serve my purposes, sir."

Thoughts were whirling through Nichol's mind. Where was Goforth? What had the man found in the room? But there was nothing to find. Very well, they'd as well have it out.

"Of what am I suspected?" he asked crisply. "And who are you to suspect me?"

The man matched his crispness. "I suspect you of being an impostor, a spy. As for me, General Negley could give a not unsatisfactory account of the service I have rendered the army as secret-service agent."

"And I," said Nichol, "am Captain Enoch Ford. My cousin Major Philip Yorke of Trenton is staying here. He can identify me. I could of course be mistaken, but I believe that General Buell would be disposed to regard my services with favor, and to resent any unnecessary annoyance offered me. Also, it might be mentioned that General Buell outranks General

Negley. Will you leave the room, sir, or shall I throw you out?"

"Major Yorke's cousin? Oh, no, you ain't. Of course you couldn't be using that to kill time knowing that Yorke will not return till night. I think I'll stay awhile. When I first saw you last night something—I don't know what it was—warned me. I didn't put on my crazy little stunt just for fun. I done it to watch you closer."

The man was talking too much. He had his suspicions but they lacked confirmation. He had not yet discovered their substance. Perhaps he could suspect better than he could ferret out.

"Will you please leave the room? My time is too valuable to be wasted. If General Negley wishes to entrust his work to bungling amateurs that is no concern of mine."

The mean light glinted again in the man's shifty eyes. "I have a directory of the men assigned to secret service. It isn't complete, but you are in it. I looked it up last night. You are thirty-eight years old. What has happened to make you fully ten years younger?"

"Indeed! I have found this life refreshing—until now. Perhaps that would account for it."

"There was also a large wart on the side of your nose but now no sign of it remains."

"The healing influence of a clear conscience is supposed to be very beneficial to warts. I have asked you to leave the room. I dislike to repeat such requests."

"It is stated that you are five feet eight inches tall. Your clear conscience seems to have lifted you fully to six feet."

"I knew that I was getting taller, but——"

"I'm going to take you to the headquarters of the provost marshal. If he finds from Major Yorke or anyone else that you are really Captain Enoch Ford no harm will have been done. If you are not, which I am convinced is the case, our cause will have been protected. Perhaps I'd better search you before we start. Get your hands up."

There was no mistaking the ruthlessness of the man and Nichol recoiled a step or two, his thoughts searching furiously for guidance. He didn't intend to go to the provost's headquarters. That would be suicide. The odds were better here. Where was Sergeant Goforth? His lunge would have to hit the man below the pistol, would have to hit him quick and hard. He summoned strength to his legs and could feel it gathering.

"When I have counted three and you have not raised your hands I shall kill you as I would a traitor."

One. . . . The word *two* formed but was not spoken. Sergeant Goforth's revolver fell crushingly upon Fisheye's head. The clerk hit the floor with such force that he almost bounced. Sergeant Goforth closed the door of the closet from which he had emerged so silently. Beasley Nichol stood looking at the man sprawled on the floor.

"You said something about thinking fast when you had to," observed Goforth dryly. "That's now."

"Why didn't you come out before? I needed you."

"It was too good a show," said the sergeant, grinning. "I knew it wasn't you when I heard him walking down the hall. When he stopped and begun to turn the knob I got in there quick." He pointed to the closet.

"So far, good, but what now, Sergeant Goforth? I fear my mind for once in my life is a bit sluggish, inadequate, as it were. Thoughts do not emerge."

"It's the wrong time for them not to. If we had the order from General Nelson for Captain Crockett we could lock him in a closet and take a chance on fast work."

He knelt by the sprawled body and ran an expert finger over

the man's head. He listened to his breathing and lifted a hand to feel the pulse better. His fingers again searched the skull, and remained there during a speculative moment.

"I expect it's cracked. I don't know for certain. I hit him plenty hard, and he's liable to be out a spell, but he won't die. No such good luck this time."

Beasley Nichol shook his head as does one who clears an inner mist from his vision. "If he were less dangerous dead, another blow on his skull would be warranted, but . . . What do you think, Sergeant?"

"I think I should lock that door." He did so.

"Still my mind does not rise. It stays below, or I would have thought of that. Woe is me that it should fail me in this case! What shall we do, Sergeant?"

"I reckon we'd better put him in the closet and lock the door. It might even be tomorrow before they find him. We got to hurry. Things has got dangerous."

"My opinion, precisely, Sergeant, but it will be calamitous if General Nelson doesn't report soon. How sorely we need the general just now!"

He bent to pick the clerk up from the floor, but just then an imperative knock sounded at the door. It was quickly repeated. The sergeant and the lieutenant stood in stark surprise looking at each other. The knock was repeated, and a voice called, "Stretcher for the sick man."

"Oh," said Nichol excitedly, but in low tones, "it's working again. I mean my mind. In a minute," he called to those at the door. "Oh, what a blessed mistake! They've got the wrong room, thank heaven. As I came up they were talking in the lobby of a sick officer. They had asked for an ambulance to take him to the hospital. Here's their sick man, right here. Follow my lead, Sergeant. Throw a blanket over him quick." Then he strode to the door and threw it wide.

Two men stood at the door with a stretcher upright between them. "We were sent here to get a sick officer. Do you know what room he's in?"

"Here he is. Right here. Get him to the hospital as quickly as you can."

"Yes, Captain, right away."

"Where is the ambulance?"

"We hitched it in the back. We'll carry him down the back stairs. Just as soon as we git this stretcher ready."

Nichol's and Goforth's luck held. They heard steps going down the back stairs and then the grind of the wheels leaving.

Two minutes later they locked the door and started down the stairs. The grinning Negro was sweeping on the stairs. "Gin'ral Nelson's back. He's at the Cunningham House now." His voice was low, almost a whisper, but they heard him clearly, though he didn't look up as they passed.

"Where's that?"

"Turn lef' as you go out the front doah, walk one square, turn lef' again, walk another square. It's a big house right across High Street."

The tempo of his sweeping increased. The eyes of both the lieutenant and the sergant searched all the vistas opening from the stairway. No one was in sight. They went on down the stairs, but very warily. The lobby was almost deserted. Two officers slept sprawled in chairs. No one was at the door. They went on out the front door onto Summer Street and turned left. They walked briskly, though avoiding very carefully all aspect of hurry.

II.

IN WHICH DIFFICULTY IS ENCOUNTERED IN SECURING INFORMATION

1

THE LADIES again were meeting at Polk Place. This time they were not making shirts but putting into order for the use of the prisoners in the Maxwell House an odd and motley assortment of trousers which they by process of insistent canvass had collected from their menfolks.

Mrs. Baker as was her wont came hurrying in a bit later than the appointed hour. She was hot and panting, but a look of triumph covered her ample face. She entered the library with a dramatic flourish and held up a bundle for all to see.

"Eight pairs," she announced proudly. "Can any lady present beat that?"

No lady could. Mrs. Baker assumed that no lady could, so she didn't wait for a reply. "I made up my mind to bring eight pairs, but it looked for a while like the most I could do was six. But I had set my mind on eight. And when I set my mind something happens, ladies. I'd even made me up a motto. *Pants for eight patriots.* Why, that's almost as good as the Declaration! Don't you think so, ladies?"

"Berrien is coming to take them to the Maxwell House at four o'clock. We must have them ready by then," suggested Mrs. Polk with becoming delicacy.

"So this morning I went out to get my other two pants, pairs of pants, I mean. I knew Brother Howell would give me a pair—that is, if he had an extra one. Well, what do you think? Brother Howell is in jail. That old scoundrel, the

Governor, had him put in because he wouldn't swear to vote for Abe Lincoln, or something. Don't try to stop me, ladies. I always say what I have on my mind. And I'd a lot sooner tell that Governor than you all. Well, on the way back from Brother Howell's house I met Mr. Watkins. He's a good man but they do say he's mighty stingy. I didn't think there was any use in beating around the bush in a worthy cause, so I just asked him then and there to give me a pair of pants. Mr. Watkins is a bachelor, you know, and I guess he's not used to frank talk. He got to blushing and I declare I thought he'd lost his power of speech. I told him how sacred the cause was and how all the men were giving their pants. And it's so! Why, Mr. Baker has given three pairs—though he don't know about one of them yet. But he'll be generous when he finds it out. He always is. I told Mr. Watkins we were expecting him to do his part, and how frightful the condition of the brave men at the Maxwell House was. You know Mr. Watkins never smiles on but one side of his face. They say that's on account of him not wanting to commit himself too freely. Well, he was still blushing, and he was smiling on both sides. . . ."

"What I want to know is did you get the pants?" asked Sallie Lindsley. And she, though with some restraint, was also smiling on both sides of her face.

"As I was saying, Mr. Watkins may be stingy but he's patriotic. So he said he would go to his house and get the pants and leave them at my house before noon. Then I had an idea. It came to me quite sudden-like—so many of my ideas come that way. . . ."

"Wouldn't it be a good idea if we got to work?" asked Mrs. Fogg. "There's quite a lot to do yet."

"So I told Mr. Watkins if he could spare two pairs it would save me a trip to Brother McFerrin's, and I wasn't sure Brother McFerrin had an extra pair anyhow. Mr. Watkins waited a minute. Then he grinned again. On both sides of his face, ladies. I wonder if I'm the only living person that ever saw him grin on both sides of his face at once? He said that if our fine men could stay outdoors for the cause he guessed he could stay indoors."

"Then you did get your pants for eight patriots?"

"Did I say eight? I mean nine. I went on to Brother Mc-Ferrin's and I guess he'll be staying indoors too."

Mrs. Baker, still wearing an aura of triumph, untied her bundle and poured nine pairs of scrambled trousers upon the table. The work of sorting for sizes, of sewing on buttons, of darning, proceeded. The hot humid winds came in through the windows. Steel-shod horses moved to and fro on Vine Street and steel-rimmed wheels crunched against gravel.

"Berrien said that the men at the Maxwell House wearing their new shirts reminded him of an Easter parade," said Mrs. Polk. "He said they were as pleased as children."

"Berrien has seen but half. He should observe them a few days from now," said Adelicia Acklen. She held up a pair. "Can you imagine any man in his right mind wearing anything of that color?"

Florence Kirkman also held up a pair for general scrutiny. "I pity the poor fellow that gets these. They're an inch thick. They'll cook him, weather like this."

"Somewhat warming now, but a real blessing when cold weather sets in."

"They say," said Mrs. Baker, "that the war will be over by cold weather. Mr. Baker always says watch out for a killing frost the twelfth of October."

"Then we're due a long hot spell," snapped Mrs. Polk, who found certain types of optimism irksome. "I don't know a thing about military strategy, but I know a great deal about people. I've traveled in the North and I've lived among Northern people. And I've kept my eyes open. It'll be God's own blessing if this war is over by cold weather next year, or the year after. I believe I'd meet what they say with deafness, my dear."

"Two years! What will happen to us here in that time?"

"Here? Precisely the same that will happen all over the South. A great deal of wretchedness of which we have not yet even dreamed will happen to us. Food will grow scarce, the pinch of poverty will be upon us, and—God help us!—a great many of our men will be killed. War, dear ladies, is no country picnic for silly people. War is a ghastly thing and we literally are in the middle of one."

There was a long moment of silence. The curtains swayed idly. Soldiers were marching on the streets as if to give verity to Mrs. Polk's words. It was Mrs. Fogg who spoke first.

"It is a year ago that Henry went away to the war. What did we do to be so punished?"

"Yes, my dear, I know. How terrible a year can be—or how incredibly lovely! But I, my dear, am of the Presbyterian faith. I do what I can and then accept the years as they are sent. I am no stranger to the terrible years. We have wars because the people are ignorant and stubborn and can think of no other means by which to gain their ends. The few who are wise are punished along with those who are stupid. It's the way of all mankind. The wise would not want it any other way."

"Ninety-nine pairs," announced Mrs. Morgan, who had been counting. "That's good indeed."

"I'll see that it's a hundred." Mrs. Baker rose promptly. "Dr. Felix Robertson hardly ever goes out any more. He's getting pretty old now but I guess he's still got pants. I'll be back in a half an hour—and it'll be a hundred if he has to stay in bed while he treats his patients. They say that . . ."

But the door closed behind her before it was fully revealed what "they" had said.

"There is still some mending to do, and some buttons to

put on. Each of you ladies take a pair and we'll have them ready by the time Berrien gets here."

"We are being punished," said Mrs. Polk, "but in war, who could or would escape? I don't know why we are punished so unevenly. I only know that is the way of war. But for that matter life itself is so uneven. Sometimes that unevenness disturbs me greatly and sometimes it inspires me." She broke off. "But who am I to pose as a sage? By the way, I saw Elizabeth Harding this morning. She came in from Belle Meade to see Governor Johnson about a pass to go visit her husband. They have him in a Northern prison, you know. But he wouldn't see her, not even for a moment. But sooner or later he will—if I know Elizabeth. The strength that the war has discovered in that woman! Condemn war however you may, it does discover strength."

There was a knock at the door. "Well," said Mrs. Polk, "she got her pants sooner than I expected."

She opened the door but it was not Mrs. Baker. It was Berrien Lindsley standing there.

"I had nothing to do. So I came a bit early, and very gladly, too. I am the bearer of news."

"What?" the Ladies asked in one voice.

"General Forrest has captured Murfreesboro and taken over a thousand prisoners."

In one voice the Ladies rejoiced.

"And last night one of General Forrest's scouting parties took five prisoners out on Mill Creek, surprising them where they were camped in Mr. Buchanan's plum orchard."

"The war *will* be over by Christmas," breathed Mrs. George Gray.

"It'll take more than the capture of one small county seat to end it."

"General Forrest will capture other places."

"I think he will," said Berrien. "He'll likely take Lebanon

in a few days though I fear it bears very little relation to the end of the war. But enough county seats would become extremely significant."

He picked up a garment and looked at it critically. "Why, excellent! If this keeps up before long it will be so that the only way to get decent clothes to wear will be to get captured and put in prison." Berrien paused considering. "I doubt if that is passable humor. I withdraw it."

A sharp peal of thunder crashed and crackled, and though in the fortnight thunder had become commonplace each woman looked at one or more neighbors with surprise in her eyes. That peal of thunder sounded personal. Mrs. Polk went to a window and looked out, her eyes slanting toward Capitol Hill. A bluish-black cloud was mounting angrily in the sky. She left the window and went into the hall and asked a servant to examine the windows, to see that they were closed against the storm. She turned back into the library and again glanced out the window.

"My goodness, she's late," she said and went to the door to admit the tardy one. A girl, one of the younger Ladies, came hurriedly into the hall.

"Oh, Mrs. Polk," she said, "I know I am awfully late, but I have been so excited. I still am. I was ready to leave when Mama said there was a Negro at the back door who wanted to see me. Mama said she thought I'd better go see him. And I did. It was one of the boys who work at the Saint Cloud— and he said, Mrs. Polk, that Hume had got out of their prison, said he was on the way back to General Forrest! He said he guessed some folks helped him out, but that was all he knew. Mrs. Polk, I forgot all about the meeting of the Ladies. I came just as soon as I remembered."

"I understand, dear. How beautiful are the ways of God! Come on into the library. We are a little behind in our work. We need you to sew on some buttons."

The Ladies looked up from their folding and sewing. "Who needs a good button-sewer most?" Mrs. Polk asked quickly. The Ladies caught the subtle command for their member's tardiness to go uncommented.

"Here," said Adelicia Acklen, holding up an ancient garment of mole-gray jeans. "This pair demands expertness. It seemingly antedates the use of buttons."

"I had a caller this morning," said Mrs. Polk in the tones of one who tastes what she is saying for further flavors, "a very interesting caller, a major in the Northern Army."

"A Yankee, Mrs. Polk?"

"Certainly, a Yankee, one named Philip Yorke. Yankees come to see me. My husband was President of their country, too. Well, there was something about this one that puzzles me. He said that he was present at Mr. Polk's inauguration and that he saw us in Washington on several occasions. He wished merely to pay his respects, but there was something, some little trace in his voice, something in his choice of words—I don't know what it was, but it was something . . ."

The door opened abruptly and Mrs. Baker came in, her features overlaid with another spread of triumph. Plainly her trip had met with merited reward.

"Did you get your pants?" several of the Ladies asked.

"Yes, I did, and guess who I saw on High Street not five minutes ago!"

No one essayed a guess.

"The identical man I saw on Lafayette Street the other day. You remember. I told you about it. The boy from Franklin. The one I knew. Well, there he was as big as life, riding down the High Street hill. There were two others along with him, and I know one of them, too, but to save me I can't think who he is. I don't think he lives here but I've seen him here in Nashville. There must be something the matter with me the way I'm forgetting things. And all three of them had on Yankee uniforms. I tried to catch his eyes but never could. You wouldn't think . . ."

Mrs. Polk's eyes were upon the girl who was sewing on buttons. She saw the girl throw a garment on the table and start to stand, her eyes blazing.

"But Mrs. Baker—" Mrs. Polk was very suave and very crisp—"what we want to know is did you get your pants?"

"I told you I did. That's what I told you when I first got back, and I just did beat that storm, too. I hope those three boys have some place to go even in Yankee uniforms."

"Let's see the pair of pants you got," said Mrs. Polk very emphatically.

Mrs. Baker placed her bundle on the table. "Don't say *the pair* to me. It surprised Dr. Robertson when I told him what I wanted. It doesn't seem as if anything would surprise a man who has had as many experiences as he has but he certainly was surprised. He said it was the first time a lady ever asked him for pants. So he gave me two pairs."

Just then the storm hit Polk Place.

2

X

AN ORDERLY met Nichol and Goforth at the door of the Cunningham House.

"I am Captain Enoch Ford, a special agent from General Buell's headquarters with a message for General Nelson. I should like to see him at once."

The orderly was sympathetic. "The general's busy now, but you won't have to wait long. Have a chair."

He came back presently and led them into the room in which General Nelson sat. The general, a massive man of three hundred pounds, overflowed his chair and it creaked loudly when he shifted position. He returned their salute, waved them to chairs and sat waiting. He was polite but pre-occupied. His eyes were on distant horizons outside the window.

"I am Captain Enoch Ford from General Buell's headquarters, and this is Sergeant Bowie."

General Nelson bowed, the faraway look still in his eyes. "I believe that you have brought a message for me, Captain Ford?"

The captain unbuttoned his blouse, reached back along his belt until he reached the flap, unbuttoned it, and handed the folded envelope to General Nelson. An open knife lay on the table and the general used it to open the envelope. He took therefrom the two sheets. He straightened the first out on the table and read it.

"I was told that we had taken one of their spies here in town, wearing our uniform. I wonder what General Buell can want with him." He studied a moment, wrinkling his brow in a gesture of thought. "All right. I'll endorse this. Carry it to the provost." He wrote his endorsement across the sheet.

Then he read the second dispatch. "What!" he said explosively, his clenched fist falling hard upon the table, his chair protesting the torture of his violent motion. "What can this mean? This changes everything. Everything, Captain Ford!"

"General Buell did not advise me of the contents of the message, General Nelson." Nichol spoke in crisp Northern accents.

"It changes everything." The general sat in silence and his brow was furrowed with deeper wrinkles. Then his voice rang through the building. "Orderly, orderly, Corporal Kelly!" The corporal came hurrying in.

"Yes sir."

"Get my staff. Get all of them you can find. Send messengers. Hurry!" His eyes again sought the dispatch. "This changes everything."

Presently he became aware of the presence of Nichol and Goforth.

"Oh, yes. Pardon me, please. This is quite disconcerting. Thank you, Captain, for your services, and my compliments to General Buell. Things seem to be going quite well with him. I shall proceed to put his orders into effect. . . . Oh, yes, the prisoner. Give this to the provost." He handed the order to Nichol. "Good afternoon." He included both men in his bow.

At the door Nichol stopped and faced General Nelson. "May I make a request, sir?"

The answering nod of the head was detached but did not lack in courtesy.

"I regret to ask it but I am sure General Buell would like to see this spy as soon as we can arrange it. He said so very positively. We need horses, sir."

"Horses?"

"We were ambushed by some Rebel soldiers, and our horses were taken. It was either lose the horses or risk almost certain capture ourselves. We naturally accepted the former. We walked the last twenty miles in six hours."

"I see," said General Nelson musingly. His mind was still deeply concerned with the fact that everything had been changed. He raised his eyes back to the two men standing before him. "I see. The Rebels have plagued us greatly in that section. Just where was this, Captain?"

"Cedar Knob, this side of Lebanon."

"Oh, yes." He was musing again. An uneasy feeling stirred within Beasley Nichol's breast. The ambulance carrying Fisheye would likely reach the hospital very soon. When it did, what would happen? Perhaps nothing immediately. But something would happen when the clerk emerged from the anesthesia of Goforth's pistol butt. That could not be doubted. They were standing there wasting time for which their lives might pay. Then he heard General Nelson speaking.

"I think horses can be provided. I will give you a note to our commissary."

He penned a few lines and handed it to Nichol, who hoped that the drumming of his heart was not audible. As the two men went out the door of the Cunningham House they heard General Nelson calling to his orderly to hurry up the summoning of his staff and remarking with emphasis that everything had been changed. The desperate creak of the chair sounded in Goforth's and Nichol's ears until they reached the street.

Out on the street Nichol's sense of magnificence rose above his awareness of the need for haste. He stopped and looked up at the Capitol and admiration kindled in his eyes. The blotches of war could not obscure the dominant stateliness with which it sat on the hill that towered high above the city. The folds of the United States flag rippled in the hot wind.

"That used to be my flag, Goforth," said Nichol with an odd wistfulness in his tones. "I still like it."

They stopped a passing soldier and asked directions to the jail. They turned north on Summer Street, passing by the Baptist Church and the fine home of Mrs. Felicia Porter. The Catholic Church gleamed white in the bright sunlight. They turned east on Cedar Street and Cousin Philip Yorke's complaint was turned into reality. The continuing rains and the interminable tramp of soldiers, the beat of horses' hoofs and the grind of wheels had laid waste not only the streets but the sidewalks as well. The sidewalks had been made of brick which yielded most disconcertingly to the impact and pressure of those walking. A pedestrian could feel the brick slipping, and he could see the mud oozing up between the joints.

An unending roll of wagons loaded with the implements of war lifted a sinister and jarring noise upon the summer afternoon. The cry of drillmasters on the Capitol grounds could be heard. The afternoon was hot and steamy and the uniforms of soldiers on the streets lay in drab limpness against their bodies. The sun which had been shining brightly dimmed and fell behind a bluish-tawny cloud. Beasley Nichol touched the sergeant's arm and pointed at the cloud, which meant that a wet night lay before them. Sergeant Goforth grunted briefly and shrugged his shoulders, which meant that the night just ahead carried more of menace than a mere rain.

They came presently to the quarters of the provost marshal, located in a squat little building sitting hard by the jail house. The marshal was out somewhere, but his deputy lolled obscenely in the office.

"We are in a very great hurry," Nichol told him. "I imagine you are authorized to act in his absence when the matter is definitely urgent."

"Oh, sure," said the deputy, vaguely complimented. He spat with emphasis into a corner.

Nichol handed him the order. The deputy squinted at it, then took from the desk a pair of heavy spectacles, which he adjusted carefully. Then he began reading the order. When he came to the signature his face brightened with pride. "Oh, signed by General Buell! Well, you can have the feller, though we aimed to hang him here."

"We would like to start immediately. This is important. General Buell is very anxious to question this man."

"Oh, sure. Come with me." He led them out into the yard, through a gateway in the side fence and then into the jail.

"Get me the feller in Number Nine," the deputy bawled to the turnkey. A few minutes later the turnkey came back bringing Hume Crockett. His face was of an ashen color, for it was in his mind that the call meant his life was at a crisis. His quick darting eyes fell upon his two friends standing in the dingy little office, and the color flowed back into his face. He started to say something but checked himself when he glimpsed their almost imperceptible gestures that he knew so well, the hands spread, palms downward, the fingers apart.

"Is your name Hume Crockett?" Nichol asked with cold formality. "Answer correctly, please."

"Yes."

"It is our mission to carry you to General Buell. I should warn you that if you make any effort to escape or if you resist commands we will be obliged to kill you. Further, if any attempt is made to rescue you our orders are to shoot you first. Is that clear?"

"Yes," said Hume Crockett, watching his captors warily, "but why am I to be taken to General Buell?"

"We were not told." He turned to the deputy. "Where is the commissary? We have orders for horses and we need them immediately."

There was no trouble about obtaining the horses, and they were reasonably good ones. They rode three abreast, west on Cedar Street.

"We've got to get out of Nashville," said Goforth. "We got to get out of here, I tell you. I feel it in my bones that there ain't much time to lose."

"It's my neck that's sensitive," said Nichol. "There's a red welt circling it now. Very prophetic, and I don't like the looks of that cloud either."

Goforth flicked a look at the inky-black cloud mounting the sky behind Capitol Hill, and as he did an ominous roll of thunder sounded among the hills that lined the lower stretches of the river. "That might help us," he said grimly, "and again it might wreck us. I'd like mighty well to be out of town when it hits."

"Did you see your girl, Crockett?" Nichol asked with curious irrelevance.

"No, I didn't," said Crockett, and with quiet sad humor he added, "I lacked just a half-hour of seeing her. I had it arranged, but . . ."

Nichol looked across at Goforth. "You know the town. What way out do you have in mind?"

"Not the way we came in, sir. If—if anything has happened they'll be watching, and I'm scared that something has happened. I've been thinking, sir, maybe we'd better go out Spruce Street, then cut across to the Nolensville Pike, and then take the Mill Creek Pike."

"Why out Spruce, Sergeant?"

"They might be watching Cherry Street, sir."

"We are in your hands, Sergeant. Only get us back to Bed Forrest. I won't be happy till you do."

"I didn't get to see my girl," said Crockett.

"I, too, met with certain frustrations, but life is like that. They will pass."

They reached High Street. "I think we'll turn here, sir. The soldiers'll be thicker on this end of Spruce. We'll cut across to it beyond Broad. It'll be safer there."

They rode by the Cunningham House, and from those milling about and going hurriedly in and out of the door they knew something exciting was finding its center there. While in front of it they stared steadily and stonily ahead. Once beyond it Nichol looked across at Goforth and winked. "This changes everything," and the voice with which he spoke was that of General William Nelson.

They crossed Church Street, and then they heard clearly borne on the tight sultry air the strains of "The Mourning Dove." Again the eyes of lieutenant and sergeant met. This was warning to all who heard and understood that danger was abroad. And then as if to give accent to the urgency of those plaintive strains the elements exploded in a terrific crash of thunder. When it echoed into silence they could still hear the song.

"Jest like I mourn for mine."

"I wish we was out o' town," said the sergeant. "They's something wrong here. I'm uneasy."

Nichol sighed. "I know a gem from Shakespeare that fits beautifully, but I guess I'd better not say it just at present. It's from *Julius Caesar,* first act, third scene. . . ."

"I guess you better not recite it," said Sergeant Goforth grimly. "They didn't have a fiddlin' man there, did they?"

"No, Sergeant. The fiddlin' man is our only improvement on the immortal Bard. I don't suppose Shakespeare ever thought of the fiddlin' man."

"I'm human," said Crockett, "and I'd like to know what is happening. I didn't think Old Bed would let them hang me, but you all have me puzzled."

"We're taking you to General Buell so he can hang you in person. That has long been his ambition. No, don't look so pained. It neutralizes your native beauty; a look of triumph is far more becoming. Maybe he'll do you a favor and have you shot. I'll request it personally. No, gentle friend, trust us a little while yet. We'll reveal everything just as soon as we are a little less hemmed in."

They rode across Broad Street. The thunder sounded almost continuously, and as they rode by South Union Street the rain fell in sudden and almost solid sheets.

"What'll we do, sir?" Sergeant Goforth lifted his voice to an urgent shout.

"We're going to stop in here," said Nichol. He pointed to Trinity Church, just before them. There dimly through the sheets of rain they could see a hitching rack at the door of the church, then required for use by the military. They threw themselves off the horses and the reins about the rack and dashed for the door, but they were drenched before they got inside.

The church was deserted as far as they could tell. They sank into seats and sat listening to the roar of the storm without.

"This perhaps is a good time to tell you our story, Crockett. Our life has not been dull."

"No," said Sergeant Goforth. He was mentioning figuratively that at times walls and floors may be sensitive to sound when a limb from a hackberry tree, torn by the power of the storm, crashed through one of the church's exquisite windows.

"There's somebody else coming," said Goforth. His keen ears had heard the splashing of horse's hoofs without.

"So there is," said Nichol. "I'll play host." He went to the door and opened it. The scene registered in an acute commingling of visibility: the rain falling in oblique sheets, the trees writhing under the twisting torture of the wind, a man running toward the doorway. And there in mid-air above the man was a great limb wrenched from a tree that stood at the corner of the church. Thoughts flashed through Nichol's mind in split seconds then. The horses! But he saw that the limb would not strike the horses. The man! Clearly the limb would strike the church steps at the instant the man reached them. At Princeton and elsewhere Nichol had played games involving the sudden and complete use of his legs. He sprang propelled by splendid muscles and struck the man below his waist, struck him with force that threw him outward and down. With a grunt that sounded above the storm the man and Nichol went down together, burrowing in the mud of the churchyard. And their fall was in unison with the crash of the limb upon the stone steps of Trinity Church. So great was its impact that twigs and leaves torn from the main body rebounded and showered upon the two men lying in the mud.

Nichol struggled to his feet. "Get up," he said. "I don't think you're killed."

The man rose on one knee, struggling audibly to recover his breath. "By Gad, sir, may I ask what——"

Nichol's peal of laughter sounded unreal and grotesque against the storm. "Of course you may ask, Cousin Philip, but let's get out of this rain first."

Then Yorke saw the great limb lying across the steps. "Oh!" he said, "oh! It's you. What are you doing here? Why, cousin, you saved my life."

"I owed you that much. I always take a personal interest in my kinfolks, and save their lives frequently. Come in or you'll drown. I'd hate to go to that much trouble for nothing."

They climbed over the fallen limb and went inside. "You saved my life," Major Yorke repeated.

"That was the Noel in me," said Nichol. "That's the part of me I use in emergencies."

"It's decidedly the better branch," said Major Yorke, wiping his face furiously.

"You met Sergeant Bowie at breakfast, cousin. Of course, you did. This is—is, why, Captain Crockett. My cousin, Major Yorke." Nichol paused, and then decided to keep on talking to provide his companions time for adjustment. "Just imagine, cousin, our meeting so surprisingly twice in the same day. I never heard of anything like it. Why, it's beyond all understanding. It's like a play. What, may I ask, brought you here, cousin?"

"What brought me here? This thunder, this lightning, this wind, this rain, this mud brought me here. They're the wretchedness of my life, the plague of my declining years. . . ."

"Declining years, my word! You're relatively a mere infant. According to your years you ought to delight in mud. What lovely things the very young can fashion of mud!"

"I never saw mud in Trenton. I knew nothing of it till I came here. Here I find nothing else."

"So I am mud, for you found me here."

"You're nothing of the kind. You're excellent flesh and blood. You're just a wallower in it as I am." His interest turned from mud to other matters. "I find you here just in the nick of time to preserve me from the wrath of my special foes, the elements. How did that happen, cousin?"

"It was arranged by the destiny of wind and rain. We were on our way to rejoin General Buell, and on most important business."

"It's about stopped," said Goforth, his ear on the storm outside. "We'd better get started. We've got to be going. It's about stopped."

"It never stops in this loblolly patch. All day I have drilled soldiers in ankle-deep—no, knee-deep mud. I ought to be entitled to a little freedom from it at night, but am I? I dismissed the men a half-hour early. I thought when I left

Fort Negley I could surely get to the Saint Cloud undrowned, but I should have judged the place better. By the by, I saw you talking to Fisheye at the hotel. What did you think of him?"

Nichol's mind staggered a bit in surprise, but he decided quickly. "He seemed a bit annoying to me."

"He'd be comfortable in mud, that snake! I wouldn't trust him even if I thought I could. I wouldn't commit myself even against this weather in his presence. Do you know what I think? Well, I think he's a spy."

"Surely not that, cousin. What kind of spy?"

"What other kind is there? I'm a bit delicate. I never look at him before I go in to eat."

"It's time to go," said Sergeant Goforth.

Nichol went to the door and looked at a drenched world and then at the sky.

"So it is. Good-by, cousin."

As they rode away from the church Nichol turned a glance back over his shoulder. His cousin was indeed an interesting man. Perhaps it was the Noel in him.

They bore to the right and presently reached Spruce Street. They had to ride carefully, for trees were lying across the streets. The late sun was breaking through the clouds, and a new freshness and buoyancy had come into the air. There was the feel of that vitality which follows every summer rain in Middle Tennessee, life and beauty combined into a single phenomenon! They watched the sun sink into the shadows behind the Belmont hill. The storm had not had its full fling yet, for the dull flame of sheet lightning was so continuous that it seemed almost to stand still in a cloud that lifted above the Litton home out on Hillsboro Road. By the time they had reached Woodstock and the Elliott home across the road shadows soft and vaguely purple had imparted to the land a sort of tranquil twilight and everywhere a million fireflies sparkled with incandescence. Everywhere growing things swung an unseen censer of fragrance.

They met many riders, all inbound, and a few foot soldiers sloshed toward town along the wet roadside. But they noticed that no one traveled to the south.

"I don't like it the way they look at us," said Sergeant Goforth. "It keeps me worried. Them officers look at us like we was a-doin' sumpin' wrong."

"I've noticed their interest, too. Well, let them look—if they'll stop at that."

As they neared Melrose they saw that their way was blocked by a soldier on horseback sitting squarely across the pike. They started to ride around him on the edge of the pike but they were halted sharply.

"Where you going?"

"We have passes issued by General Buell. We are on special service for him."

"General Buell? Where is he?"

"Stevenson, Alabama, or near."

"This isn't the way to Stevenson, Alabama."

"I was afraid we had taken the wrong road. Will you direct us, please?"

"I'll direct you back to town. You won't be seeing General Buell yet awhile. All passes are canceled."

"Canceled? Why?"

"General Forrest's on a rampage. May be going to attack the town. That's all I know."

"General Forrest! Where is he?"

"He was out on the Murfreesboro Pike before the storm. All I know now is he ain't passed here."

"I'm sorry but you must let us by."

"I ain't got the right."

"Well, maybe you haven't, but we have," said Nichol, and brought his whip stingingly down upon the hindquarters of the soldier's horse. The startled animal wheeled with such sudden violence that its riders was thrown clear of the saddle. He grabbed frantically at the horn of the saddle, missed, and fell shoulders first into the roadside mud. By then the three men were galloping furiously out the Franklin Pike.

"You're in charge, Sergeant. You get us to Bed Forrest, soon and safe."

"I ain't a bit popeyed about tonight," said the sergeant grimly. "It's got me puzzled pretty bad. I never yet seen things so mixed up."

"That turnkey at the jail had me scared," said Hume Crockett. "It looked like——"

"You looked like they always look just before," said Nichol. "The very presentiment of woe."

"But all the time I knew that General Forrest would be sending somebody after me. I figured it might be you. But even if he did I couldn't imagine what you'd do."

"We have had some funny luck," said Nichol. "You don't think it's about to run out, do you, Sergeant?"

"It might be," answered Goforth gloomily. "It sure might be." Then he essayed a touch of humor. "It's mighty nigh got me buffaloed."

They rode on at a gallop. "Here's where we turn," said Goforth. They turned in at Thompson's Lane.

"If General Forrest was on the Murfreesboro Pike this afternoon, where would he be now?" Nichol was asking the question as much of himself as of the others.

"Just as soon as we get out where it's safe I'm a-goin' to start finding out."

"There's one pleasing augury," said Nichol. "All the Yankees seem to be going into town. I could be wrong, as I have been so oft before, but it's my guess Bed's got them buffaloed. What's that?"

"That" was the faint crackle of musketry perhaps two miles ahead of them.

"If I ain't turned around purty bad that'd be on Mill Creek Pike just about the church," said the sergeant. "Maybe our luck ain't a-goin' to run out."

But it had—at least for the time being. They rounded a curve in the road, and suddenly saw the dim sinister outlines of men on horseback by the margins of the road. There were fully a dozen of them. Then, as their eyes adjusted to the darkness, the figures moved across Thompson's Lane, blocking it, and a harsh voice called, "Stop! Stop, I say. Stop, or we'll fire!"

This might be Bed Forrest's men. They slowed to a canter, approaching warily.

"Drop your guns or we'll blow your heads off." They knew then that their luck had run out. It was a voice that never belonged to one of Forrest's men.

"Ride through them," said Nichol with sharp savagery in his voice. Those were good horses which General Nelson had provided. They hit the group blocking the road with the impact of a cavalry charge. A gun went off aimlessly.

"Kill them. Don't let them by!" the voice yelled. Crockett and the sergeant bored their way through. Nichol's horse was better blocked. His horse was almost clear, but the last man he had to pass swung at him with a clubbed musket. In the darkness he sensed rather than saw the descending rifle butt. He leaned to one side, and the blow fell upon his horse. The outraged horse reared, then plunged, but by that time a trooper reined in and grabbed the bridle. Nichol saw that the man's hold on the reins would not be broken. He swung off the horse, landing on his feet in the middle of the road. A shadowy figure also dismounted and rushed upon him. Nichol's fist crashed home to the jaw and the man went down with a grunt. That threw Nichol off balance and while he was recovering another man spurred in and clubbed him hard and effectively on the head. And as his mind faded into unconsciousness he heard the hoarse voice yelling, "Get the other two. Don't let them get away." Dimly, he heard horses galloping out the road in pursuit of his friends.

THE crude ambulance jolted its way south on Summer Street to Broad, then to Market, then south to the main University of Nashville building which at the time was used as a hospital for Union troops. They climbed the hill crowned on the right by the Howard School, and on the left by Cherry Hill. The horses were hot and weary and wet with sweat which in spots the harness had churned to a foam.

"He ain't stirred a finger. Reckon he's dead?" asked the ambulance driver.

"Saves a passel o' trouble when they die quick," answered the driver's companion. "I ain't for draggin' such things out myself."

"Must be terrible onhealthy here. Looks like a lot o' 'em gettin' free rides gratis in this half-breed hearse we usin'. Five already today."

"There'll be more'n this if they don't keep General Forrest away. They say there was a snake bit him once and died immediately. Yes sir, five already and when we unload him we got to go to Fort Negley for a couple more. Mighty on-healthy!"

"Fort Negley! Looks like it'd be plain civil to start a spell o' sickness where we could get to 'em without too much trouble. At Fort Negley we have to carry 'em half a mile, and practically down a bluff at that."

"We goes where we're told," said the other sententiously. "In this army a man ain't got no rights."

"I think a foot soldier's got a flowery bed o' ease compared with us. They can get sick and get a free ride to a hospital and the doctors cut off their laigs and won't charge 'em a cent. We ain't even entitled to get sick. I say it's a funny war."

"Anyhow it's better'n some. In the Revolutionary War wasn't anybody entitled to get sick."

"What'd they do if you did?"

"A man got sick and he had General Gawge Washington in person to deal with. After that he got well mighty sudden-like and then he didn't try it no more."

"What's the matter? Ain't we got no good generals? Oh, so he's startin' up."

His reference was to a deep groan which emerged from the rear of the ambulance. There followed a second groan and then a third one even deeper.

"Look out. Better watch him. He's liable to get vi'lent. They do sometimes."

He did get violent. The sheets were convulsed, thrown aside, and the figure with a sort of lunge sat bolt upright in the bed of the spring wagon which necessity had metamor-phosed into an ambulance. The man's hair was sparse and sandy and in advanced disarrangement. His eyes were bulg-ing, and his face was brick-red.

"What am I doing here?" he yelled.

"Just a-takin' a nice ride," the driver of the ambulance

said soothingly. "We'll be there drekly. Just you don't go and get excited."

"Where was I? Where'd you get me? Was I at the Saint Cloud Hotel?"

The driver's assistant saw that the sick man was about to spring from the wagon, so he quickly climbed to the back of the wagon and with a brawny hand pushed the struggling man back on the mattress. "You be quiet," he growled. "I don't want to be rough with a sick man. We're about there."

"Let me out." Memory was returning. "They tried to kill me, that's what they done, tried to kill me. I'll hang 'em! Let me out. I'm with General Negley."

"Oh, he is! Well, that's relievin'," said the man who was driving. "I was afraid he was with General Napoleon Bonaparte. Still, I'm glad we're just about rid o' him."

They drove up to the front of the stone building. An officer came hurrying to meet them.

"Who is this man?" he asked crisply. "He's not the one for whom you were sent."

"Yes sir, Colonel. We got him at the Saint Cloud Hotel."

"Let me loose," yelled Fisheye. "Let me loose, I tell you. Send for General Negley."

"There has been some mistake," said the colonel. "This man is not Captain Joynes."

"He's the one we got at the Saint Cloud."

"What sort of foolish mistake is this? This is not the one we sent you for. It's not Captain Joynes." He turned to the man struggling to leave the ambulance. "Who are you?"

"Send for General Negley. Send for him. He knows who I am. He'll tell you."

"Let him out. We'll find out who he is. You go back immediately to the Saint Cloud and bring Captain Joynes. And hurry! I don't want any mistake this time."

"But we got orders to go to Fort Negley for two sick men there," said the driver.

"You have orders to get Captain Joynes at the Saint Cloud. Go get him."

"Yes sir, Colonel."

"Take me back with you!" yelled the man. "I've got to get back, I tell you. I've got to. They tried to murder me."

He took a folder from his pocket and from it a card which he handed to the colonel. The colonel, obviously puzzled, read it.

" I don't understand this at all. But I want Captain Joynes here quickly. If this man wants to go back with you, take him. I'm going to find out what this means. It won't hurt to stir those nags out of a walk. I want Captain Joynes brought back here and I'll wait till you bring him."

They turned the ambulance around and left in a trot. There was more need for hurry than the mingled pleas and commands from the rear of the wagon. An angry cloud was mounting rapidly in the southwest.

"I know now how it happened," the man shouted. "I know now. One of them was hiding in the closet. I hadn't got to search it yet. This is one hanging I wouldn't miss. Can't those plugs go any faster? They tried to kill me. Good God, how my head aches!"

The driver of the ambulance called back over his shoulder, "What happened to you, anyhow? You were deader'n a kite when we carried you out."

"They tried to murder me. Can't you go any faster?"

"Who tried to murder you?"

"Two Rebel spies. I'll watch 'em hang."

The rain hit them halfway up the hill after they crossed Broad Street. And all three were drenched when they entered the Saint Cloud. Fisheye was unsteady on his feet and the two men helped him. The clerk at the desk looked curiously at his colleague, then his gaze shifted to the waiting ambulance men.

"You certainly take your time," he said in tones edged with sarcasm. "They've been waiting for two hours for you to pick up that sick captain in Number 30. Maybe he's dead by now. He could be as far as anything you've done."

"We got the man we thought was him. Anyhow, we can't take him out in this weather."

"If he's still living you can take him. Put a tarpaulin over him. You get him to that hospital." The men went up the stairs. Fisheye sat down on a chair in the lobby.

"Where've you been?" the other clerk asked him, regarding him with interest. "What on earth happened to you? You look like a couple o' barns fell on you."

"Where's Otis?"

"Don't know where he is. Haven't seen him for—well, maybe two hours. The way you're looking you better get you a dram. There he is now coming in at the door."

A man came down the hall, raindrops showering from him at every step he took. He stopped at the desk. "What happened to you, Bailey? You look——"

"Let's go to the room. I want to talk to you."

The two sat in Fisheye's room.

"And what have you to report?"

Otis shrugged his shoulder, waiving further interest in Bailey's looks. "I stayed here like you told me. One of the men came and went upstairs. Maybe ten minutes later, maybe it was fifteen, I don't know, both of them come down. They went from here to headquarters at the Cunningham House."

"What for?"

"How should I know? They went in but they didn't stay very long. Then from there they went to the jail, and when they come away from there there was another man with them. . . ."

"Who was he?"

"How should I know? I never saw him before. Then they went to the commissary and got horses, and I borrowed one and rode along after them. I couldn't make heads or tails out of the way they went. It didn't make no sense to me. It started pouring cats and dogs and they hitched their horses and went inside the stone church at High and Ewing. I left them there and come on back here to tell you. I guess they're still there. That's all I know."

"That's plenty," said Bailey grimly. "I don't know what happened, but I'll find out. Otis, you take four or five good men and get out to that church fast. If they are still there you get them. Don't kill them if you can help it. I got other uses for them, but dead or alive, you get them. I doubt if they are there, though. But go see."

Otis left. Fisheye stood musing. "They were afraid to leave by the Lebanon or Murfreesboro Pikes. They thought these might be too well watched. They might try the Nolensville Pike, but I doubt it. More likely they'd go out Spruce till they got clear out of the town and then bend east to join General Forrest. Why, Thompson's Lane, of course! Now, who was the one they got at the jail? The jail! Why, we had a spy there. It was him, of course. Why, of course, it was. That'll make a real hanging. But what'd they want at the Cunningham House? Oh, yes, he said he was wanting to see General Nelson. And the general was there then! Well, I'll find out."

He studied a map on the wall. "They won't use either the Franklin or Nolensville Pike very far. That isn't where they are going. But it's the best way to get out of town, anyhow the Franklin Pike is. Then when they're out of town they'll bear east till they get to the Rebels. Let's see, there's

Thompson's Lane. . . . That's the place. That makes sense.
Where's Herb? I want Herb and his men. We've got to
catch 'em. Where's Herb? Oh, I know where he is." He left
the hotel, walking in a curious but rapid hobble.

"Light that lantern," commanded the rough voice. A sudden
light flickered in the darkness, and one of the men handed
the lighted lantern to the popeyed clerk at the Saint Cloud.
He smiled evilly as the light fell upon the face of the unconscious man lying in the mud of Thompson's Lane.

"It's him, all right. Well, I thought it would be," he said
with obvious satisfaction. "And tell them at the jail I'll have
the man shot who lets him get away. They won't have to
keep him long," he added as a grim postscript. "Who went
after them others?"

"Cal and Aleck and two more," one of the men told him.

"They have good horses?"

"The best we got."

"They'll catch 'em. We'll wait here awhile and see. Herb,
you and Frank get this feller to jail. Your horse'll carry
double, Herb. Don't let him die. I want to hang him myself.
Tell them at the jail what I said." He mused a moment. "I
wonder how they got by that sentry? Maybe they killed him.
How much start did they have on Cal and Aleck?"

"Maybe three hundred yards. Things happened right fast.
They ought to catch 'em somewhere clost to the church."

"They'd better catch 'em. I want both of them. I want

them mighty bad. We'll wait here till they git back. Take this one on to jail. Shoot him if he tries to get loose. We'll bring the other two when the men get back. Tomorrow or next day this town is going to see a first-rate hanging."

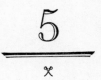

CAPTAIN CROCKETT and Sergeant Goforth were old hands at a military adaptation of the game of hare and hounds. Presently, they rode into a side road and waited until their pursuers had clattered by. They knew they would run a risk going on ahead. The rifle fire out by the church had indicated the presence of the enemy there in force. It would be suicidal to be caught between two bodies of the enemy.

"On a guess where'd you say Bed is?"

"Well," said Goforth, "if I was a hound and he was a fox I'd say somewheres about Kingsley."

"I suppose they got Nichol," said Crockett.

"It looked like they had him hemmed in. What do you think we ought to do?"

"Later we'll have to go get him back. I knew we couldn't stop then. Right now we must get to General Forrest just as soon as we can. We both know some things that he needs to. I guess you're right about Kingsley. If he isn't there he isn't far away. Now, I know a side road that the Yankees never heard of. What's that?"

They sat on their horses listening. From the road came the sound of a few shots and some shouting. Crockett slapped the mane of his horse in a joyful gesture.

"A good old Forrest trick. We've seen him do it twenty times, Sergeant."

"It works," said the sergeant dryly. "Block them in front and maneuver some men behind 'em. It's worked before. Sounds like it worked this time."

"It isn't a bit safe to gallop merrily on when Bed Forrest is just ahead."

"Because you might find that he's just behind you, too. Bed can be in two places any time."

"Precisely, Sergeant. Let's go hunt up the general now. We have another assignment a little later on. Nichol quote any Shakespeare for you, Sergeant?"

"Listen," said the sergeant, "that man can talk wilder'n a bat and crazier than a hoot owl."

They knew General Forrest and his ways and means; so they found him exactly where they figured they would, at Kingsley, the home of the Weaver Coles. The general, with Captain Morton and Dr. Plunkett, both old friends of the owners of Kingsley and in the days of peace frequent visitors to the place, was sitting with Mrs. Cole. Crockett and Goforth were conducted to the house by the sergeant whom they had first encountered.

"Two men to see you, General."

General Forrest came out into the yard. The light from the chandelier in the hall fell upon the faces of the two men in blue uniforms.

"Well, I'll be kicked by a five-legged steer!" said the general with sudden and strong emotion. "Couldn't be two fellers anywhere I'd ruther see. Where's that Beasley Nichol?"

"They got him, General."

"Got him? Who got him? You mean the Yankees?"

"Yes sir."

"Sometime them Yankees goin' to make me mad! Then watch out! You have any news for me?"

"I've got what you wanted to know, General."

They went out to the stile block and the general sat on it while Crockett told him what Nichol had found out. When he had finished General Forrest shook his head with solemn vigor.

"I didn't make any mistake when I sent you. And I didn't when I sent Nichol after you. This is worth a gold mine to me. When do you want to start back?"

"You mean to get Nichols?"

"He's the only one you lost, ain't he? He got that dispatch from Buell, didn't he? We can't let 'em hang a feller like that. Don't leave the sergeant with them this time. Sometime I might think up some use for him, too. I've been trying and sometime it'll come to me jest like a flash."

"I don't suppose they killed Nichol. He wouldn't be easy to kill. I suppose they'd rather take him prisoner. Then they'd take him to jail. That's where we'll find him."

"Any idea how, Captain?"

"Well, to save trouble I was thinking of trading them the sergeant for him, but if you want to keep Goforth, I suppose I'll have to think up something else."

"The time might come when you'd need me," said Goforth humorously. "I'm getting to be a reg'lar expert at rescuin'."

"If we went in by the Murfreesboro Pike, where would we first find the Yankees, General?"

"I'd say at Lafayette Street. They're too scared to come this side of it."

"I'm thinking," said Crockett, "that we'll approach them from the north. They won't be expecting visitors from that direction. By doing an extra bit of riding we can come in by the Buena Vista Pike. That'd make us real Yankees, wouldn't it?"

Presently Crockett and Goforth mounted their horses and rode away into the darkness of the little side road that Goforth knew about but the Yankees didn't. It was raining steadily.

BEASLEY NICHOL knew that something was wrong long before he returned to consciousness. It was as if all of the ache in the world had gathered in his head. He knew that he tossed interminably on his bed—or was it a bed?—but he couldn't think why or where. Vaguely he was afraid that he had been groaning. Echoes of something that sounded like groans dinned fitfully in his ears. He hoped he hadn't been groaning because he didn't like to groan, or to hear people who did. But he felt sure that he had been groaning. He was sure he wouldn't groan without a good reason. All right, but what was his reason? He stirred, and found another acute and overwhelming pain spreading across his middle. The dim foggy notion came to him that someone had been carrying him face downward across a horse, and that the swaying motion of the horse had caused the horn of the saddle to wear itself into his vitals. He tried to think but thoughts wouldn't penetrate that barrier of pain.

He couldn't get his eyes open but he knew that it wasn't night. He felt rather than saw the light of day. Another pain came from somewhere and distressed him sorely. He searched for it and discovered that it was thirst. He turned this way and that, struggling to get up but couldn't quite make it. When he moved the pain in his body was more agonizing than that in his head. It must have been the horn of a saddle. The notion persisted.

Then he remembered. And as he did his eyes opened and he saw where he was. In the cell of a jail, a wretched cell. It was a filthy rag covering some filthier straw that he had been lying on. He sat up as memory flooded back into him. Where were Crockett and Goforth? That would mean that they had escaped. If he could judge those two hardy spirits aright they were back with General Forrest by now. That was fine—but it left him in a precarious plight. The Yankees might get to use some of their hanging rope after all. Well, he wouldn't mount that scaffold until they built it. Besides, it wouldn't be like General Forrest to take no steps in such an emergency. Crockett and Goforth would not remain idle. He laughed suddenly.

"Traded Crockett for me! Why, it's as good as a play. It *is* a play. How does it end, I wonder?"

He stood up carefully, went to the window and peered out between the bars. *"The gray-eyed morn smiles on the frowning night,"* he said, and there was music in the tones. And then the sun broke from behind the clouds and brightness flooded the world.

"Why, gray-eyed no longer! It's an omen. All is well. My head aches no longer." He drew his hand across his front and grimaced. "Now where did I get that? Did the withers of a horse have to do with that bruise? Of course! I was brought here on a horse. Before that . . . we were going out Thompson's Lane and we ran into them. I was thrown off my horse. And one of them struck me with a rifle stock. Whose voice was that I seem to remember? Aha, so he was there waiting. Well, he's got a solid head, the way the sergeant struck him. And he was there waiting! The man *is* positively cunning. He's more dangerous than we thought. How does one get out of here?" He looked carefully around the room, and sighed his answer, "One doesn't." Then his native optimism reasserted itself, and he said, "But, of course, one does."

He sat down on the cell's lone and rickety chair, and as he bent a sharp and involuntary groan escaped him, the protest of bruised flesh against the twist and strain of bending.

"I must be out of here before Fisheye shows up. He will presently and I don't want to see him. His manners are atrocious. He would annoy me."

Keys jangled at the door and one grated in the lock. It opened and a man came in, a tin plate held in his hand and on the plate a slab of fried salt meat and a hunk of bread.

Inspiration flashed into Nichol's mind, flashed hard and bright. This was his chance. If it failed he had nothing to lose. He rose to his feet and stood erect, and though the movement cost him breath-gripping pain, no hint of it crossed his face. He had played roles for the admiration and wonder of audiences, but now his role was for his life. Get the act over before Fisheye came! He ignored the proffered food.

"Take that stuff away. I wouldn't touch it. Stand aside."

"Ef you don't like these fine vittles you don't have to eat 'em. But you ain't a-goin' nowhere." The man's free hand strayed toward a pistol, all too visible in a holster at his right side.

"Listen," said Nichol and there was patient pleading in his voice: "I know it's a good joke but it has gone far enough. If I am held here longer I shall be compelled to tell the whole story to General Buell, and that would cause somebody trouble."

"It's you that's in trouble." There was a leer on the man's face, and a gesture to the throat.

Nichol remained patient. "You know why I am here, don't you?"

"Course I do. Here's where they put spies—till they hang 'em."

"All right. Save your jail for spies. Go ahead and hang them if you want to. Will you stand aside?"

"You ain't a-goin' nowhere till they h'ist you up. So you don't want them fancy vittles! Well, it's that much saved. We'll feed 'em to the next spy."

"Spies! Spies!" There was drama in the way those words rose and fell in the dingy cell. "What have spies to do with me? I am no spy. Don't you know that I am an officer in the Union army—your army? Stand aside."

"Now, me," said the man with a show of mock modesty, "I ain't a-claimin' I'm Jeff Davis. But if I was a Reb spy I might. Sometimes they ack funny."

"Did someone tell you I was a spy?"

"That's what they said and I reckon that's what they aim to hang you fer."

"Are you serious?" Incredulity was in Nichol's eyes.

"Me, I'd call it ser'us. Any time I'm three or four hours from havin' my neck stretched—yes sir, ser'us is what I'd call it."

"Spies! Spies! So I am a spy!" There was art in the way his words rose and fell in that dingy cell. "So General Buell gives a pass signed by himself to a spy!" With a magnificent gesture he brought from his pocket an envelope. "So General Buell sends a Rebel spy on an important errand to Nashville! So General Buell—wait till he hears of this. . . ."

And now the man was puzzled. "You plain out o' yo' head."

"Listen: I don't know whether you know this is all a stupid joke or not but you're wasting my time. I was sent to Nashville by General Buell on urgent business. I must get back to him. Immediately!"

"They said for me to stick to you like you was glue."

"Of course they did. It was their notion of a joke. They were friends of mine—but no longer. I had, God forgive me, drunk too much. They brought me here. I was half unconscious but it all comes back to me. General Buell shall hear the whole story. Let me out, I tell you."

The man was impressed. "They'll be back drekly. Ef you ain't no spy they can let you out then."

"*Then!* And the minutes stretching into hours!" He took the pass from the envelope, unfolded it and held it before the man's eyes. "Read that!" he cried. "That says pass me. Look whose signature that is. It is General Buell's. Now, will you let me out of here?"

"They's a sergeant in the office, but he's asleep. I'll wake him up ef you say so."

"Look at that pass. Would I have it if I was a Rebel spy? I haven't time to wait for you to rouse your sergeant. A pass like that gives you just as much right to let me out as President Lincoln has."

"Orders is orders."

"Not when they are part of a silly joke. Think how much time I've already lost. *Tomorrow, and tomorrow, and tomorrow, creeps in this petty pace from day to day.*" He stopped suddenly and his voice dropped from rich melancholy to a deadly intensity. "For the last time I tell you that I am on General Buell's staff. For the last time I show you the pass he signed. Will you permit me to leave now?"

The gesture was convincing. The man hesitated a little, then held the door open.

"Go on," he said. "I guess they'll skin me alive when they find out about it."

"Never! They'll thank you. They would not care to face me. You have, my dear sir, rendered fine service to our cause. I shall henceforth remain sober."

He walked rapidly to the street. He continued to walk

rapidly south on Market Street. But he slowed his gait abruptly when it occurred to him that too many others had seen
him, had seen him walk. Presently everyone on the streets
would be under scrutiny. He smiled and nodded his head in
assent. The idea pleased him. He proceeded on down Market
Street but there was a dragging limp in his walk, and a hint
of pain crossed his face to accent the downbeat of his left
leg. Several whom he passed looked at him with compassion
in their glances. Doubtless a hero from the wars. One officer
paused, bowed courteously, and said, "Shiloh, Captain?"

"Not at all, sir. I was at Shiloh but it was a picnic compared
with the rebel Forrest in the mountains. I am fortunate, sir,
to be alive."

"They say he is bad medicine."

"You don't get well of anything you take him for." He
murmured a mild little "ouch" and grabbed his leg.

"War is bad business. I wish you well, sir." The man
bowed politely and passed on.

A few steps later Nichol turned right on Union Street. He
knew where he was going. The idea had wandered around
the periphery of his mind while he was engaged in the ha-
rangue with the jailer, and it had met with firm resolve while
he had been verifying the reports current of General Forrest.
He was going to pay another visit to the cobbler on Cherry
Street. Perhaps forgery was not the sole art practiced there.
He was concerned with an art at which he had certain dex-
terity if only the materials were provided. He turned on
Union Street, and he was very alert then, his senses sharp.
He wished to hurry but caution held him to normal progress.
The little beads of perspiration that stood thickly upon his
face as he turned into the cobbler's shop were not from the
heat, nor wholly from the dull ache in his head and the gall-
ing pain across his middle.

The cobbler looked up from his work, tacks held between his lips. He turned back and drove home a half-dozen tacks. He took the rest from his lips and said, "I thought you got him out."

"We did. Shall we talk here?"

The man put his tools aside and led the way into the little room which he had visited the day before. He motioned Nichol to speak.

When the story had been told the cobbler sat for a moment in silence. Then he said, "You can stay here till things are safer."

"Thank you, but I think they'd be worse. I expect Captain Crockett and the sergeant to be coming for me and I want to get out of town and back to General Forrest before things get all mixed up again."

"What do you want, Lieutenant?"

"First, some salve. They carried me across a horse last night and left the front part of me practically a pulp. Second, I need a disguise. They'll be watching for me. Without one I doubt if I'd get out of town."

"Aaron isn't here."

"He's the one who helped me before?"

"Yes, he'll be here after a while."

"Has he any beards or false hair? I could put them on myself. I must hurry."

The cobbler's eyes searched the face of the other as if to pry loose any hidden thoughts. He motioned Nichol to follow him. He moved aside some chairs, a table and a tall mirror, and a door stood revealed. The cobbler rapped once, then opened the door and went inside.

A girl sat at a table sewing, and Beasley Nichol's quick eyes saw that the garment upon which she was working was the blouse of a Union uniform. After his first glance he knew

that the effect of this girl upon his vision was extremely pleasing. He was conscious of the brightness which her red hair
and blue eyes imparted to the dingy little room. He heard
the voice of the cobbler saying, "Miss Hunter, you can help
this gentleman. Miss Hunter Cragwall, Lieutenant Beasley
Nichol of General Forrest's command."

Surely this was no ordinary cobbler. And then he heard
the voice that belonged to that hair, that face, those eyes, saying, "I shall do what I can to help, and with pleasure. How
do you do, Lieutenant Nichol?"

Nichol's eyes widened and his hands lifted in a gesture of
great surprise, and when he spoke it was in the tones of in-
finite wonder and pleading, *"She speaks:—O speak again,
bright angel!"*

"I have heard much of Lieutenant Nichol. I believe, Lieutenant, that you formerly played with Forrest."

"Oh," he said, "oh! That I played with Forrest! How did
you hear that?"

"Lucy Stratton told me. You made a deep impression on
her, Lieutenant Nichol."

"Lieutenant Nichol wishes to be disguised," said the cobbler dryly.

"I could try, but it would be difficult," said Hunter Cragwall. "Lieutenant Nichol's personality would be hard to
obscure. It is indeed very vivid. I would have known him
anywhere from Lucy's description. I imagine you wish to get
back through the enemy's lines, Lieutenant."

"Yes, back to General Forrest."

"Will the enemy be looking for you quite diligently, Lieutenant Nichol?"

"Very. I would, I fear, provide them with the diversion of
a public hanging."

She looked at him gravely. "I doubt if you hang easily,

Lieutenant. The enemy would, I think, find you troublesome. Lucy seemed to think that you are quite resourceful."

"When did you see her?"

"Why, yesterday. Yes, it was yesterday. She would be most excited if she knew you were in Nashville. She is—oh, so deeply in love with a Southern officer."

"Who?" His voice was hoarse.

"I am not at liberty to say, but she would be delighted to tell you."

"Lieutenant Nichol is in a hurry," said the cobbler and left the room.

"Of course! How silly of me to waste his time." She opened a drawer and placed on the table before her an assortment of wigs and hair, pieces of cork for burning, and a bottle partly filled with a tincture of black-walnut hulls.

A half-hour later Lieutenant Nichol looked into a cracked mirror and gasped, for it was another man he saw there, a bewhiskered, swarthy man. Even his nose bore an alien cast.

"Disguises aren't my specialty, though I have worked a little at them. I am really much better at uniforms. I spend most of my time on them. By the way, Lieutenant, that uniform you are wearing is good. May I ask who made it?"

"I don't know," he said soberly, and there was for the instant in the mind's eye the picture of a grave between the stones among the cedars. "But it ought to be a good one. I got it from a Yankee officer."

"Oh," she said, and there was a pause full of strain. He turned from the mirror and stood looking at her. His eyes were bright and his breathing a trifle irregular. She was very beautiful, more beautiful than anyone he had ever seen. He knew that the whole course of his life had been changed while she adjusted sideburns and complexion, and recast his nose.

"Lucy talks about you all the time," she said. "Well, most

of the time. How long has it been since you saw her, Lieutenant? Oh, I know, two years. It was the summer she spent at Beersheba Springs. I should think you'd have been to Nashville long before this. I don't understand it at all. Such inaction doesn't become you, Lieutenant Nichol."

"My inactive days are over. Hereafter . . ."

"Are you in very grave danger?"

"Yes," he said huskily, "I think I am, and my life is much more precious to me than it was an hour ago."

"Oh, since you have heard from Lucy?"

"No, since I have seen you."

"Since your life has become so precious, shouldn't you be going?"

"Yes," he said, "but I'll be back. And when I come will I find you here?"

"I work here whenever I am needed. I'll be at my home if I'm not here—of course, that is, if I'm not staying with the Yankees then."

"I'll find you, my dear, even if you are—are staying with the Yankees."

"Leave the Yankees alone, Lieutenant. The less you have to do with them the better."

"Better for whom?"

"For all of us. I should like for you to come to my home. There are only my father and mother there, but I'd ask Lucy, so it wouldn't be lonesome."

"What about her Southern officer? Couldn't you ask him? If I could get there, couldn't he?"

"Why, yes, I think he could. Yes, I think he'd love to come. You really must go now."

He moved a reluctant step toward the camouflaged door. Then with sudden and strong decision he turned, pivoting about, and caught her fiercely into his arms and held her, held her with his lips firmly pressed against hers, held her while the golden seconds passed. After a little while he released her.

"When may I come back?"

"Whenever you can—whenever you can come safely," she said a little breathlessly.

Again he paused at the door, his tongue feeling and tasting and longing to utter the song from *Love's Labour's Lost,* *"Love . . . spied a blossom passing fair,"* but thought better of it and went hurriedly out the door, leaving the girl standing there, breathing in little gasps, her eyes shining. Then she closed her eyes and stood a moment longer. Presently she returned to the table and began to sew on the blouse.

Beasley Nichol stopped before the cobbler. The gaunt man studied him in minute detail.

"Very good indeed, Lieutenant. I doubt if General Forrest would know you. Here's the salve. Wouldn't you like to apply it before you leave?"

"No," said Beasley Nichol. "I do not need it now. The pain is entirely gone. I don't even remember where it was. I don't remember that I ever felt it."

The gaunt man looked after Nichol's retreating figure. Almost he permitted himself to smile.

THE weather was still hot, and the feel of rain was in the still sultry air. White feathery clouds, fragments of heavier clouds that lay banked against the horizon, scudded from the southwest.

Out on Cherry Street Nichol fell into his dragging limp. It was the sort of thing he had seen Edwin Forrest do in *Richard III,* and he felt with a tingling of pride that his act would not shame his old preceptor. But his pain was coming back. He got along well for more than a block, but something went wrong, some mist was before his eyes and he stumbled and saved himself by grasping firmly a young sycamore tree standing at the margin of the street. He had said at the cobbler's that his bruises were well. That was because he was then numb to pain. But now his bruises hurt him so horribly that he steadied himself by holding onto the tree.

An old man, tall and angular, with the strength of the pioneer in his seamed face, witnessed the little scene from his doorway. He walked quickly out to the gate and said courteously, "I fear you have been wounded. I am a physician. May I offer my services, sir?"

"You are very kind, but I am all right."

The old gentleman was watching him keenly. "No," he said, "I fear that you are not all right. I am Dr. Felix Robertson. Will you not come into my house for a few minutes? Very possibly I could be of help."

Suddenly Beasley Nichol knew that he needed help. That rifle butt had not yet taken its full toll, for there was a roaring in his head, and it felt crowded with pain. Something in the twist of his clutching the sycamore tree had reloosed all the agony of his bruises. He followed Dr. Robertson inside and sat in the chair to which the physician motioned. A moment later he slumped forward, and that was the last he knew until he awoke in a strange bed in a strange room. At first his memory was blank and he didn't remember the tall, gray, grave old man who sat so quietly at his bedside. But the sound of the man speaking revived memory.

"I imagine you feel better now, Captain."

"Yes, I feel better, much better, indeed. Tell me, please, how long have I been here?"

"To be exact, twenty-two hours. A part of that time you have been quite restless, tossing and muttering. But," he added with a touch of wry humor, "so was the night. It rained and thundered all night long."

"I am indeed grateful, sir. I must be going now." He sat up in bed.

"No, Captain, not yet awhile. I do not practice regularly any longer, but I am acquainted with your condition. I have in my practice encountered it several times. Your fever has dropped but it could rise again."

"I am grateful," Nichol repeated, "but I must leave the first moment I can. It is important."

"I thought so. Is there any message you would like to have sent to anyone?"

"No," said Nichol sharply. "No."

"I thought not. Very well, sir. Your presence here will remain uncommented on."

Nichol said nothing. He lay there staring at the seamed face.

The physician tapped the floor gently with the walking cane he held in his hand. "I am eighty-one years old," he said. "My father was the founder of this settlement. I was the first child born in Nashville. I have been a physician here for fifty-seven years. I do not have much time left and so am not so much concerned for it as are those who are younger. Is there anything which you should tell me?"

"Do you know who I am, sir?"

"Not exactly. I do know that you have been struck a violent blow upon the head, though I find no evidence of a fracture. I do know that you are severely bruised across your stomach and upper abdomen. I do know that you are wearing a very effective disguise. That is all I know. I have not looked in your pockets. I have, however, made some inferences. If I can give you aid you have but to command me."

"Thank you, sir."

"There is no news in which you would likely be particularly interested. There is a great hue and cry about a Southern spy who escaped in curious circumstances yesterday. There was something of the kind the day before but there seems to be some mystery about it. Anyhow, the Union forces are, I understand, disposed to take no chances hereafter. They intend to hang anyone under suspicion and hold his trial later."

Nichol smiled wanly. "An economical idea, but even then there might be slips."

"This spy was captured in the outskirts of the city. He was struck on the head with a rifle and swung upon a horse in front of a trooper and carried to jail. It isn't very clear what happened after that."

Oddly Nichol felt better. "Perhaps the prisoner outtalked someone."

"To outtalk someone, particularly an enemy, is indeed held an art among some Southerners."

For a full minute nothing further was said. Then Dr. Robertson went on, "I do not have any part in this war. It is the most terrible and senseless thing I have ever known, so I go my way and join with neither side. My family naturally is committed to the South. It is our home. I myself feel an odd and stirring pride when the South wins a victory and yet I cannot hope for ultimate victory. I cannot bear to think of the dismemberment of our Union. It is all most tragic indeed." There was another pause, and then the grave voice continued. "You may trust me, Captain."

"Thank you, sir. I think that I shall have to now. In fact, I think I want to."

"Why did you come into Nashville, Captain?"

"I was sent, Dr. Robertson, to rescue the officer who escaped day before yesterday."

"So. Well, that is about the way I thought it was. Did he get away?"

"I don't know. I think so. There were two of them, one a sergeant who came with me."

"But you did not get away. And now what is your most immediate problem, sir?"

"To leave Nashville. I am almost sure that my friends will come back to help me if they can. If they are here, and they may be by now, I must get word to them that I am no longer in jail."

"How could word reach them, Captain?"

Nichol thought for a moment. No, he could not betray the cobbler's shop. But he could mention the grinning Negro at the Saint Cloud. General Forrest would surely have sent Crockett to him also. Oh, yes, the fiddlin' man! But he would take the first chance with the Negro.

"I wonder whether you sometimes visit the Saint Cloud Hotel, Dr. Robertson?"

"I have not been there for months. It is usually crowded with swashbuckling Union officers. I could, I believe, send word to anyone there."

"I would like to leave immediately. I know that my life is in danger as long as I am in Nashville. Isn't it possible for me to go? I walked some yesterday without much discomfort."

"I know. It was then you had your disguise put on, was it not? You will forgive an old man's curiosity, but that disguise interests me. Usually they are clumsy, but not yours. It has a certain art about it. I should imagine, Captain, that your disguise was done by a lady."

Nichol said nothing.

"What, may I ask, is your name, Captain?"

It was on Nichol's tongue to say that he was Captain Enoch Ford, but he stopped in time. This man was dealing fairly with him.

"I am Beasley Nichol, Lieutenant Beasley Nichol of General Forrest's command. This uniform, sir, is one I acquired."

"Yours is one of the best of our names, Lieutenant Nichol."

"I am not a Tennessean, Dr. Robertson. I am from Florence, Alabama."

"It's the same name, the same blood. I believe a great deal in family, Lieutenant Nichol. I am proud of my family. My father was a personal friend of General George Washington. But I fear I am becoming garrulous. To whom at the Saint Cloud should your message be carried?"

Nichol told him.

"I shall see that he is told immediately, and with all discretion. I shall do that within an hour. As your physician, however, I could not permit you to leave my house at the earliest before tomorrow."

"Do you think I could get out of the city?"

"I don't think so—yet. Every exit is guarded in strength. They are out to catch their spy. At any rate, that's the way I have heard it. They will relax their vigilance before long. I'll leave you now so that you may take a little rest. You may consider yourself safe here, Lieutenant." At the door he turned. "I imagine you would like to sit up awhile. Don't try it till late this afternoon. Try to sleep now. Why, it's raining again."

It was raining. There was a monotonous sort of music in the slow and ordered beat of rain upon the roof and Beasley Nichol went to sleep and dreamed of Cousin Philip Yorke

wading mud to his knees and boasting plaintively that there
was no mud in Trenton. That dream faded, then there was
peace again in the land and he was walking down a country
lane, and at his side was Hunter Cragwall.

WHEN he awoke, light was streaming in at the window. He
listened for the beat of rain upon the roof, but failed to hear
it. He lay there looking at the window. Somehow the light
surprised him. It was too mellow for sunlight and too full
and rich for the gaslights on the streets. He knew then that
it was the moon. Why, then, the rain was no longer falling.

He lay there, he did not know how long, looking at the
light and remembering. There were many things to remember. Everything was so peaceful. The night had about it a
calm that was almost unearthly. It was curious that so
ghastly a thing as war could obtrude itself upon such serenity.

Then he heard steps. Someone was coming down Cherry
Street. There was nothing muffled or surreptitious about the
sound but there was purpose in it. Someone was on a mission
that involved decision and reasonable haste. Nichol arose and
stood tentatively by his bed. He was all right. He was steady
on his legs, his head clear.

He went quietly to the window and looked out. As he did
so a man came into his field of vision, a man not fifteen feet
away from him. He was not walking so rapidly. Nichol
couldn't see him very well for the shadow of the building

across the street was on him, but he could see that the man was of medium height and build and plainly dressed. He wore a crumpled hat, and in his right hand carried a whip, the loose part of it looped and held in the hand that grasped the stock.

Nichol saw the man stop for a moment and look intently at the house. Then he walked up the steps and rapped sharply on the door. The sound rang through the house, accented by the stillness of the night. There was no response and after waiting a moment the man rapped again. Presently there came from Dr. Robertson's room the sound of one getting out of bed. A few moments later Nichol heard him cautiously open the front door.

"Yes?" the physician said inquiringly.

"You Dr. Robertson?"

"Yes. What is it, please?"

"I seen you a lot o' times but the light ain't very good. I wouldn't wish to trouble you, sir, but I heard some talk that I reckon I better tell you."

There was silence, but Dr. Felix Robertson decided quickly. "Please come in," he said gravely.

Nichol heard the man cross the threshold and close the door.

"Now, tell me please what it was that you heard."

"I'm a-stayin' at the coach barn," said the man. "My trade's drivin' but they ain't no bizness, and I bin thinkin' some about j'inin' up with the South, and I expect that's what I'm a-goin' to do."

"Yes?" A hint of impatience was in the voice.

"I might have a little trouble a-gettin' out o' town, but I reckon I could make it effn I set my mind to. I bin thinkin' o' j'inin' up with Frank Cheatham."

"Hold on a minute," said Dr. Robertson a bit excitedly. "Haven't I seen you before?"

"Well, I ain't a-sayin' that you couldn't have. . . ."

"Aren't you the man who did such fancy driving at the State Fair five or six years ago? Why, of course you are. I remember that afternoon well."

"Thank you, suh. I had a lot to do with hosses in my time. But as I was a-sayin', I sleep down at the coach barn. The Yankees don't pay me no mind, though they ain't no tellin' when they might. They's several fellers stayin' there now. One o' 'em bunks right clost to me. He's trashy-like. He whooped and hollered for the South till the Yankees got here. Then he done forgot all about 'em. He drinks a lot and to-night he come in after midnight all lickered up and his tongue loose and a-hangin' out. He said to wake him up real early 'cause they's sure goin' to have a hangin' tomorrer. I ast him who they goin' to hang and he said they goin' to hang the spy that bruk jail. I ast where they catch him. He said they ain't yet, but Friday they's a man saw the spy go in at Dr. Robertson's house on Cherry Street jest afore it started rainin'. He took the news to headquarters but the way he told it the man don't look anything like the spy. They bin watchin', but the man ain't come out yet. That sounds funny to them and they're takin' the posse down there to git him jest as soon as it gits back from another trip. That ol' drunk scounderl said the spy'd be back in jail long afore daylight, and after that it wouldn't take 'em long to git aroun' to the hangin'. I got to thinkin' and when he drapped off to sleep I come down here. I had to dodge a Yankee soldier or two but that wasn't much trouble."

It was then that Beasley Nichol opened the door and stepped out into the hall fully dressed.

"You will pardon me, sir. I didn't intend to eavesdrop, but I couldn't help hearing. I don't want to cause you any trouble, Dr. Robertson, and I think I'd better be going now."

"Yes, perhaps you should. I imagine you wouldn't run as much risk by leaving as by staying. Let me feel that pulse. Well, well, how hard to kill some folks are! It is very reassuring. Southern men are well put together." He turned to the man standing there. "I remember you very well now. My wife and I rode to Louisville once in the coach you drove. We were on our way to Maryland to visit her people. I remember how pleasant you made the trip. You are a gentleman, sir."

"I ain't a-denyin' it, but then I ain't a-takin' sides with you neither. Anyhow, I like to give gentlemen help when they's in the kind o' trouble I don't like. I'd be right glad to try to help this gentleman. That drunk scounderl don't need to see no hangin'. Besides, I reckon it's time for me to be a-j'inin' up with Frank Cheatham."

"I don't want either of you here when the posse comes. I don't like hangings either."

The driver and Beasley Nichol left together, walking toward Broadway. In the air was the feeling of early morning, fresh, with a little touch of coolness, a bit dewy and expectant. A moon sinking toward the western horizon touched the streets with a soft half-light. Out across Broadway somewhere a rooster was crowing hysterically. There was yet no hint of glow in the eastern sky.

They reached Broadway. "I think I'd better leave you here," Nichol said. "I don't intend for them to get me, but if they do I'd prefer to be alone. You are my friend, sir. I wouldn't want you to catch the plague from me."

"Mebbe you got the wrong idee. What I needs is protection. The hosts of wickedness is done pursuin' me and effn you'll tag along to see I ain't overcome by the Philisteens I'll be right thankful."

Beasley Nichol grinned broadly. "What chance would

the—er, Philisteens have against us? If you have any ideas what to do, my friend, lead on."

"Effn I had a team of hosses that'd be one thing. Yes sir, hosses is a real shelter in time o' storm. But with jest legs I reckon it's another thing. Anyhow, I got a plumb good notion for some fancy shenanigan and it might work. You don't skeer easy, do you?"

"Well, I always count ten before I start running."

"It might be good sense to start quicker'n that this time. Maybe you better start when you count one. I done tried plenty things in my time, but this one's brand-new."

"Again I say, lead on. I'm in your hands, General."

The coach driver led on. He led east on Broadway to Spring Street and there turned right. A cloud had risen and obscured the moon, and a heavy shadow lay over everything.

"Wait a minute," said Nichol. "Where are we going?"

"Mebbe we goin' to take a ride. Le's stop and I'll tell you what I been a-thinkin'."

They stopped there on Spring Street and the driver spoke in guarded tones. He had loafed a bit that afternoon down at the river. Some wagons were being placed for loading. The driver of one had handled his team so badly that it became unmanageable. He had had a way with hosses since he was waist-high to a gosling. So he had ventured over and straightened matters out. That gave him some standing, so he had stayed around and watched what happened. The driver by putting two and two together had reached the belief that the wagons were to provide supplies for a detachment of soldiers who the next day were to go out and give battle to Bed Forrest. He had heard it expressly stated that the wagons would leave at sunrise. He didn't know where they would be going. His bones told him somewhere about Lavergne. His bones had previously been dependable.

Then something happened which had given him considerable thought. The wagon which an hour before he had helped to rescue from the confusion was fully loaded. The driver of the wagon, who "didn't have bat sense," locked the door of the wagon and put the key in his pocket. That is, he thought he'd put it in his pocket. But his effort was so clumsy that the key had missed the pocket and had fallen to the wet ground, an inadvertence which the man never noticed. A moment later he had gone around to the front of the wagon and the driver with one quick motion had lifted the key from the ground and dropped it into his pocket. He didn't know why he had taken the key, but a little later the thought had occurred to him that if he were in that wagon at sunrise he could likely get out of Nashville and so jine up with Frank Cheatham. Reflection, however, had confirmed the unsoundness of the idea. By himself he felt he wouldn't have a chance. But now, the two of them . . . !

"What kind of wagon is it?"

"It's a box wagon, with a back door. They got a few guns in it and some other gimcracks and lots o' ammunition. It's got enough cracks so one wouldn't smother."

"I think," said Beasley Nichol, "that I'll enjoy the ride. Why, it's as good as a play!"

They continued out Front Street and came to a great lot by the riverside. Nichol could see on it the dim shapes of wagons, a great number of them.

Suddenly the driver laid a restraining hand on the lieutenant's arms. He stopped quickly and noiselessly. Then Nichol heard it, the crunch of heavy steps.

"The sentry," said the driver. "Le's get out o' sight till he gits by."

The sentry was coming along the side of Spring Street nearest the wagons. The two men crossed to the opposite side. They went a dozen yards inside a vacant lot and crouched low on the ground. The sentry continued his walk almost to Broad Street. There he stopped and waited, evidently resting. For full two minutes he stood there. Then they heard him resume his march. He passed the lot, and they crouched lower, fearing that quick eyes might discover them, but the sound of his steps never varied its beat. Presently his footsteps on out Spring Street softened into the silence of the night.

"Now," said the driver. They walked rapidly and with as little sound as possible across the street. Unerringly, the driver found the wagon he was looking for.

"This here's our chari-ot," he said. He fitted the key into the lock, spreading his hand to muffle as best he could the grating sound of the turning key. The east was pearl then, and deepening, and more roosters were crowing.

"Lovely, lovely," said Nichol, taking a long look and breathing deeply before they entered the cavernous darkness of the wagon. *"But, look, the morn, in russet mantle clad, walks o'er the dew of yon high eastward hill."* Then he crawled into the darkness of the wagon and the driver followed.

"There he comes," whispered the driver. Again they heard the crunch of the sentry's step. "When he gets out o' hearin' again I'm a-goin' to lock that door from the inside. You can't tell what one o' the Philisteens might try. When we get started I'll unlock it. It might be safer then."

The light brightened into day, and almost with suddenness the lot became alive with horses and men. Harness creaked and chains clanked and orders were shouted. Then somewhere the wheels of one wagon began to turn, then of another. They heard someone mount to the wagon's seat, and after some adjustment bawl hoarse and uncouth commands to the team. A whip slapped viciously against horseflesh and Nichol felt the driver at his side shudder. Then they were moving. The horses strained, and they heard the crack of the wheels unsucking from the mud in which they had settled. The wagon reached the street and the wheels ground harshly against stone.

The cracks along the sides of the wagon were enough to let in a little of the deepening daylight without, enough to dilute vaguely the shadows within, but no more. They could see that some wooden cases and many sacks were in the wagon and guns were in racks along the sides. The two men sat on sacks but they had to hold their heads forward, so low was the top. Outside the driver of the wagon spoke almost continuously to the horses. The man who sat inside with Nichol had loved and lived with horses from childhood and the hoarse growl and vile threatening words were to him an accumulating offense.

"It's the identical feller that got 'em mired up yestidy," he whispered. "Someday I aim to learn him better, and I hope that day ain't long off."

For a while he said nothing more, listening, waiting for something, his whole body tense with alertness. He relaxed. "The Murfreesboro Pike suits me. I thought that's the way they'd go, but I wasn't sartin."

They sat there, hunched forward, and the cramp of their posture wore on them. They could lean back to straighten out a bit, but that too was tiring.

"That's the University we passin' now," Nichol's companion said, and a little later, "That's Chicken Pike." The man had a cat's sense of direction.

Their driver seemed to be annoyed by the sluggishness of the wagon ahead. "If you can't travel any faster'n a mud turkle," he yelled, "git out o' the way and let somebody git ahead who can."

Apparently his exhortation went unheeded. "Git up, le's git to the battle!" shouted the hoarse voice. There was the slashing, stinging sound of a whip striking fiercely against horseflesh. They could feel the vehicle surge forward. Through the cracks they could see their wagon inching forward against the other. Then the rate of advance diminished, for the other team had accepted the challenge. This angered the teamster and his hoarse voice grew more violent and profane. Upon the horses the whip fell unmercifully. Nichol could feel his companion shiver in futile outrage. A more violent blow struck the horse on the right and it sprang forward with such force as to cut the wagon sharply to the left. The two men behind could feel the wheels leave the turnpike and slice into the mud of the road's shoulder. There was the sound of hoofs sinking in the mud and suddenly pulled loose, of horses scrambling aimlessly and hysterically about in the mud. Then progress ceased and they knew that they were stalled.

"Hey, you there, help me out o' here. I'm stuck. Help me out," the hoarse voice yelled.

The other wagon moved on to an accompaniment of blasphemy and vituperation. The teamster was still slashing at the horses and dividing his profanity between them and the teamster ahead.

The horses were plunging about in terror.

"I reckon I better git out and stop him," said the driver. He opened the door and climbed out. No other wagons were in sight. With the agility of a cat he hoisted himself to the top of the wagon and crawled toward the front. He took from his shirt the whip he always carried. He lay there looking at it. He decided that the handle would serve him best. The teamster aimed a blow at the lead horse but it never landed. Even while it was in motion the butt of the driver's whip struck him behind the ear with such force that the whip fell aimlessly from his hand, and he collapsed into the seat and rolled out, striking the wheel and bouncing to the ground where he lay in the mud churned by the struggling horses.

"Very commendable!" said Beasley Nichol, coming around the side of the wagon. "A thing of beauty! The neatest performance I've seen in many a day, but to be followed by appropriate haste. We've got to get away from here. Change clothes with him quick, and we'll be going."

The driver pondered the shift of clothes. "A good idee," he said. "Yes sir, a fust-rate idee. We ain't out o' the woods yet." Deftly he removed the teamster's uniform and put it on over the clothes he wore. "That makes a Reb spy out o' me, too, don't it?" he asked quizzically.

"Certainly," said Nichol. "It's your great chance to share fame with me." At that moment Nichol was galvanized into action. "Let's get him in the wagon! Quick!" He pointed. A soldier was galloping over the brow of the hill toward them. He seized the man's shoulders and the driver his feet, and a moment later they had him inside and the door closed.

"Quick, on the seat," Nichol called. "You drive!" They vaulted into the seat. The soldier then was not more than three hundred feet away.

The driver clucked to the horses, "Come on now, come on, come on, boy. Le's get out o' here." He talked quietly, continuously, persuasively to the horses and they strained at the traces with a steady pull. They were back on the pike by the time the soldier reached them.

"Turn around!" he shouted. "Take your wagon back to Nashville!" The horseman, a colonel by his insignia, spurred his mount and galloped on toward town.

"I'm a-thinkin'," said the driver, "that now's a right good time to go away from here and do it quick." But his quick eye caught sight of other horsemen topping the rise. He grinned wryly. "I reckon we better stay. Frank Cheatham's goin' to have to wait."

"They come not singly but in solid phalanx," said Nichol almost gaily. "That's the trouble with the Yankees—no finesse, no strategy, always a show of force. Yes, I suppose we'd better stay."

The horsemen, all officers, rode up. "Turn your wagon around and take it back to the lot," one called. "Wait there for further orders." They started to leave.

"What has happened?" asked Nichol.

The officer then saw the insignia he wore and reined in his horse. "The Rebels have dodged us. We don't know where they are. They're likely to attack Nashville from some other direction." They rode on toward town.

Other wagons were coming over the hill.

"Nashville, how can I leave thee? Well, I can't. I'm coming back," said Nichol. "It's as good as a play. It *is* a play, a lovely play. I wonder how it will end."

They headed back to Nashville, leading the line of supply wagons returning from their game of hare and hounds with Bed Forrest. They drove past the Chicken Pike.

Beasley Nichol said crisply, "Maneuver somehow to get behind. I'm not going to return to that wagon lot." He jerked his head back toward the wagon. "How hard did you hit him?"

"He'll sleep a while yet," said the driver serenely. "Oncet when we fit agin' Mexico . . ."

"Get us behind," said Nichol. "I have a prophetic cramp in my neck," he added grimly.

The driver used song as a medium for repartee.

> "They hung Old Pink Eye 'way above the ground
> But his neck it stretched till it let him down."

He drove the team to the side of the road, sprang out and began fingering the harness. A wagon drew up alongside and proffered assistance.

"Jest a busted hamestring," said the driver cheerfully. "I'll have it fixed drekly. You jest drive on."

The other wagons passed them. The driver and the captain looked at each other and grinned.

"This trip was a good idea while it lasted," said the captain, "But it just didn't last. Got any more good ideas? We could use a few."

"Idees ain't what I run out of fust. I got a few mo'. Do you remember seein' anythin' special in there where he is?" He pointed to the wagon bed.

"A lot of boxes and sacks, and some rifles swung up against the wall."

"And one saddle and bridle," said the driver, "and it look like a right good saddle, too. I been thinkin' mebbe you better take a ride. Walkin' 's right tirin'."

"And where, wise sir, would I ride to?"

"Sence you asts me, pardner, I guess I'll have to tell you the whole truth. I jest plain don't know, but I don't know where-at you'd walk to neither."

His whip hissed through the summer air and a fly gorging upon the flank of the lead horse died suddenly and fell slanting to the ground. "Hossfly," he said plaintively, "don't you come around me when I'm puzzled."

"We can't leave this wagon here. We're in sight of a dozen houses. Drive on slowly. I have to decide on something quickly. Pardner, I'm worse puzzled than you are."

The driver offered a tall tale in rebuttal. "My mind's done got filled up with caterpillars that eat idees jest like leaves."

"My caterpillars eat more leaves than yours, or perhaps I don't have leaves any more. Listen, friend, I'm reasonably certain that two of the best soldiers in General Forrest's army are in Nashville looking for me. If this keeps up, something bad is going to happen. For all I know they think I'm still in jail. They'll be watching the building and it's dangerous to watch that jail just now. I must get word to them somehow. And I don't know how."

"Mebbe I could get 'em word you ain't a-livin' in that jail house no mo'."

"There's a Negro boy at the Saint Cloud who used to belong to General Forrest; in fact, I suppose he still does. He's the grinning one. They have one who doesn't grin but this boy does. Tell him that I'm out of that jail. I believe he can get word to Crockett." He started to say, "or to the fiddlin' man," but checked himself in time. It would be discreet not to mention all sources of help even to one as trustworthy as he instinctively felt the driver to be.

"I'll get him word."

"Where are you going?" Nichol asked sharply. Evidently they were going somewhere.

The driver had guided the team into a lane that seemed deserted.

"There's an old field down here clost to Fairfield we can do our changin' in. I'm headin' for it."

"I believe I could get through all right, but I can't leave Nashville till I hear something about Crockett and Goforth. My word, this is lonely."

"For a town Nashville is right funny," observed the driver. "You can hunt rabbits not a quarter o' a mile from some o' the best streets."

"You know people here pretty well?"

"Well, I wouldn't prezactly say I do, but I bin here a right smart while. Yes sir, I been aroun'."

"Do you know a lady named Hunter Cragwall?"

"I don't reckon I know her but I know where she lives."

"Oh! Where?"

"Right clost to Mrs. Polk."

"Oh, Mrs. Polk? I remember her place well. You say she lives close to Mrs. Polk?"

"Not fur. Well, here we are," said the driver. The team turned into a little opening in the hedge that lined the road, and they entered a small field covered with sage grass dotted with straggling clumps of saplings. The driver drew the team to a stop and swung himself to the ground. He went quickly to the rear of the wagon and opened the door. He climbed in but reappeared a moment later.

"He's a-sleepin' like a baby," he announced. "It's purty hard to kill a feller as onery as he is. I'm a-goin' to leave him his clothes. I might get in trouble with 'em on; besides they are too hot."

He peeled off the teamster's shabby uniform and flung it into the wagon. "It's shore relievin' to get that thing off. Which hoss you want to ride?"

"That one," said Nichol, pointing. "People would be less likely to notice it."

The driver took the harness off the roan and turned it loose in the field. He unharnessed the bay and put the saddle on it and shifted bridles.

"Your fleet-footed Arabian is done ready and a-waitin', Captain. I wish you well, suh. I'll get your word to the boy at the Saint Cloud."

"Where are you going?"

"I reckon back to the coach barn. They don't notice much there. That's the safest place till the fuss dies down. But I'm a-goin' to jine with the South jest as soon as I can. I ain't a-aimin' to disapp'int Frank Cheatham. I ain't a-aimin' nei-ther to get took while a-tryin'."

"Listen," said Nichol earnestly. "Do you know where the stone church is on South High Street?"

"I've driv by it a hundred time."

"Get word to Captain Crockett, if you can, that I'll ride down there just before dark."

"I'll tell that boy at the Saint Cloud hotel about you-all afore I go to the çoach barn."

"Be careful. That hotel has keen ears and a mean heart. One of the clerks, the one with fisheyes, is a spy for General Negley. He's the one who got us in this mess. I have some very bad thoughts about him, pardner."

"I've seen him. I didn't know he was that, but I did know he was mighty trashy."

"One more thing. That girl, Hunter Cragwall. Go see her if you can. Tell her . . . well, tell her that you saw me. Tell her anything. Tell her . . ."

"Jest so I tell her? Cap'n, she's the same as told. Well, so long, Cap'n. I wish you well." He walked through the opening in the hedge, snapping his whip at caterpillars that lay in clusters upon the leaves of a stunted walnut tree and singing merrily:

> "It may rain and it may hail
> But I've got a home in the Bowling Green jail."

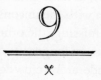

BEASLEY NICHOL opened the door of the wagon. The man inside was breathing heavily but with regularity. Nichol stood for a moment in the posture of thought. Having matured his ideas, he disengaged a piece of rope from the harness which lay in disorder where it had fallen on the wagon tongue. He crawled inside the wagon and tied the man's hands securely together. The loose end that remained of the rope he looped tightly around one of the racks.

"I wouldn't want you to leave here too soon," he informed the unconscious man. He climbed crabwise out of the wagon and closed the door. He stood there regarding the portion of the world in view with appreciative eyes.

There was beauty in the old field itself, the light green of the sage grass that rippled in the slow summer wind, the clumps of saplings which flecked the field with their darker green. Against the tiers of the upper river hills which lay gently etched against the eastern horizon was a diaphany of faintly purple haze. There was no sound except those which were almost a part of sight itself. There was nothing to tell that a city lay just beyond the slope of that hill, no hint of the traffic that moved on streets not far away. There was none of those hostile sounds that are a part of the slaughter of men and the desolation of men's homes. There was none of those angry sounds which arise from the pursuit of an escaped spy. It was strangely quiet with a sort of olden serenity.

For a moment the thought clung to Nichol that this would be the best place to stay, at least until evening. But he quickly rejected it. The wagon with the unconscious and bound teamster within, one horse missing, the other bridled and saddled! No, it wouldn't do to tarry longer. Boldness for the time was his best ally. On moderately crowded streets, not the deserted ones, he would attract less attention. And then toward night he would go to the stone church on High Street.

He rode through the opening in the hedge into the lonely lane and turned toward the Murfreesboro Pike. Presently he

was riding along Lafayette Street, and not much later he
reached Broad. His horse, though fairly brisk, was not one
he would have chosen. Its clumping gait offered little ease
to the rider. Obviously its career had been committed to a
wagon, and a saddle was alien equipment.

He turned north into Cherry Street, and then he was passing Dr. Felix Robertson's house, though he saw no one. Ahead
of him the great bulk of the Maxwell House was in plain
view. Just beyond that would be the cobbler's shop. No, he
would not be stopping this time, but his eyes would search
and long for the sight of red, red hair, and sky-blue eyes,
and the sound of a voice that was as music played at twilight
on a summer evening. But the cobbler's shop had about it
the stillness of death. He rode to Union Street and a minute
later turned south on Summer. He passed the Saint Cloud,
and his alert eyes swept the front of it. Officers were going
in and coming out but he saw no one he knew. He turned
west on Church Street, and then he heard the music of the
fiddlin' man. It was a fast and merry piece he did not know.
He rode down the middle of the street, eyes straight ahead.
At High Street he turned south toward the stone church. He
looked at the sun. It would not set for two hours, but he
knew nothing to do until someone or something gave him his
cue. A vague faintness seized him. He wondered if the
blow on his head had not yet exacted full payment. How
odd that he had forgotten it! He ran his hand over his dia-
phragm and found that the most of the soreness had van-
ished. Then he realized it was hunger that assailed him.
Presently he saw a flaring sign:

RIDDLEBURGER'S OLD STANDBY RESTAURANT

"To suit the taste of the most fastidious epicures."

Nichol tied his horse securely to the hitching rack and boldly walked into the room. It occurred to him as he was eating that fastidious epicures must be weakening if that fare suited them. But he was hungry and he ate it. He was preparing to leave but conversation among some soldiers at the adjoining table caused him to delay a bit.

"There's the very devil to pay at the wagon yard," a soldier said loudly. "One of them wagons never did get back. Looks mighty queer to me."

"What became of it?" inquired his companion.

"That's what I don't understand. The colonel sent two of us back to look for it. We went to where it turned around to come back to town, but we didn't see hide nor hair of it a-tall. It looks like it's plumb disappeared. And there's another thing that looks funny to me. Two or three other drivers say they'll swear on a stack of Bibles they was a officer settin' on the seat with Red Link, but they ain't found nobody who knows who the officer was or what he was doing up there with Red. And some say it wasn't Red nohow. It's all mixed up."

Beasley Nichol paid his bill, left the restaurant, mounted and rode on. At the church he tied his horse to the hitching rack in the rear. That horse might have some distinguishing mark upon it, and he suspected there would begin presently a sharp scrutiny of all horseflesh. He placed it out of public view as well as he could, and walked around to the front of the church. There was the gaping hole in the stained window, and there was the limb which had missed Cousin Philip by the barest margin, its leaves lying withered and limp in the churchyard mud. There were still traces of the imprint made by Cousin Philip when he had been so rudely hurled to the ground.

He went into the church and sat in one of the pews. He

was alone in the church, and it was quiet and restful there. So he sat and thought of many things. The altar door of the church opened and two brawny soldiers entered, carrying a side of beef. They laid it on a huge block which stood in front of the pulpit. From under a bench they took butchers' saws and knives and cleavers and proceeded to dismember the carcass. Nichol shuddered at the sacrilege, but this was war! The men finished their work, put the chunks of meat into hampers, placed their saws and knives back under the bench, and carried the hampers out by the door they had entered. If they had caught sight of the lone man sitting in the rear of the church they made no sign.

NICHOL remained there, thinking of many things. Idly the notion came to him that Hunter Cragwall might sometime have sat in that very pew. His eyes rested upon a stained-glass window, and he found that he was matching her hair against its glory. Involuntarily his hand touched his face. The beard that she had fitted upon it was still there. His experience in disguises had not met with such permanency. There must be, he felt, something symbolic in its remaining so long. The day before at Dr. Robertson's he had with soap and water cleansed the unbearded parts of his face. For him cleanliness was an ideal. He yearned for it. He thought whimsically that when peace had come again he would wash hourly until he had overcome the accumulated deposits of war.

He shrugged his shoulders. The war wasn't over. It didn't show any signs of being over. Over! One wrong step, one wrong word, one wrong glance; to be somewhere one moment too early, or one moment too late . . . ! He shrugged his shoulders again. He had invited danger when he joined with General Bedford Forrest. Whatever came he'd accept with such wit and grace as he could summon.

Then his thoughts reverted to the cobbler's shop, and to the girl in the dingy back room. What was it she had said about Lucy Stratton? How long ago seemed that summer at Beersheba! He felt an odd sense of resentment. Why hadn't Hunter Cragwall been at Beersheba Springs then so he could have met her that much earlier? He was conscious that somebody had come into the church. He emerged from his preoccupation and saw Hume Crockett standing in the aisle by him. They looked long and steadily at each other and there was warning in the eyes of each. The walls of that silent church could prove treasonable.

"Good afternoon, Captain," said Nichol in brittle tones. "Is there any late word of the Rebels?"

"Yes," said Crockett in his husky tones. "Part of them have been cornered." He covered with an audible shifting of his feet the half-whispered postscript, "Where on earth did you get the whiskers?"

"I have an idea about where the Rebels will attack us. Let me show you, Captain."

Nichol led the way down the aisle and out the door used by the butchers. A swarm of flies arose and buzzed in angry protest as they passed the block on which meat had been cut. They stood under a hackberry tree at the back of the church, not in unobstructed view of passers-by along the streets, and yet avoiding any hint of concealment.

"Where's Goforth?"

"They've got him," said Crockett soberly. "They've got him. I guess I'm weakening."

"The Yankees?"

"Yes, the Yankees. It was my fault. I don't know what's the matter with me. I guess I don't think well any more. I led the boy right into them."

"If they took him, how'd you get away?"

"Sometimes I wish I hadn't. Well, that night we got back to General Forrest. We found him at Kingsley and talked with him. He sent us back to get you——"

"I wasn't worth all that trouble," interrupted Nichol; "still my heart leaps up when I behold your honest face. What about Goforth?"

"I thought the Yankees might be watching out for us on that side of town. So we took all night and rode clear around Nashville and were coming in by the Buena Vista Pike. We had just crossed a little bridge and there were thick trees on both sides of the pike just ahead. I saw something over at the side. I don't know yet what it was. I yelled to Goforth. It was too late to do anything but go ahead, for they were coming out of their hiding places then. There must have been a dozen of them. They took some shots at me but the horse I was riding was fast as a streak and I got through them. I don't know what happened to the sergeant, except that they got him. Maybe he didn't understand me. Maybe his horse was unmanageable. I don't know what happened. Anyhow, they didn't try to follow me and when I got out of sight I circled back and from a clump of trees I watched them riding back to town. They had the sergeant all right. What happened to you?"

"Many things, all different. I'll unfold my harrowing tale later. Right now, what about Goforth? What should we do about him? Is there a plan?"

"Well, it's in my mind that General Forrest will expect us to bring him along when we go back."

"Strange, isn't it, how I keep thinking the same? General Forrest would never want the sergeant hanged."

"I haven't had a glimpse of my girl yet."

"That's not critical at all. You can see her after the war. Right now we'd better try to humor the general. Where are they keeping the sergeant?"

"I don't know. I guess we'll learn before long. General Forrest's boy is trying to find out."

"How is he going to let you know?"

"I'm going to see him, before bedtime. He's likely to discover where they have him. Suppose you come back here at nine o'clock. If I'm not here, then try in the morning a little while after sunup. I'll come then for sure—if I'm not in with the sergeant."

"Keep out of there. To rescue both of you would be taxing even for me. Really at the moment I don't see how I'd do it. You don't think we'd better stay together then?"

"No, that'd only multiply the danger. Take care of yourself, Nichol."

He was walking away when an exclamation from Nichol stopped him. A man had come in at the front gate of the churchyard and in the waning light he saw that it was the driver. "I'll tell you about him later," said Nichol.

The driver's alert eyes caught sight of the two men and he came on around the church to them. He had not seen Hume Crockett before but he knew instinctively who he was and that the boy at the Saint Cloud had performed his assignment. He nodded to them inclusively but directed his statement to Beasley Nichol.

"He says they got him in the jail, the same place they had you."

"You?" said Hume Crockett, surprised, looking at Nichol.

"My dear fellow, don't be snobbish about your jail. Aren't you willing to divide it with me? Or perhaps you underestimate me. Of course I've been in jail."

"How did you get out?"

"A matter of righteous indignation. I boiled over and they let me go. Boiling over seems very convincing to the Yankees. But a little patience, dear friend. You shall be told all presently." He turned to the driver. "What else did you hear?"

"Nothing, suh, only that they's keepin' him there. That's all the boy told me."

"Thank you. Your service will be known in high places. General Forrest's blessing will supplement ours."

The driver started to leave but as he passed Nichol he handed him an envelope. "Something for you, suh."

It was some word from General Forrest's boy. He would read it presently. The driver was saying very casually, "I walk around a right smart. It sort o' keeps my mind offn how I miss the hosses. I guess if nothing happens I'll be passin' here about dinnertime tomorrer." He left, singing plaintively:

> "I got no fo'ks an' I got no home
> All I do is to travel and roam."

The two men stood in the thickening dark.

Hume Crockett said presently and with irrelevance, "That's a first-rate disguise. Where'd you get it? I'd feel safer if I had one. This uniform is running out. Too many have seen me wearing it. I need some sort of change."

"Why haven't you been to see your girl?" Nichol also was irrelevant.

"See her! Good God, what opportunity have I had to see

her? Don't you think I would have seen her if I'd had a ghost of a chance? But I intend to see her before I leave Nashville."

"Then you'd better hurry up. I think we should be departing soon." He paused. "Not too soon, though. I have an errand myself."

Again Crockett said nothing, his eyes resting speculatively on the gaslight beginning to glow in the town beyond Broadway.

"It's dark," he said. "Do you suppose we can talk safely here?"

"I think so. I doubt if anyone would notice two Yankee officers in conference."

They stood and talked, but their speech was abrupt and disjointed. Their obligation was clear—to get Sergeant Goforth out of prison and to rejoin General Forrest with all possible haste. The latter they thought would not be difficult. But they were baffled by the first problem. That cell had yielded its prisoner too often. The authorities had felt their outrage too keenly not to imbue their underlings with deadly alertness. Crockett and Nichol were ingenious and daring men, but the task ahead gave them pause.

"We've got to get the sergeant out," said Crockett doggedly.

"Yes," said Nichol in the monotone of one whose thoughts are far away. "We must. Can you think how?"

"Whatever we do must be done pretty soon. He was wearing a Yankee uniform when they took him. He won't have a chance if we put it off much longer."

"No, not a single chance. They'll hang him for you and me both."

"I've thought that maybe we could somehow get the word started that General Forrest was on his way to the city—say, by the Charlotte Pike. That might cause a diversion we could turn to some use."

Nichol drummed the fence with his finger. "It might," he said. "It might be done. It might be done, but. . . ."

11

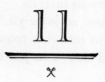

SOMEONE was coming in the church gate. The flickering gaslight a block away illumined the darkness enough for them to see that the figure was a Negro. Then they recognized the boy who belonged to General Forrest. Nichol touched Crockett on the arm and led the way, keeping close to the building. The boy saw them. Nichol motioned and they moved into the shadow of a tree near the church.

"I didn't know yo'd be here, but I come in hopes." His eyes glanced warily about.

"All right, what is it?"

"They havin' a meetin' tonight at the ho-tel. Maybe I can fix it fo' you to lissen."

"Something that we should hear?"

"Yas suh. I don't know for certain but I thinks mebbe it is. They havin' the meetin' in one o' the rooms and the one next to it ain't got nobody in it."

"But the hotel might put someone in it."

"Yas suh, might put you two gemmun. It's General Nelson's room an' he's off summers in Alabam'. Won't be back tonight nohow. Won't nobody else be put in 'cept you two gemmun."

"What are they having the meeting for?"

"They's troubled 'bout things here. Say they can't keep no secrets no mo', say it looks like the Rebs fin' out things as soon as they do, say they can't plan nothin' like things is, say mebbe the man they got in jail could tell 'em what they want to know, say——"

"What time are they to meet?"

"Half after ten, 'bout an hour yit."

"Can you smuggle us into that room?"

"Yas suh, I thinks I can. You jest foller me but don't git too clost."

They followed him, keeping at a discreet distance but within sight. He led them along alleys. He came to Broad Street. He walked boldly across it and a minute later they followed him. They went through some more alleys and then they came to Church Street. Between Church and Union he turned into an alley, and two or three minutes later he waited for them to come up. They saw they were at the rear entrance to the Saint Cloud Hotel. The boy listened a moment. Then he said, "You gemmun wait here till I gits back."

They waited, standing in the deep shadow, everything enlarged against their acute alertness. They did not hear General Forrest's boy until he stood again at their side.

"I thinks we can git in now."

They followed him up the back stairs, stepping with great care. As they neared the hall a gesture held them rigid in their tracks. He disappeared for a moment, then again stood at the head of the stairs, grinning broadly. Again he crooked a beckoning finger, and within a brief moment they were in a dark room.

They heard General Forrest's boy walking away down the hall, his footsteps muffled by the shreds of carpet that remained. The sound died away as he went down the stairs.

Nichol closed the door and the room was enveloped in darkness except for a few dim streaks of light that filtered through
the dirty windowpanes. Nichol felt for the lock, found the
key, and turned it. To his relief it turned easily, without rasping. It was intolerably hot in the room but they could not risk
opening the window. This was not the live heat which carries
a sort of vitality, but heat dead and oppressive, a ghostly heat
that remained long after the fuel creating it had been consumed. A stifling smell of air dead for days hung in the room,
and as one breathed, the air touched his tongue so he could
taste it as well. The meaning of that hot dead air was plain.
When the occupant had left his room the window and door
had been closed. The heat from without had come in and
compounded itself with the lifeless heat inside the room, and
no air from without entered to cleanse the foulness within.

Crockett saw the outline of a chair, groped toward it and sat
down. It squeaked in momentary protest and then was silent.
Nichol started to sit upon the bed but checked himself. Hotel
beds were not committed to silence. So he sat upon the floor.
They sat there half panting while the minutes stretched out
interminably. They could not talk; they even breathed most
guardedly. They could only wait. They could feel that the air
they were drawing into their lungs served little purpose but
to leave them stricken with a numb but strangling nausea.

Footsteps mounted the stairs and the two men grew rigid,
but whoever it was turned down the opposite hall and in a
moment or two they heard a key grating in a lock and a door
pulled open. They had not heard the fiddlin' man. The hour
likely was a bit inconvenient for him. Still, it wasn't late.
Perhaps ten o'clock. A half-hour to wait! Too long to wait
when lungs were panting futilely for one bit of freshness!
Nichol tried to beguile the time by thoughts of home but they
faded in the hot, airless room. He tried to think of Hunter

Cragwall but couldn't. He looked angrily at the window. Only the thickness of thin glass partitioned him off from heaven's pure air. Crockett bent over, touching his sleeve.

"What time is it?" he whispered.

"I don't know. After ten, I think."

They heard the imperative shrill of a whistle but it sounded far away. Now and then the beat of horses' hoofs sounded on the cobblestones without. Somewhere there arose the long musical chime of a steamboat calling for the landing. They knew that it was one of those boats from St. Louis that daily added to the vast accumulation of supplies which grew so amazingly upon the wharf.

Then they heard men coming up the stairs and an accompaniment of voices. The steps reached the head of the stairs and this time they did not turn down the hall. The men—there must have been four or five of them from their voices and steps—came down the hall past their door. They heard a key search for the keyhole, then turn, and the party enter the adjoining room. They heard the splutter of a match, and here and there pinpoints of light showed through cracks or nail holes in the flimsy wall. Crockett and Nichol were then standing in the darkness, tense and alert, panting a little but no longer conscious of the heat or lack of air. They must hear what was said. General Forrest's boy had considered the gathering in the next room as significant, significant enough to risk their lives to hear what was said.

"Have seats, gentlemen," said a voice, distinct and clear, crisp with authority.

There were the sounds of feet scuffing, of chairs drawn about a table and of men occupying them.

"You will pardon me, General Negley, if I may seem a trifle overdiscreet, but may I inquire whose room that is?" The speaker was obviously pointing.

"That is my room," said a third voice. "It is locked and

the key is in my pocket. I can vouch that there are no ears
in it."

"Thanks, Colonel Walter. And on the other side, please?"

The voice that replied was General Negley's. "That's
General Nelson's room."

"Then there are no ears in it either," commented the in-
quirer with a brief laugh.

"I doubt if General Nelson will require the room much
longer," said General Negley. "He was in it awhile Monday
night, but not for days before that. He is exceedingly busy
just now assembling his troops for transfer. It is imperative
for us to get troops into Kentucky immediately."

"I suppose he'll move from here to the Galt House in
Louisville. That's their best place."

"Perhaps General Nelson should stay away from Louisville. I hear that he has sorely offended the Indiana troops."

The words spoken jestingly went without comment, but
one replied seriously.

"He will not go to Louisville, certainly not at first. He
probably will move east from here, stabbing at General Forrest along the way, then into central Kentucky. I should
imagine that the danger lies there, say about Lexington or
Richmond."

"General Nelson has been under considerable strain for
a month. He has definite orders to follow the Rebels into
Kentucky, but everything seems to go wrong. General Forrest seems to have foreknowledge of our every movement.
He pounces with uncanny accuracy upon every regiment as it
moves toward the assembling point. He is working havoc
with both our plans and our *esprit de corps*. He has captured
more than three thousand of our soldiers."

"We should pounce upon General Forrest," said one.
"Haven't we some officers with foresight, too?"

"There seems to be some difficulty involved with our foresight," said General Negley dryly. "It has lately seemed somewhat dimmed. Gentlemen, I should like to review briefly some very puzzling events which have added lately to our confusion." There were the sounds of chairs moved closer to a table and the creak of the table under the weight of elbows.

"Eight days ago," continued General Negley, "General Buell at Stevenson, Alabama, sent Captain Enoch Ford with an orderly to Nashville bearing a very important message to General Nelson. On last Monday evening Captain Ford and his attendant arrived at the Saint Cloud Hotel. In conditions such as surround us it is important to acquire information which too often escapes our usual military intelligence. We therefore try to secure men of special fitness and place them in strategic civilian service. One of those we have with us tonight. He is Mr. Calvin Bailey, ordinarily a clerk in this hotel, whom doubtless you all know.

"Fortunately—I presume fortunately—Mr. Bailey was on duty when Captain Ford and the orderly arrived. He suspected something then, and his suspicions were strengthened to the point of his entering their room the next day for purposes of search. While he was engaged they returned and assaulted him so violently that one less hardy would likely not have survived. We do not have a clear picture of what followed, but at any rate Bailey returned to consciousness in an ambulance that had been sent to the hotel for Captain Joynes who was sick and needed care in a hospital.

"The bogus pair next appeared at the Cunningham House where General Nelson was dispatching some business. They delivered the message from General Buell, undoubtedly genuine, and also an order for a spy whom we had captured a few days before and whom we were then holding in prison, to be handed over to them and brought by them to headquarters for personal questioning by General Buell. I have the order here and it is the most remarkable forgery I have ever seen. General Nelson was greatly preoccupied at the time, so no question was raised, and the spy was turned over to them.

"Very fortunately, Mr. Bailey regained complete control of his faculties and himself and by some quick thinking was able to intercept them as they left the city. Two of them escaped, but the third—apparently the one who had impersonated Captain Ford—was taken and placed in prison. Something— again we do not know quite what—happened at the prison early the next morning and he was released, too. Since he was wearing our uniform the guard with criminal stupidity let him go, evidently thinking some mistake had been made. We have reason to believe that a little later the spy entered the home of a Dr. Robertson on South Cherry. He is reported to have been in some distress at the time—which would seem to be natural since he was knocked unconscious when captured. A watch was kept upon the house for twenty-four hours and since he did not reappear it was assumed that his injury was serious.

"When the guard went off at midnight last night, through an unfortunate omission it was not replaced. But a little later we decided to search Dr. Robertson's house, which was done. No trace of the spy was found. Dr. Robertson when questioned said that it was his custom to treat anyone in need of his services. He never inquired as to the political preferences of a patient. He had treated a man but had not even asked his name. He was vague as to the time of his departure, vague as to any details regarding the man, and did not know where he went when he left. The standing of this physician in the town, and for that matter with us, is of the highest and it does not seem wise to press the matter on him any further."

"We have made quite eloquent examples of some men of high standing."

"Quite so, Colonel Walter, but this physician as far as we know has remained strictly neutral. It would, I believe, be unwise to carry the matter further. The professional ethics of a physician is a most sensitive matter.

"But let me drop back a little. It seemed reasonable to Mr. Bailey that the two Rebels who escaped would make some effort to rescue their comrade. They are extremely sentimental in such matters. So men were posted to watch the various approaches to the city. It proved a move of wisdom. The two men were found long after midnight approaching Nashville. They were followed far enough to determine their intentions. So, when they arrived, Mr. Bailey and some soldiers were awaiting them. But our bad luck persisted and only one was taken. The other escaped and we think is in the city now, though as a matter of fact we have no idea where or in what disguise.

"Then there is another matter which I cannot explain at all, a baffling matter indeed. One of the wagons which we sent out a bit prematurely to engage the Rebels was found late in the afternoon in an old field in the eastern borders of the city. The teamster was inside the wagon, tied, with his clothes removed but left in the wagon with him. One horse was grazing near by; the other has not been found. What sense can be made of that? We have witnesses who state that, when the trip was called off and the wagons turned back, there were two men on the driver's seat. We know of but one, the teamster we found in the wagon, but the description of neither man seen by the witnesses fits him. Furthermore, the description of neither man fits the spy who escaped. What sense can be made of that either? It leaves us all most uncomfortable. Mr. Bailey has some theories, but frankly I am not able to put much credence in them."

"Pardon me, General, but are you sure that all of this is very serious?"

"I certainly am. It is extremely serious for the Rebels to frustrate our efforts as they have been doing. Besides, any leak or any weakness is always likely to spread. Also, there are dangerous possibilities in this forgery, that appalls me by its very perfection."

"Has anyone questioned the spy now in our custody?"

"No, and I have it on my mind that it should be done. He will be tried before our court tomorrow. There is not much doubt what the judgment of the court will be, but doubtless some lighter punishment could be arranged in return for the information we need, which he probably can give."

"I have never seen a Rebel spy. Why not send for him and question him here?"

"That is precisely what I intend to do, and I'll trade him his life for any worth-while information."

"I doubt very much if you would get anything worth while out of him," said a voice that had not spoken before. "I've had a lot of experience with these Rebels and they can be as closemouthed as any clam."

"They'd be willing to open them to save their necks," said Colonel Walter.

"We will see," said General Negley. "I'd rather this fellow would go unhung than his story remain untold. It would serve our purposes better. Are there a couple of dependable soldiers here we could send to the jail for him?"

Each of the men standing in the dark room felt the other stiffen. Colonel Walter was saying, "I have two excellent men here in the lobby. One is Lieutenant Kirby whom you know. He is entirely trustworthy."

"Wait a moment, and I'll write the order. Please give it to Lieutenant Kirby. Tell them to use every care. They should be back within a half-hour. Tell them to bring the prisoner handcuffed. They should take no chances. If you will excuse me, gentlemen . . ."

Crockett and Nichol heard a pen scratching across paper. It was time for them to go.

"Get your shoes off," whispered Crockett. "We've got to get away from here. Easy with that door, for God's sake, Nichol. Don't let it squeak."

Nichol's hand was trembling when he first touched the key but he steadied himself. He knew he had to. Three lives were depending on it. He put his shoes on the floor and held his free hand over the lock, muffling sound as far as he could. Then his thumb and forefinger which gripped the key went limp and his hand fell to his side. Three lives could well depend on the smoothness with which that key turned.

"Hurry," whispered Crockett, "it's our chance to get the sergeant." Nichol's fingers firmed and turned the key without sound. The knob turned without squeaking. They pulled the door open and then they were out in the hall.

They looked toward the back stairs but Crockett shook his head. It would be far more dangerous to be noticed going down the back stairs than the front. They stopped halfway down and hurriedly put on their shoes. Their starved lungs were panting for fresher air. Two soldiers sat in the lobby and slept soundly. Otherwise the hotel seemed deserted. They started out the main entrance that opened on Summer Street. The door was locked. Again their eyes met. That was an odd thing, to lock the main door of a hotel. The windows were barred, so there was nothing to do except use the back door—unless it too was locked. But it wasn't. They passed through it and down the back steps. They reached the little courtyard and stopped for a brief instant to fill their lungs to overflowing with fresh sweet air. Then they walked hurriedly along the alleyway to Summer Street.

"We'd better wait here to see which way they go," said Crockett in low tones. "We mustn't lose them." They

crossed to the east side of the street and stood in a shadow
watching, still panting for air.

One minute, two minutes, three they waited, and no sounds
came from the hotel. Then they heard men descending the
back steps. They heard them reach the ground. They heard
the crunching of heavy shoes on the gravel of the hotel's
courtyard. Then they heard something—they could not recog-
nize the sound—followed by two dull, muffled thuds, then
a low, quick gasp, finally silence.

NICHOL and Crockett stood in the shadow of a Summer Street
building and waited, breathing in the pure air of a summer
night. Something unexpected had happened. Steps sounded
again, coming out the alley. But only one man made the
steps they heard then. He appeared in the mouth of the alley,
and stood there, his eyes evidently searching the streets. Apparently he saw the two men standing in the shadow and
started across the street toward them. When he was halfway
across Nichol uttered a sharp exclamation, for he knew that
walk. He couldn't see the man's face but he knew that form.
It was his cousin Philip Yorke.

Quick, sharp thoughts flashed through Nichol's mind.
Was Yorke an advance guard for the men sent to bring
Goforth? If so, what was the meaning of those confused,
inarticulate sounds they had heard some seconds before? In
any case he was an officer in the Northern army. Suddenly in

that brief space of time he was conscious that somehow he liked the man. But this was war, a state involving terrible obligations, and they were faced then by one of them. Crockett's arm moved and a pistol appeared in his hand. They heard Cousin Philip speaking in clear but guarded tones.

"Peace, gentlemen, peace. Put aside that ungodly thing. It disturbs my poise! I suppose you want the order for the sergeant. Isn't that it?"

They said nothing, merely stared at him through the darkness.

"Well, here it is." He had reached them by this time and held out something dull-white in the shadows. Crockett took the paper with his left hand, but the pistol in his right still menaced.

"I fear we left those poor fellows pretty much damaged, the Negro boy and I, but there seemed no way out of it. Surprised, aren't you, Cousin Enoch?"

Beasley Nichol didn't understand the turn matters had taken. There were many things he didn't understand, but he was himself again. "Oh, quite, Cousin Philip. But we're in a bit of hurry. The snake is merely scotched."

"Too true. How golden are the minutes! Put up that pistol, please, Captain Crockett. Its appearance is unseemly among friends. Really it's an ugly thing."

"Friends?" It was Crockett who asked the question.

"Oh, indeed. I am fairly well acquainted with your reputation, sir. I am told you stand well with General Forrest. That for me is an excellent recommendation. Here are the handcuffs they had, and this is the key. Don't fail to put the handcuffs on him as the order says, but hold onto the key. You can free him the moment you get off the premises. The Negro is placing the poor fellows in the basement now. Very regrettable, but so is war. Well, good-by, cousin, not of the

blood, but of the cause. Good-by, Captain." He turned but
remained for one more word with Cousin Enoch. "When we
meet again—as we may presently—don't fail to remind me,
though most tactfully, how I dislike mud."

13

✗

NICHOL and Crockett walked rapidly out Summer to Deader-
ick but a squadron of soldiers was coming noisily up the
street, so they turned back to Union and proceeded east on
it. They came presently to the jail and entered it. At the
office they handed the order to the sergeant on duty. He
read it through and drew his brow into a tight frown.

"This seems to be in order," he said, "but we've had some
bad luck lately. I imagine you've heard about it. We have to
be extremely careful."

"We have to be careful, too. That's the reason for the
handcuffs," said Crockett.

"You will of course sign a receipt for him."

"Of course."

"I'll go get him. You wait here." He took a pistol from
the table and a key from the hook on the wall, and disappeared through a back door.

They stood there waiting. The sergeant seemed absent a
long time, for Nichol and Crockett knew that soon those
who also waited at the Saint Cloud would become impatient,
knew the action that would attend their impatience. The

front door opened and a soldier came into the office. He regarded the two men with interest. He saw their insignia and
saluted.

"Did you wish to see the sergeant?" Nichol asked easily.

"I'm to relieve him, sir, at midnight. It's beginning to
rain so I came early."

Rain! Crockett and Nichol looked at each other. The rear
door opened then and Sergeant Goforth came into the room.
His face was darkened by deep bruises and his eyes were
bloodshot. He saw his two comrades and for a split second
one foot stopped almost in mid-air, a split second and no
longer. Then he continued with firm step until he came to
the middle of the office. There he stood waiting.

"Hold out your hands," said Crockett sharply. The handcuffs were placed on his wrists.

"Where you goin' to take me?" asked Goforth hoarsely.

"To General Negley for questioning," answered Crockett.

"There's plenty I can tell him."

Crockett made no comment. He signed in a ledger book
a receipt for the prisoner. Then, with Goforth walking two
paces ahead, they left the office.

No one was in sight in the jail yard.

"My idea," said Crockett, "is to go out Market Street. If
we can get past Broad we'll make it. All right, Sergeant, hold
up a moment and we'll remove your jewelry." He fumbled it
seemed for minutes but finally unlocked the handcuffs and
dropped them to the street. Then he stooped and picked them
up.

"No," he said, "my Scotch-Irish soul rebels against such
waste. I'll take them along as a reminder of your captivity,
Sergeant."

"I knew you'd come," croaked the sergeant.

"My God! He knew we would come! Did you hear that, Nichol? He knew we would come for him. Did you hear it, he knew it! Sergeant, there are times when your faith is touching."

"I ain't so sure about Market Street. Maybe they aren't watching it too close," said Goforth. "But I'll bet a Yankee dime they got Broad Street sealed up tight."

"We've got to get across it sooner or later. Perhaps this rain may help."

They started south on Market. The night was hot and steamy and a slow, even fall of rain had set in. Lightning veined the sky directly ahead, and seconds later sounded the low hoarse rumble of distant thunder.

They walked a block in silence. Then Beasley Nichol laughed with restrained heartiness.

"I was just thinking how lovely is the night for Cousin Philip—mud everywhere."

"Who is your Cousin Philip?" asked Crockett.

"I haven't any idea. I met him at the Saint Cloud the night we came. I was supposed to be Captain Enoch Ford of Philadelphia. He said he was Enoch's cousin. It was a very cousinly reunion. But now I'm becoming suspicious. I doubt if he's anybody's cousin."

Suddenly the town awoke from its sleep. Whistles blew shrilly back at the Saint Cloud. Orders were shouted and the streets became alive with the sounds of soldiers marching rapidly. Soldiers were desperately searching for something, searching along all the streets back there and their search was spreading.

Ahead was Broad Street, and as the three men neared it a squadron went by, moving rapidly toward the river. The three men pressed against a wall until the soldiers had passed beyond view. They stood there uncertain, breathing a bit hard, still hugging the shadowed wall. Broad Street had become perilous, and yet beyond it lay their best chance for freedom.

Their irresolution was broken by the ominous sound of another group of soldiers coming down Market Street toward them. Though the Southerners could not see yet who was approaching, the cadence of the footsteps was unmistakably military. Now the soldiers were just reaching Union Street. Fortunately they were coming down the west side, opposite where the three men stood. It was raining a little harder and the lightning burned at briefer intervals in the sky to the south.

Crockett, Nichol and Goforth knew their peril. Broad Street was under patrol. They could not go on—and they couldn't stay where they were. The night was dark but the gaslight at Broad thinned the darkness to give the men visibility. They knew too that the night, rain or no rain, would grow brighter, for an hour or so later the moon would be rising. Of course, they couldn't retreat up Market Street. They were caught.

"Something has happened. I wonder what," said Nichol.

"Well, it happened," said Crockett.

"There's a vacant lot yonder," said Goforth, pointing down the street. "Let's climb that fence. It'll be dark in there. They haven't seen us yet."

It was perhaps thirty feet to the south corner of the building against which they crouched. From it a paling fence continued down the street. They edged along the wall, Goforth ahead. He placed his hand on the runner of the fence and vaulted easily to the other side. The others followed. They were then in the vacant space between two brick buildings. They could see the dim bulk of trees toward the rear. Under the largest tree they paused and as they did so the patrol passed down Market. If there were orders to comb the town systematically, and there likely were, the soldiers would come back up the east side. In that case their hiding place would surely meet with some scrutiny.

"We haven't a chance like this," said Crockett. "We've got to break up. I imagine they are all over town." And as if to confirm his pessimism there sounded the fierce blowing of whistles from somewhere up toward the Capitol. "Together we haven't a chance; singly perhaps we have. And if one of us, or two, gets away this time we won't be coming back on any rescue party—unless the general sends us. This hide-and-seek business is about played out."

"No, we can't stay together," agreed Nichol. "It's every man for himself, but if any of us does get through tonight he will go first to Les Campbell's and wait there a little while for the others to come. They'll know at Campbell's where General Forrest is. Listen!"

They didn't have to listen. The sounds were audible enough. Soldiers were approaching. But it was not the squad. From the sound there were only two of them. Their *tramp, tramp* came steadily up Market Street.

"They've been sent back to search this lot," whispered Crockett. "Each one behind a tree. Quick!"

The two soldiers stopped by the paling fence. The three men could see that each held a pistol in one hand and a lighted but well-smoked lantern in the other.

"I'll look through here," said one. "You take the lot up the street." His companion went on up Market Street. The remaining soldier placed his lantern on the brick sidewalk and swung himself over the low fence. He reached back and got the lantern and proceeded, moving with caution, through the lot. He reached first the tree behind which Sergeant Goforth was sheltered. It was the largest of the trees and the ser-

geant's outlines did not too greatly overflow its shadowy bulk.
The soldier held his lantern out ahead for a clearer view. He
both heard and saw the sergeant's quick move but not in
time for the shout which welled in his throat to become
audible. One of Goforth's hands covered the soldier's mouth,
cutting off all sound but the threshing of his feet. By then
Nichol was pinning the man's flailing arms behind his back,
as if in a vise, and Crockett was holding his feet immobile.

"Here's where my frugality is rewarded," said Crockett
whimsically. "I knew I'd need those handcuffs. My thanks
to my Scotch-Irish ancestors."

Nichol pulled the man's hands behind the tree and Crockett
snapped on the handcuffs, dropping the key to the ground.

"Fix his mouth so he can't yell for an hour or two. I wish
we had some rope for his feet." They had no rope, but Nichol
by process of choking opened the man's mouth and stuffed
inside one handkerchief. He tied Crockett's securely over the
Yankee's mouth.

He addressed the soldier wryly. "Better be thankful, Bud.
I've seen 'em worse off."

Then they stood stock-still in the dark, held rigid by the
sound of steps of the other Yankee returning. He stopped at
the fence and waited a moment. Then he called, "Hey,
there!" No one answered him, and his grumbling voice came
through the dark. "I thought he was going to wait for me."
He moved briskly on toward Broad Street.

"It's time to go," said Crockett. "I'm going to try it by
the river. See you at Les Campbell's. Good-by." They heard
him swing over the back fence.

"I've an idea," said Nichol. "The soldiers are down the
street. Let's go back up Market together for a piece. We've
got to get away from here. We could act like a searching

party and when it looks safe make a break for it. Wait a minute. I want that fellow's pistol. It might come in handy."

The sergeant nodded and a second later they were over the fence on the sidewalk. They marched together boldly up the street. As they neared Union their hearts missed a beat, for another outfit of soldiers was coming down the street on the other side. There was no option for them but to continue their show of boldness. As they passed the leader of the group called to them, "No luck?"

"No luck yet," answered Nichol and the brittle touches in his speech would have satisfied the demands of the most exacting Yankee.

The two men paused at Union. "Let's go that way," said Nichol, pointing to the west. "I've a notion that for us the boldest way is the safest. Bright lights for those whose consciences are bright, eh, Sergeant?"

The sergeant nodded assent and they turned out Union Street. Midway of the block they passed more soldiers and exchanged greetings and at Cherry another squad came from the south.

Nichol took the initiative. "No luck?"

"No," said the leader of the squad. "I don't think they're in this section. Where have you been?"

"Down on the river front. We saw nothing suspicious except that one boat is missing."

"You've reported it?"

"Of course. They've sent us to go through the railroad yards next."

"Luck to you, but I don't believe they'd go that way. If a boat's gone I'd watch up the river mighty close. That's the way they'd try to go."

They continued west on Union Street. They passed the

Cunningham House where a few days before they had visited General Nelson himself. The house was lighted and
the signs of activity were obvious. They passed the Union
Street side of the house with seeming assurance but the little
drops that stood on their faces were not from the rain that
fell with slow and dogged determination. An officer came
down the steps at a run. He saw the men passing and called
out to them, "Something's happened on Lower Market. You
heard anything?"

"Not a thing," said Nichol. "They've sent us to search the
railroad yards."

The officer unhitched a horse from the rack and rode away
in a clatter.

"They annoy me," said Nichol. "They are too eager.
Their whole philosophy is out of balance. I've a notion to go
away and leave them." A minute later he pointed. "Look,
Sergeant, there's Polk Place. I saw it when I was here before.
I never thought . . ." He stopped suddenly.

He remembered that the driver had said Hunter Cragwall
lived near Polk Place. His heart was beating faster. If he
only knew where, he'd walk by her house even if the enemy
opposed in force.

And the enemy did oppose. A shrill but determined voice
sang out suddenly, "Halt!"

They saw soldiers standing at the mouth of Polk Alley.
There was but one thing to do and they did it. They ran with
all the speed they could summon across Union Street and into
the alley that lay behind the Adams house. They could hear
the soldiers running after them, splashing through the wet
dark alley. Only a scant veneer of gravel coated the mud
and there was much sloshing as they stumbled into water-
filled holes. They could plainly hear their pursuers behind
them.

"Here's where I leave you, Sergeant. Make as much noise as you can for a little while, then dodge them. Report at Les Campbell's the first minute you can. In the meantime be a good soldier. Good luck."

NICHOL swung lightly over a fence into the darkness of a back yard. Sergeant Goforth continued to slosh along the alley. A rifle cracked and echoed but the sounds of Goforth's flight continued. The Yankees rushed by the place where Nichol crouched. When they were fifty yards farther on he vaulted the fence back into the alley. He rapidly and quietly retraced his way, crossed Union Street and entered Polk Alley. There would hardly be more than one outfit of Yankees assigned to it. But again he underestimated the enemy. A gaslight burned on Church Street and he could see a squadron posted at the end of the alley there. He turned and started back toward Union and heard as he did so the soldiers returning from their fruitless chase of Sergeant Goforth. Very well. They didn't have the sergeant. They could never have taken him in that time. They had simply lost him, encouraged to that end no doubt by a certain cunning on the part of the sergeant. They would now go to headquarters, perhaps at the Cunningham House, to report. He wondered if they could see him from Church Street and decided that he was safe since no light was behind him. But

the men coming back from their chase of the sergeant could
see him. He would be clearly outlined against the light on
Church. He stood for an instant undecided, and while he did
so a clock somewhere tolled midnight. He could hear across
town near Lower Market a confusion of whistles blowing and
a general tumult.

"It's a lovely night," he said to himself, "for jumping
fences." So he jumped another. And then he realized that
he was standing on the lawn of Polk Place. Very well, one
used even Polk Place in such an emergency. He moved deeper
into the yard. There were sounds of excitement over the city,
but the grounds of the big house seemed curiously serene and
apart. He could see down by the corner the dim outlines of
the tomb of President Polk. It was raining gently but insist-
ently. The soldiers crossed Union Street and turned toward
the Cunningham House. They were marching rapidly, in a
hurry to make their report, Nichol thought. More soldiers
would be concentrated in this section presently. It was in his
mind to try again the alley which he had just left when a
voice, a woman's voice, spoke from the side porch of the
house.

"Won't you come in out of the rain? I'm afraid you'll get
wet out there."

He hesitated for a brief instant, then walked toward the
house. A woman was standing at the steps.

"I am Mrs. Polk. Welcome to Polk Place. Come in,
please."

Again he hesitated, then he said, "Good evening, Mrs.
Polk. I am Lieutenant Beasley Nichol of General Forrest's
army. I apologize for my intrusion. It was forced upon me.
But if my presence might mean any trouble for your home I
should prefer to leave."

"Let that risk be mine," said Mrs. Polk. "I have offered

sanctuary before. Come on in." He went up on the porch. "You must be sopping wet," she said. "I think we'd better go inside. Someone might be flashing a lantern on the porch. They seem to be using a lot of lanterns tonight."

Nichol followed her inside the house. She led the way into the library.

"Sit in that chair." She pointed. "Your wet clothes will do no harm to the leather." He sat and Mrs. Polk looked at him intently. "I am indeed very glad to see you. Curiously, you look almost as I expected. I have heard some unusually favorable things of you. Welcome to Polk Place."

"Heard of me?" he asked sharply. "Surely you must be . . ."

"No, I am not mistaken," she said calmly. "I was sure that sooner or later you would come to see me, but really I didn't expect your visit quite so soon. Still, promptness is a most commendable virtue."

"I must explain," he said. "I am in Nashville on a mission for General Forrest and I was trying desperately to get out of town and back to the general. But my departure met with some opposition from the Yankees. They have seemed determined to keep me in their midst. In fact, I entered your yard to escape their . . . er . . . hospitality."

"That's the way I thought it was," she said. "Well, in any event you'd have come back unless there has been some miscarriage of, shall we say, the mail?"

He looked at her dumbly.

"And I was assured that the delivery had been made promptly and in person."

He sat looking at her, surprise but not understanding written on his face.

"Perhaps we should change the subject," she said gently. "We can revert to it when it seems more timely. Tell me about your general. He interests me greatly, but I have never seen him. He seems to be quite a miracle worker. People here seem to expect him to win the war."

"He will have to have a lot of help," said Nichol, "though I do think that General Forrest is one of the most remarkable men I ever saw."

"Where are you from, Lieutenant?"

"From Florence, Alabama, Mrs. Polk, though I have kins-people in this section."

"It's one of our good names. Florence is a delightful place. I've been there. Mr. Polk and I made a brief visit there once. Dr. Elliott, president of our Female Academy, came from Florence. He's a very distinguished man. Your disguise inter-ests me, Lieutenant. But the rain wasn't good for it."

Nichol didn't understand the turn matters had taken.

He said, "I think that I must be going now. I must get out of Nashville tonight."

"You couldn't leave tonight, or tomorrow. Perhaps you don't understand, Lieutenant Nichol, how desperate the— well, your enemy is. They do not intend for you to get away this time. Perhaps you'd better move your chair over there. It is so hot that I left the window open, and the shutters might not wholly obstruct the view of anyone unduly inquisitive, and sometimes sounds carry surprisingly. I hear there are people specially trained to listen."

"I do not like to put this risk upon your home."

"The honor overbalances the risk. I must repeat that I have heard some charming things said of you." She changed the subject abruptly. "War is an exorbitant price to pay for anything, Lieutenant Nichol."

"Yes," he said. "I have thought of that, too."

"Too high," she said, striking the arm of the chair with a clenched hand.

"What else could we do, Mrs. Polk?"

"Nothing, I suppose, since human nature is what it is. But where is Henry Fogg, the finest boy I ever knew in Nashville? Where is he? Dead! Where is Francis McNairy? Dead! Where is James Cooper? In such a makeshift for a hospital as they provide for wounded Southern men! Where is Randall McGavock? In prison! Where is Bailley Peyton? Dead! Where is William Harding? Where is Byrd Douglas? In prison! Where are our ministers? In prison! What about our churches? Nailed shut! Why all that whistling and hubbub on our streets in the dead of night? They wish to hang some of our Southern boys for being adventurous and breaking some of war's silly rules. And what will we get for the price paid? Some lovely examples of heroism and a lot of new graveyards, and what else God only knows!"

"Life, Mrs. Polk, is sweet for all of us. I do not want to die, let alone be hanged. I have much to live for. But you, too, Mrs. Polk, would I am sure rather die than not give what your country needs."

"Of course, and yet what you have said has always been the precise formula for war. *My country needs me!* What is my country? My husband was president of both North and South. Of course, this is my home. And all those of my name and blood have answered the same call you did. But whatever good war may bring, the price is too high."

"The precious things of life such as freedom always come high. It is the law."

"Yes, I suppose they do," she said a bit sadly.

And then a stick cracked outside by the window. Mrs. Polk stiffened. Beasley Nichol was standing, his every sense poured into alertness.

"Sit down, Major," said Mrs. Polk in a voice sharp and distinct. "Can you not stay awhile longer? I may not get to see you again. I have found your conversation intensely interesting. I have not been in New York since the last year of Mr. Polk's Presidency. I found it such an interesting place."

Cues belonged as a part of Beasley Nichol's life. He caught this one. "One may be fond of New York, but for relaxation only. For sheer beauty, madam, I do not know the equal of New England in October, particularly Connecticut. The state is a panorama of all the russets and gold that God ever made." His voice was pure deep Yankee.

"Perhaps," she said, "but Middle Tennessee does not depend on autumn. It doesn't even depend on spring. Beauty here is timeless, sir."

"It is possible that the October beauty of Connecticut and Massachusetts maples might go unnoted in war, when one's mind is held to grosser things, but I shall never forget one day when I rode from Danbury to New Britain . . ."

There was another sound at the window, and then farther away a muffled step. The visitor was leaving. Mrs. Polk motioned with her eyes for Nichol to continue. His disquisition on New England beauty shouldn't close too abruptly.

"Or in Massachusetts, take Lexington, and Concord and Framingham. I think that in the countryside thereabouts is the most glorious scarlet in the world. Ah, but Indian summer in New England!"

"Ah, but Indian summer in Maury County. . . . I think our visitor has gone. You can leave New England now, Lieutenant Nichol."

"It's time," he said, wiping his brow. "My invention was running low."

"They are becoming more and more inquisitive. It must have been the light in the house so late."

"You are a gracious and generous lady, but I still think I should leave. I have two comrades out there. I don't want to be protected when they are in danger. Also, I don't want in any way to embarrass you."

"You won't, except by leaving. Believe me, I am glad to meet you. I have thought of you quite often today. This is more than a mere coincidence, sir. It has about it a sort of fitness that pleases me greatly."

"Tell me, please, Mrs. Polk, how did you even hear of me? I can't imagine . . ."

"Dear me, my memory is so unreliable. It couldn't have been General Forrest because I have never seen him. It couldn't have been General Kirby Smith either. I haven't seen him since before the war. By the way, they say he has marched into Kentucky, and that the Yankees here after a lot of false starts are about to go after him. I wonder some about those false starts. Don't you, Lieutenant Nichol?"

"Yes," he said, "I do too—some."

"I think it's about time for you to go to bed, Lieutenant. Now, listen to me, sir. I don't expect you to leave my house tonight or tomorrow. Perhaps day after tomorrow we can see how the wind is blowing. I do not wish to appear discourteous but just now hospitality must yield to discretion. You will lock your door from the inside and not open it until you are convinced that I wish it. Simply say nothing, make no noise. Ordinarily my servants are trustworthy and so are the guests in my home. But matters have become a bit changed; otherwise, we would not have been visited tonight. Perhaps I am under suspicion but the time has not come when I'll refuse help to those in distress—particularly my friends. As long as this house is mine I'll be its mistress. But do not tempt trouble, Lieutenant Nichol. Stay away from windows and keep that door locked. There are some very good books in the room. I'll show you to it now. And tomorrow we'll talk again perhaps."

His eyes were on the beauty of the house as they went up the stairs. "How lovely! Such a home is not to be shared with mere strangers."

"You are no stranger, sir. Quite the contrary. It would surprise you to know how little a stranger you are."

"Tell me, please, who was it mentioned me to you?"

"Of such matters, Lieutenant Nichol, we'll talk perhaps tomorrow. Good night, sir. Oh, one other thing—don't use the lamp if you can help it. It's late and someone might become inquisitive again."

Beasley Nichol stood in the room into which Mrs. Polk had shown him. "Ah," he said in tones touched with music. "Ah! *We have scotch'd the snake, not kill'd it.*"

15

✗

HE WALKED to the window and peered through the shutters. "It's an omen," he said, "an omen." The rain no longer fell and a wind that blew briskly was clearing the clouds from the sky. The moon was shining brightly and its light gilded the slender rifts of retreating clouds. High on its hill he could see the Capitol bathed in soft moonlight. He could hear far out toward the Charlotte Road a heavy wagon lumbering over cobblestones. There was the sound of some movement on the streets but the blowing of whistles had ceased. It had turned cooler and a gust of fresh wind from the north swept into the room. Oddly enough his anxiety for his two companions quieted. They were men of wit and daring, fully competent in any emergency. There'd be a reunion presently at Les Campbell's. He went promptly to sleep, and when he awoke a new day had come and the sun was stealing glancingly into the room between the half-closed shutters.

He went to the window and looked out through the cracks in the shutters at a shining world. There was not a cloud in the sky. He looked up at the Capitol, etched against a sky velvety and deep blue. He could see the Stars and Stripes whipping in a brisk breeze. It was a world upon which the blight of war had not laid its cruel hand.

But it had! His gaze fell to the level of the streets. The war had come back. There at the corner of Union and Vine stood a soldier, his musket resting on his shoulder. He was not there casually. There was intentness in the way he stood, and his eyes were on Polk Place.

"They must miss me," said Nichol humorously to himself. And then he found further testimony of the way they missed him, for up Union Street at the mouth of the alley behind the house stood another soldier and a musket rested on his shoulder and his eyes too were fixed upon Polk Place. He knew then that other soldiers were posted at the corners he could not see. He would not be leaving Polk Place that day.

Of course, though, he might be leaving! If the Yankees became bold enough to search the home of a President of the country . . . But he'd cross that bridge when he reached it. He glanced at himself in a mirror and the glance became a long and surprised look. He didn't know he could be that dirty. His face seemed to be a scrambled mass of altered and obscured features and dirt, old mottled walnut stain, and frayed and tangled fragments of beard. He proceeded to a diligent use of soap and water for the first time since he had left Dr. Robertson's. Half an hour later Beasley Nichol was restored in part to his own image and to a state of moderate general cleanliness.

He looked through the shutters again. The two soldiers

were still standing their posts, and their scrutiny of Polk Place never seemed to waver.

He turned away from the window. There upon a table rested a large book. He knew what it must be before he read the title. It was the *Complete Works of William Shakespeare*. Hungrily, he picked it up. It fell open, but at a play he did not know. It was *Hamlet* he wanted. He thumbed the pages expertly and they opened upon the strange and stirring tale of the Danish Prince. Then Beasley Nichol was home again from the wars, and he knew that Edwin Forrest would be playing the title role that night, and that he would be Laertes.

His voice rang like tragic music through the room.

> *"How now! What noise is that?*
> *O heat, dry up my brains! Tears seven times salt*
> *Burn out the sense and virtue of mine eye!"*

There was a succession of knocks at the door, and when he opened it Mrs. Polk came in. She looked about the room with surprise in her eyes.

"Mercy!" she said. "From the noise I thought there must be a troupe of players in here. Did you have a good night, Lieutenant Nichol?"

"I was reading your book, Mrs. Polk. It was thoughtful of you to leave it for me. It is one of my favorites."

"Oh," she said, her eyes regarding him meditatively, "one of your favorites? Most interesting, indeed."

After a while he said, "Yes, I slept well. Thank you, Mrs. Polk."

"Well, I didn't. After I left you I couldn't sleep so I went out and sat on the porch again. The town was still in a turmoil when I went to bed. I forgot to tell you that I had already had one visitor before you came. I practically spent the night receiving those who were guests under compulsion."

"Another Yankee?"

"Quite the contrary. Another Rebel."

"Oh," he said, "oh! Do you mean Captain Crockett?"

"No, but I should like to see Captain Crockett. I really wish he had come too. I've heard about him, too. In fact, I've seen him. But my visitor that time wasn't a soldier."

"But you said a Rebel. Were they after him, too?"

"Oh, yes, they were after him indeed. The Yankees are getting ambitious. Someday they may capture a Rebel and hold him. I'd be careful myself. Aren't you hungry, Lieutenant Nichol?"

"Yes, ravenously."

"Malachi will bring you breakfast right away. You can let him in. He's entirely dependable, but I'm afraid I can't say the same for all my servants. My first visitor arrived about an hour before you came. He jumped the fence too, only he jumped the front-yard fence. And then this morning a Yankee did visit me, a very nice Yankee. He came in by the gate."

"He was looking for me?"

"Not at all, or at least he didn't mention it. He was looking for my first visitor. And he didn't find him. Still, I think he was a nice Yankee and I liked him. . . . We can still do very well with breakfasts here but the time will come, I'm afraid, when . . . Anyhow you shall have yours."

It was a satisfying breakfast and moved Nichol to a Shakesperean outburst.

> "*. . . And he that doth the ravens feed,*
> *Yea, providently caters for the sparrow. . . .*"

He finished his breakfast and sat in silence, thinking. Mrs. Polk had told him too little. Who had told her of him? But, of course, Randall McGavock. And that was odd. She couldn't have seen Randall since Christmas, and he was at home only one short day then. Seven months, and yet she had talked as if the conversation in which he had been mentioned was fresh in her mind. He knew Henry Fogg, but Henry Fogg was dead. He knew Henry Maney, but Henry was dead, too. How pitifully transient was life! The thought came to him that Dr. Robertson had told Mrs. Polk of him. But a moment later he dismissed that idea. It didn't seem to fit. It was most improbable that either Dr. Robertson or Mrs. Polk had left home the day before.

Then he tingled a bit, for he suddenly knew that Lucy Stratton had told her. Of course, it was Lucy. He remembered that it was she who had told Hunter Cragwall of him. And that was a bit odd, too. She wouldn't have known that he might visit Mrs. Polk. It had been two years since he had seen Lucy. He had heard from her but once and then merely a skimpy little note. After that the fullness of life had crowded her out and he had proceeded to forget her.

No, he hadn't forgotten her! It was she he had thought of first when General Forrest had ordered him to Nashville. But Lucy was in love with a soldier. Hunter had said so. Well, he was a soldier himself. But he wasn't that soldier. One skimpy, tepid, well-wishing note would never bear the true love of a girl like Lucy Stratton. Not if followed by two years of silence. Oh, he had flirted outrageously with Lucy that time in Beersheba Springs and she with him—though, of course, with the reticence becoming such a lady. And then he had gone back home and written her a flaming letter which too long after had elicited from her the skimpy note, polite, well phrased—and meaningless. The fires of his love could never burn without fuel, and there wasn't much fuel in the few words she had sent. So, the fires had gradually grown cold and dwindled to ashes.

Then his mind jumped again. Maybe Mrs. Polk had but recently talked with Hunter Cragwall. The driver had said that the Cragwalls lived near Polk Place. Hunter Cragwall! His mind was whirling indeed. His hand went to his face and found the beard she had so carefully placed there missing. His clenched hand struck the arm of the chair in disappointment. What mattered a little dirt and disarray against the presence of her artistry? His heart was beating faster, for he remembered that Mrs. Polk had indicated the favor of the report for him.

His dreaming came to a sudden close. Strains of music drifted through the window, something elemental and primitive and sweetly poignant. Little shivers tingled along his spine. It was "The Mourning Dove" that he heard. He looked through the shutter. He could see the fiddlin' man plainly sitting there on Union Street, grim and gaunt. He could see that inspired bow as it rose and fell. What was he doing away from his stand at the Methodist Church? Then he knew. The fiddlin' man was playing a warning to him. The enemy was waiting, waiting at all of the exits to Polk Place and he was being told not to try to leave.

Five minutes perhaps the fiddlin' man played those plaintive strains. Then a rough voice shouted a command and the fiddlin' man carefully put his fiddle in a wooden case and, carrying it in one hand and a stool in the other, went on down the street. Beasley Nichol looked with warm eyes at the retreating musician. The fiddlin' man was a part of the daily routine on Church Street, taken for granted, even expected, even perhaps desired. His appearance on Union Street would not go unnoted. And its proximity to Polk Place would surely be added to the suspicions of the enemy.

Nichol, standing by the window and looking through a thin crack in the shutters, could see the soldier still at Union and Vine. An exclamation escaped him, for there talking with the soldier was Fisheye. The man's uncouth face was rigid with determination and as he talked his eyes would fix on Polk Place, dwell there, leave as though with reluctance, then come back to the house with such intentness as though he would send his vision through the brick walls and shuttered windows. After a while Fisheye went along Vine, to confer with a sentinel farther down, Nichol thought.

Then a sudden bright smile covered his face. "It's as good as a play! It's the second act, the villain is rampant, and the hero—that's me—is in a jam." He decided to threaten Fisheye. "Just wait till the third act, you scoundrel!" He smiled a bit ruefully. "I wish we'd hurry up with that act. Stagemaster, the third act, please."

His thoughts moved on to Crockett and Goforth. If they had had luck they were at Les Campbell's by then. Again the tremors went up his spine. Somewhere in the house he heard a man's voice gently echoing through the empty halls, and he knew that voice, or had known it. The words were indistinct, but he knew that voice, knew it but couldn't identify it, matched it against other voices, but still couldn't find one to fit it. He hadn't heard the words at all, only the quality of the voice. A woman's voice had answered, undoubtedly Mrs. Polk's. And then silence had closed in on Polk Place as a door closes on a room.

It was not Crockett's voice, or Goforth's, or Fisheye's, or Cousin Philip's. There was something about that voice very personal and not too far in the past. Whose was it?

Cousin Philip came into his mind. Who was Cousin Philip anyhow? What did he want? What was he trying to find out? He had been helpful once, but for what purpose? An interesting man, but one to be regarded thoughtfully.

With quick nervous steps Nichol was pacing the carpeted

floor. Unconsciously his hand slipped into his pocket, and without noting that he did so, he drew out of it a crumpled envelope. He stood staring at it. What was he doing with it? Then he remembered that the driver had handed it to him in the churchyard the evening before. He tore it open and unfolded the sheet of paper he took from it. He stood stock-still there in the middle of the room and read the lines on that paper. For him every letter was traced in pure gold. It said:

If you are still in Nashville tomorrow night and your whiskers need a bit of care be at Mrs. Polk's a little after dark.

H. C.

P. S. But don't risk too much and do be cautious.

Tonight! Here! Hunter Cragwall coming here! To see him! The soul of Beasley Nichol overflowed in Lorenzo's lyric.

> *"The moon shines bright. In such a night as this,*
> *When the sweet wind did gently kiss the trees*
> *And they did make no noise . . ."*

Then he laughed. There'd be no moon tonight, not till late. Well, moon or not, there'd be no lack of light. And the wind would gently kiss the trees. And again the spirit of Lorenzo was upon him.

> *". . . In such a night*
> *Stood Dido with a willow in her hand*
> *Upon the wild sea-banks, and waft her love*
> *To come again to Carthage.*

"It's better than a play," he said, "far better than any. How

Shakespeare could have written about it! I have a royal command to come here tonight, but I obey the summons and hours afterward read it. It's better than any play. When I am through with all this I'll write the play myself. I'll call it *'Tis Coincidence That Shapes Our Ends.* How pleasing is the countenance of Coincidence! How pleasing and how purposeful! How she has smiled at me! Tonight!"

Then Reality thrust Coincidence momentarily aside and strode upon the stage. "Tonight—why, 'tis seven hours away! Seven long and dreary hours! Can seven such hours ever pass?" But at that moment it seemed revealed to him that they could. "Forgive me, my dear," he asked in melting tones. "Of course they can pass. And what hour could be tedious or dreary when filled with blessed thoughts of you?"

Again the little tingles played about his spine. For then curiously and without reason there came from nowhere and recreated itself that familiar voice he had heard. And he knew whose it was. It was the driver's, the bearer of the note he held in his hand. So he had been here in Polk Place. Could it be the driver who had told Mrs. Polk of him? Their acquaintance had been abrupt, brief, and only on terms of danger. But what was the driver doing here? Obviously he had made a trip to the Cragwall home. Nichol knew that the time had come when danger challenged the driver every time he walked along a street. Perhaps the driver had come to get him away from the coils which the Yankees were drawing ever tighter about the home. Well, what was to be would be. If only the hours were less sluggish.

He tried to remember how Hunter Cragwall looked when she was touching his face with gentle daubs of walnut stain, but he couldn't put his glimpses together into one picture of her. The glints of fine gold in her hair he could see clearly; her cheeks—their loveliness was bright before his vision; her eyes were azure pools whose heavenly charm no sky could ever match, and her movements had the grace of wheatfields moved by the slow winds. But he could not put them together. Well, her presence would compose them into a blessed unity.

For a long time he sat recreating his lady's beauty. Then a knock sounded at the door. He sat waiting, for Mrs. Polk had cautioned him. There were those in her own household whose loyalty she did not fully accept.

The knock sounded again and a low voice said, "I got yo' dinnuh, suh."

He opened the door and the old Negro came in with the tray. He placed it on a table, adjusted the various dishes, and said, "I'll be back fo' de dishes, suh, in about an houah."

He made a courtly bow and withdrew from the room. Nichol locked the door after him. Neither danger nor the vision of a radiant lady could lay a restraining hand upon his hunger. So he sat and ate with keen relish.

His grace was a touch of Falstaffian wisdom. *"Wherein neat and cleanly, but to carve a capon and eat it?"*

16

HE ATE and sat musing. A knock sounded. It was not the old Negro but Mrs. Polk.

"May I come in?" she asked.

"I would be unhappy if you did not," he said, bowing.

She sat in a chair by the shuttered window.

"Thank you for the food you sent me, Mrs. Polk. It was excellent and I was very hungry."

She withdrew her eyes from a brief glimpse of the world without. "Tell me, Lieutenant Nichol, just what you were sent to Nashville to do. I know that General Forrest sent you, but for what?"

He sat for a moment gazing into space, then he told her.

"I didn't ask out of mere curiosity. Oh, I am curious enough—indeed curiosity is quite a part of me—but this time I was trying to tie some loose ends together."

"Tell me," he said very gently, "about Hunter Cragwall."

"Hunter Cragwall?" She smiled oddly. "So you know Hunter, Lieutenant?"

"I have seen her once, Mrs. Polk."

"Only once? Something about your request surprises me. Should I be surprised, Lieutenant?"

"Only once, Mrs. Polk. And having seen her, wouldn't it be the more surprising if I didn't ask?"

"Perhaps then some other loose ends are falling together. Hunter sent me word an hour ago that she would call on me tonight. Could she know that you are here?"

"No, but she could know that I would be here then."

"Oh," she said. "Where did you see Hunter that one time?"

He told her.

"Only once." Mrs. Polk was smiling and her head was cocked characteristically to one side.

"So it was that driver who brought you the note. And who else would it be? I wonder how much you know of him?"

"Only that he helped me get out of town—and then back in. And that he devised the means for my present liberty. And that he brought me the note."

"So you saw Hunter only once! It's an interesting generation. It grows on me. Well, sir, the gentleman who helped you get out of town and then back in is a remarkable person. Did you ever hear of General William Walker?"

"The Gray-eyed Man of Destiny? Of course."

"This driver was with him on his last expedition, was with General Walker when they shot him. During those terrible days of our capture no one was more helpful than the man who brought you your note. He is truly a very remarkable gentleman. Would it surprise you, Lieutenant Nichol, to know that he came to my house before you did?"

"No. I heard his voice. That surprised me."

"Well, he was the one. The Yankees caught him down on Market Street. It must have been right after he saw you at the church. They put him in jail on some pretext and he promptly cut his way out with a pocketknife. And when they got after him he ran in here. It seems that I am conducting an asylum for pursued Southerners. I think I'll put a sign up—IF THE YANKEES ARE AFTER YOU COME RIGHT IN."

"The sign would be unnecessary. We do anyway."

As he spoke there came from the Capitol the sound of trumpet and drum and marching men. Nichol went and stood by one of the windows and Mrs. Polk sat at the other. They could see soldiers milling about on the terrace of the Capitol, then falling into place, the drum beating furiously all of the time.

"I know what it is," said Mrs. Polk. "I heard the news awhile ago. It's General Nelson and his men on their way to Kentucky. The Southern troops are making some headway there so the Yankees have to go. I heard that they were to leave two days ago, then yesterday . . . and today they are at last on their way."

"Does it mean the Yankees are getting out of Nashville?"

"Oh, my goodness, no. Not all of them. Nashville is too

important for that. There will be plenty of them left to annoy us greatly. It means that they must do something about General Kirby Smith. They can't have him rampaging about over Kentucky without opposition. Bad for their morale."

The column came marching out of the Capitol grounds into Vine Street. General Nelson, dwarfing his horse, rode at the column's head, and as they passed Polk Place he turned his face to the right and saluted the home of a President of the nation. It was a gracious gesture. And the soldiers, too, passed with their eyes on Polk Place. Somehow the sight thrilled Beasley Nichol, but at that moment he happened to glance at the sentinel and there again stood Fisheye. He was talking with the soldier but barely taking his eyes from the house.

Nichol pointed. "Mrs. Polk, do you know that man?"

"Yes," she said, "I know him. I hate to admit it, but I know him. To my discredit I can call his name. The Saint Cloud Hotel has sunk pretty low to use the likes of him."

"Or does he use the Saint Cloud?"

"I have been told that he's a clerk there. That would be merely an excuse to compound his villainy better. He has always been low and cunning. He is from moderately good people, and I feel sorry for them. He has been tied up with more meanness than any man in Nashville. What is he doing out there?"

"He is carrying on his meanness, though I hope it will not be long continued. But I must see——"

"Oh, yes, you must see Hunter. Your disguise, I do believe, needs redoing. Why, of course it does. And she's the only one you could trust it to. Well, in that emergency I shall fetch Hunter up to a little parlor I have on this floor. I often bring company there. Then I'll come for you."

She paused at the door, stood for a moment as if in indecision. Then she said, "It was your friend, the driver, who told me about you. He liked the trip you took together, said he really enjoyed it. He said he had just talked with someone and from what was said he thought it very probable that you would visit me soon. Well, here you are." She closed the door and left.

17

BEASLEY NICHOL sat at the window and watched the minutes as they slowly fell into the past from Time's unending store. For a long period Time had seemed a miser. Somewhere an unseen Joshua had commanded the hoarding of minutes. But then the grudging had relaxed, and again the sun moved. Slowly at first, then with gathering speed it fell into the west. Long after he could see it no more Nichol watched it gild with glory the Capitol's Lantern of Demosthenes.

Then the solemn hush of twilight came upon the city and the yards and open places sparkled with fireflies. He could see dimly the soldiers guarding the corners. The departure of General Nelson's army had not weakened the watch upon Polk Place. That evening the war was silent. The sounds that drifted through the windows at Polk Place were compounded of music and tranquillity, the low sigh of the summer wind, and over by the sulphur spring the plaintive cry of a whippoorwill, repeated over and over again. The softened rumble of wagons could be heard along the distant streets. From everywhere came the lazy drone of katydids.

There was a knock at his door. He opened it and found

Mrs. Polk standing there at the threshold. She came into the room.

"Well, sir," she said, "your friend the driver has gone. Just a few minutes ago. Who do you suppose made it possible for him to leave?"

Nichol stared at her, saying nothing.

"The Yankee officer who came here searching for him—and likely for you, too. I like this Yankee very much. I met him before the war began. He was on a visit here and saw one of our finest girls at the Presbyterian Church—only once, Lieutenant, only once—and fell in love with her and she with him. It is a very pretty story, Lieutenant Nichol. I was interested in them, much interested, for I perceived in them a certain fitness, each for the other. But it was this driver—the one who brought you the note, Lieutenant—who gave them precious help. Wasn't it curious that with a town full of officers they picked this particular one to search my house? There's a destiny that shapes such things. I do not doubt it. Well, this Yankee knew, I think, that the driver was here, though I doubt if he knew about you. And he knew how much he owed the driver, and being a gentleman, he paid it. He gave me for him tonight's password about the city, and some clothes. That Yankee is a gentleman, Lieutenant."

"It's as good as a play, Mrs. Polk."

"Oh, much better. God can think up more interesting things than people can."

"Yes," he said, "it was He who thought up my meeting with Hunter Cragwall."

"So there was divinity in that meeting. Well, it wouldn't surprise me if there was. Hunter is one of our finest, Lieutenant. I suspect, sir, that you are quite demanding. And yet you couldn't ask for more than Hunter Cragwall can give. We somehow take beauty and goodness for granted in such girls as Hunter. But beyond that she has a strange resource-fulness. She has always had. Whatever needs to be done is in Hunter's routine, always has been. I knew that she was giving some sort of service to the cause, but I didn't know what."

"Do you know Lucy Stratton?"

"Oh, yes, since she was a week old. So you know Lucy, too! You met her only once, Lieutenant?"

"Daily," he said, "for three days at Beersheba Springs, two years ago."

"Your choice is excellent, sir. You do choose our best. But Lucy wouldn't please you so well as Hunter. Her beauty is a little less vivid, and she wouldn't surprise you so often. I think, Lieutenant, it must delight you to be surprised. Lucy wouldn't be coming, too, tonight, would she?"

"If she is I do not know it."

"I've heard that she has a devoted lover in the army."

"Hunter said she had."

"*Hunter!* This generation never fails to interest me. You saw her only once, and she only smeared your face then! And yet you say so glibly 'Hunter.' "

"Mrs. Polk, I want the war to close. Tell me, please, will it be over soon?"

"No, not soon. We have already been through some awful days, but nothing to match those to come. People should not go to war who flinch at the sight of blood, and grow weary of wretchedness, and are greatly disturbed by the presence of death. And this time there will be so much blood, so much wretchedness!"

"And so much death?"

"Yes, Lieutenant, so much."

"But we will win, won't we?"

"Do not say what I tell you to others, Lieutenant Nichol.

They would not understand me. No, we will not win. Except for spirit and gallantry we have not the wherewithal. The North is slower in action then we are. No Yankee can in swiftness of action match your General Forrest. No Yankee can in military skill match several of our generals. But they are a terribly determined people, and they have resources we can never equal. In the end they will wear us down, grind us to nothing except in spirit."

Her seriousness sobered him. "In the end, Mrs. Polk? How long will that be?"

"Only God knows. I do not have that vision, Lieutenant, but much too long."

"They do not have the generals. All of the geniuses are on our side."

"Oh, I know we say that. But what is a genius? Is it one who performs brilliantly for a while, to go down later in defeat? Or is it one who, though uninspired, takes great odds and dogged determination and with them wins in the end? Genius is not entirely detached from supplies, Lieutenant. A genius needs food for his soldiers, and swords. Besides, I am not too sure that Northern generals are without talent. I know that some of them are greatly gifted. I have met their General Thomas and I should reckon him as an able officer and a gentleman. But forgive me, Lieutenant. I fear that I am becoming a garrulous old lady. . . ."

"Then," he said, "the two adjectives you just used have gained a charm I never dreamed of."

"There is something about you that baffles me, Lieutenant. You always leave me a bit mystified. What did you do before you became a soldier with Forrest?"

"Before I was a soldier under Forrest I was an actor under Forrest. But different Forrests, Mrs. Polk." He sketched that phase of his life. As he was talking Mrs. Polk rose from her chair.

"There is someone at the door downstairs," she said. "I must see who it is. We must talk again of the two Forrests. Excuse me, please."

Presently she returned. She held a finger to lips indicating silence, and he followed her along the hall, all sound deadened by the thick carpet that lay on the floor.

She rapped once and opened a door. It was the little parlor that she had spoken of. He followed her into the lighted room. The picture of that parlor would remain in his memory as long as he lived. It was not only parlor, but library and study as well. Shelves of books rose to the ceiling. There was about the books a quality of russet richness. Somehow they bespoke old truth, ripened by time. There were some chairs and they looked old like the books. Some books, too, were on the table, companions to a vase of zinnias. A lighted lamp on a smaller table mellowed the room with golden light.

But his eyes did not dwell on those things, for there standing by the larger table, one hand resting gently on its polished surface, stood Hunter Cragwall. All of this he saw in an instant, but that was enough. That glimpse would hold through life. Beasley Nichol knew the picture would never fade from his memory.

Mrs. Polk was saying with wry humor, "My dear, I should like to present my friend, Lieutenant Beasley Nichol of General Forrest's army. Lieutenant Nichol, my very dear friend, Hunter Cragwall. Oh, but how forgetful I must have grown! I remember now that you have met before—once, I believe."

"I knew he would come," said Hunter Cragwall, her eyes never leaving his face, the lamplight catching and revealing the fine gold of her hair.

"Oh, my dear, how could you know it?" asked Mrs. Polk. "He didn't know that he was coming himself till he learned it from the Yankees. Aside from—well, shall we say their suggestion?—you would never have thought of paying me your respects, would you, Lieutenant?"

"The Yankees were purely accidental. They merely happened. I'd be here tonight even if there were no Yankees. This was an order of the Great General."

Mrs. Polk smiled tolerantly at his grandiloquence. "I do find this generation most exciting. I wouldn't have missed it."

"I knew all the time you'd be here," repeated Hunter Cragwall, her eyes still fixed on his face, "and yet I was almost afraid you would."

"I came before I read your note," he said.

"I told that man—the one who tried to get out of Nashville with you—to tell you that I would come here tonight. That didn't seem right, so I wrote the note."

"And I, a perfect imbecile, stuck it in my pocket and forgot all about it till a little while ago."

"In that case I think I'd better go and read the *Dispatch*," said Mrs. Polk. "One should read it sometimes even though a lot of it is most distasteful. I'll be back when I finish it, but I do read slowly."

She closed the door softly behind her. A faint gentle smile played upon Hunter Cragwall's face. "I've been trying to remember," she said. "Wasn't it from Shakespeare you quoted at the cobbler's shop?" she asked. "Have you any other quotations ready, or did that time exhaust your store?"

"Exhaust it!" he exclaimed in low intense tones. "Exhaust it! It but multiplied it. Now I have hundreds." He stood looking at her hungrily. Then he spoke. *"I have had a dream, past the wit of man to say what dream it was."*

"You should not dream so vaguely, Lieutenant Nichol. My dreams are much clearer."

"And so are mine. My quotation was inept now that I

think of it. And what are your dreams? Shouldn't I be told of them?"

"I have heard it said often that it is bad luck to tell one's dreams."

"Bad luck only when told to those who have no part in them. You can tell yours to me."

"Lucy said you were an actor. There are times when you should play no part."

"Your presence strips away all pretense. I play no role but mine when I see you."

"I am glad you came to Mrs. Polk's, whatever the role," she said.

"So am I, but as soon as it seems at all safe I must get back to General Forrest."

"I know you must. But dreadful things can happen to those who fail to get back to General Forrest."

"More dreadful now than ever, and yet its most dreadful moment would be brightened by a lovely dream. But dreadful things were not a part of your dream, were they?"

She shivered. "No, in my dreams we were safe. I, too, am in danger, you know."

"I know," he said, "and you are braver than I am. I have excitement to dull the edge of danger, but you——".

"It was very exciting when you came to the cobbler's shop. I forgot about danger, too. Sooner or later the enemy will find out about the cobbler's shop."

"I wish you wouldn't go back to it," he said. "It's unsafe there."

"I have been repaid for the danger," she said quietly.

"I know that you have served the South there. . . ."

"It was there I met you." There was another pause. Then she asked, "When will I see you again?"

"You haven't finished seeing me this time, my dear," he said almost gaily.

"I must leave soon. There is curfew presently. I must be at home before then. When do you think the war will be over? Will it be much longer?"

It was the same question he had asked but a little while before. "I don't know," he said soberly. "My thoughts about it were happier till I talked with Mrs. Polk."

"I have been fearing it." Her voice was touched with sadness. "Years, perhaps, and so many dead . . ."

And then she was in his arms, held tightly. "I'll not be dead. In my heart I know it. Years, perhaps. They will pass. Will you wait, Hunter?"

"All the years there are if at the end you will be coming back to me."

"I think that I shall come often before then. Death alone could prevent my coming, and with such a motive I could defeat death."

"Would memory depend on our meeting again?"

"Memory needs only one meeting. I have had two."

"Then why would you risk so much?"

"Not for memory, but for me."

"Was it unbecoming for me to come here? My friends would think so."

"Your heart is the wiser counselor."

"You are the only lover I ever had."

"I do not wish a well-practiced sweetheart."

"Nor I to be one link in a chain of conquests."

"One link! My dear, you're the chain and each time I've heard your voice is one link. If I do not leave here till tomorrow night could you come again?"

"No," she said. "It would risk too much. They would be noticing. I must miss being with you a little while now to be with you longer—someday."

"Much longer, my dear, much longer. As long as always."

Mrs. Polk was humming a bright little tune as she came

down the hall. They were standing discreetly apart when she entered the room.

"It does seem," said Mrs. Polk crisply, "that as much as the *Dispatch* costs they ought to put some news in it. And the best they could do for the reading public today was a brief notice that General Nelson accompanied by his army had left for Kentucky. We're likely to learn about the surrender of Fort Donelson any issue now." Her eyes rested speculatively first on Hunter Cragwall, then on Beasley Nichol. "I trust, my dears, that time did not hang heavily on your hands."

"You could not have even looked at the *Dispatch* in that time," said Beasley Nichol. "You merely went out into the hall and then came back in."

"Time is so relative," said Mrs. Polk musingly. "To one reading the *Dispatch* it moves with leaden feet, grudging each step it takes. To others, perhaps in the same house, it speeds by so fast that one may not taste a minute fully until it is gone. Well, I have some chores to do downstairs. Save a few moments to spend with me, Hunter, as you leave. I need to absorb a little of your youth and hope. You, sir, will then go back to your room and do nothing to draw any attention. We must return you safely to General Forrest."

She went on down the stairs.

"I must go now. It is almost nine. When you come back I'll be waiting."

Then again she was in his arms. For a long instant there was no war, no sentries posted outside Polk Place, no cobbler's shop masking its military partisanship, no make-believe hospitals filled with broken and dull-eyed men, no Maxwell Houses to shut the sunlight from hungry eyes, no graves under the cedar trees, no desolation, no lists of the dead. And in their stead two lovers in the upstairs parlor at Polk Place, the cry of the whippoorwill outside and the gentle movement of the summer night wind. Then the war returned and somewhere General Forrest waited impatiently for him, and the little room off the cobbler's shop waited for her.

Beasley Nichol heard the door close and her light steps as they ran down the walk toward Vine Street. Their sound diminished into silence, and she was gone.

18

HE WENT down the hall to his room. But before he had closed the door he heard the knocker at the main entrance to the house fall imperatively, once, twice, three times. Standing there tense, he waited. A few seconds later the door opened and there was tentativeness and caution in the sound.

Then Mrs. Polk's voice asked crisply, "Yes? What is it, please?"

A man's voice replied. "Good evening, Mrs. Polk. May we come in, please?"

The little tingles were playing on Beasley Nichol's spine. It was Cousin Philip's voice he heard.

For a second or two there was no answer. Then she said, "Certainly, sir. Come in."

From the sounds there were two visitors. Cousin Philip spoke again.

"I am presumably Major Philip Yorke of the Union army. Really, Mrs. Polk, I am quite the contrary. Would you care if I withhold for the present any further details of my identity? This gentleman is presumably another officer of the Union army. Actually, he is Captain Hume Crockett from this section and at present of General Forrest's command."

"Why, Hume Crockett, of course. I have seen you several

times, sir. I thought as you came in that you were somebody I knew. Pay no attention to my smile. I apologize for it. I happened to think of something quite amusing. I'll tell you what presently. You are both very welcome."

"An hour ago I met Captain Crockett on the way out of town—at least he hoped he was on the way out. I knew of some dangers which he would encounter, so I was watching for him and I took charge of him. His customary discretion seemed a bit dulled, so to speak."

"Won't you come into the library?"

"First, let me ask whether by any chance Lieutenant Beasley Nichol is in your home or has been here. The possibility had occurred to me."

Mrs. Polk hesitated again, but not for long. "Come with me, please," she said.

Beasley Nichol heard them coming up the stairs and closed the door to his room and stood waiting, his heart drumming, for here was a turn of affairs which he had not foreseen and which he could not interpret.

He opened the door in response to a gentle knock.

"Come in, gentlemen," said Mrs. Polk. Enough light came in from the hall for her to see Nichol standing in the middle of the room. "You have visitors, Lieutenant Nichol. I think we'd all better go to the parlor on this floor. We'd like to see one another and light in that room would be less noticed. We have some inquisitive neighbors."

She led the way into the parlor, closed the door and motioned the three men to sit down.

"Well," she said, her bright eyes darting inquiringly around the group, her head cocked wontedly a bit to one side, "Such a nice reunion of old friends! Though I must admit that some of its phases escape me."

"I apologize, Mrs. Polk, for disturbing you like this," said Hume Crockett. "The visit wasn't my idea."

"Of course—" Cousin Philip's clipped voice was dry and whimsical—"of course, I could have left you and Nichol to your own devices, but it didn't seem quite fair to General Forrest to lose you too easily. We owed him some effort."

"We?"

"Yes—well, call it that."

"Where have you been, Crockett?" asked Nichol.

"At my girl's house till afternoon today."

"Crockett, I'll never trust you again. Did you go directly there when you left us?"

"Well, not quite directly, not right then. I had some trouble making it."

"His escape from his girl—naturally, I mean from her home—was a piece of art," said Cousin Philip. "One of our men was watching from upstairs across the street. We knew where he was but the Yankees only suspected. They kept a man marching up and down in front of the house—and perhaps behind it—all morning. He went off, I suppose to eat, and out came the captain as big as life and twice as natural. He held his head high and walked right on down toward Broad and on across it, just as if he were an intimate friend of General George H. Thomas. Then is when I caught up with him. They've all sort of fancy traps set out at the edge of the city. So I kept him with me till a while ago and then we came on here."

"You knew I was here?" asked Beasley Nichol.

"Oh, yes, you might say we did, and I think the Yankees know it too. We watched you pretty closely last night after you left the hotel. We knew the danger you were in. By the way, I think it's a neat joke the way the Yankees blamed you for those two soldiers at the hotel. Oh, but they were indignant!"

"Dead?"

"Oh, no. Skulls cracked, perhaps, and otherwise indisposed, but they'll live to annoy patriots like us still further. Someone saw you two in the lobby. He didn't know who you were but his description was good enough for Satan's first assistant who clerks there. He showed up right away and started blaming you the minute he arrived. One would rarely hear better blaming."

"I see," said Mrs. Polk dryly, who didn't see at all. "And what now, gentlemen?"

"As soon as they change guards—which they will at ten o'clock—I'm going to take your guests out of town and wash my hands of them. Oh, I'll not withdraw my good will entirely. You see, one of them was formerly my cousin, and besides that he very rudely saved my life once. To be killed by a limb from a hackberry tree would be no fitting exit for a gallant Yankee major. I'll get them out of town. But that'll be all the time I can spare them. I have other obligations, you know."

Beasley Nichol had been watching him closely. "Did you send the fiddlin' man to warn me?"

"Oh, naturally. You add two and two very well, Lieutenant. It was merely a hint that rashness might be unbecoming, you know. I hope you gentlemen will understand that I have had to temper my movements with great caution. I am here to give support to a matter of considerable delicacy, so to speak, and other than the fact that it concerns our common cause, quite apart from the welfare of you gentlemen. I should mention, though, that my stated duties include any help I can render General Forrest. In the routine of my rounds, I learned that you, Captain, had been taken prisoner. Naturally I wished to aid you but no way seemed feasible. But I did know that it would be quite like General Forrest to send representatives to the hanging. So I kept my eyes open. I spotted you, Lieutenant, when you first arrived, and

I maneuvered to be with you at breakfast the next morning.
You play a good part, sir. You were a stranger, playing the
Yankee, but something about you, some stray wisp of something, was Southern, very vague, sir, but persistent. Your
voice was good quality Yankee. I was puzzled but once you
let your guard down. It was when you used the word 'Philadelphia.' No native of the City of Brotherly Love ever pronounced the word as you did. I have sensitive ears and when
you used that word I could hear the Negroes singing in the
cotton fields—if I make myself clear."

"Good heavens, and on the way in I lectured the sergeant
on his wretched pronunciation!"

"It was in the final part of the word—the 'phia.' The way
one uses those four letters is most revealing. No, I would
have taken my oath that you weren't from Philadelphia. But
it was a moment later that you pulled me out of my seat. I
wonder whether you noticed, sir?"

"No."

"Well, it was when you said you were Captain Enoch Ford.
We had been advised that Captain Enoch Ford was en route
to Nashville with a message which then was of great concern
to us, and we awaited his arrival. You interested me the moment you came into the Saint Cloud, and later in a little conversation we had at breakfast you added to that interest. But
when you named Philadelphia as would any one of General
Forrest's better-grade soldiers, and still later announced that
you were Captain Ford, I knew things were coming to a head
fast, so we moved a trifle quickly then, too. That Negro boy
sent you to the cobbler's shop and everything turned out fine.
Well, that's my story, cousin. I fancy they've changed senti-
nels by now."

"I doubt if it is quite all of your story, Cousin Philip. It
wasn't quite an accident that you came to the church during
the storm, was it?"

"Oh, no, no accident at all, though I assure you I had nothing whatever to do with the limb. I've always excluded falling limbs from my plans. I wished only to find out how your withdrawal from the city was proceeding."

"You underestimated Fisheye."

"I underestimate him invariably. He has caused us a great deal of trouble. We shall, I think, have to do away with him, but that will require care."

"Where is Sergeant Goforth?"

"Most regrettably, we do not know. It was either keep track of him or you. We chose to keep track of you. We think the sergeant got away. We fumbled badly once, though. That was when we let you take French leave from that house on lower Cherry. Dr. What's-His-Name's."

"Dr. Robertson's."

"Quite true, Dr. Robertson's. We knew you were there. So we planned to go down there before daylight and presumably under Yankee orders search for you, and, finding you, march you presumably back to prison. You see, I am Major Philip Yorke of the Union army, and as such I am entitled to such errands. Well, we arrived while another searching party, this time genuine Yankee, was having a hectic time of it. They couldn't find you at all and they were annoyed no end. So was I. In the first place, where were you and why had you gone there? In the second, what about the posse that beat us to the doctor's? Something had slipped or I'd have known about that. The doctor's answers were polite, professional and exceedingly uninformational. We were all in quite a commotion until that coach driver hunted up the Negro boy at the hotel and told him the tale. From the word passed on to me I got the idea that driver can handle himself."

"Yes," said Mrs. Polk, "he can handle himself most admirably and all the others who happen to be around and in need of handling."

Major Yorke looked at her surprised. "Oh, indeed! My impression of him deepens. Undoubtedly a most competent fellow. I really must see him."

"You're a little late, sir. He left my house earlier this evening. He hoped to get through and enlist under General Frank Cheatham. General Cheatham, it seems, loves horses and that accounts for the driver's preference for him. He had some excitement, as he called it, after he carried the word around yesterday. The Yankees put him in jail, so he cut his way out with a pocketknife. He arrived here quite unexpectedly two hours before Lieutenant Nichol did. The Yankees looked for him here the next morning but they managed not to see him."

"How'd he get away?"

"I suppose he used the password for tonight."

"Password!" exclaimed Major Yorke. "You mean he had it? Where'd he get their password?"

"It's an interesting story how he got it, Major Yorke, in fact charming. Someday I'll tell it to you. It's something like 'Old Abe Lincoln,' isn't it?"

Major Yorke wiped his brow. "There are canoes being paddled hereabout that I seem to have missed. Mrs. Polk, I have made it a point to know something of both the Childresses and the Polks. Without doubt you compound their better qualities. May I mention our gratitude for your hospitality? It seemed the simplest way for me to bring Captain Crockett here. I know the password and used it on the sentinel and he politely waved me in. If he saw me coming out with two he might wonder a bit. But the one on now is a dear friend of mine. I maneuvered him on this shift. We'll be going now, I think. Ready, gentlemen?"

They were. But Nichol had a word with Mrs. Polk.

"May I come again when the war is over?"

"Certainly, Lieutenant. I should be very happy for you to

come. Or during the war, if you happen to be in town, though, my dear, I do not suggest that."

"Mrs. Polk, tell her . . . tell her . . ."

"I will, Lieutenant. When I see her I shall certainly tell her. Have no concern about that. She shall surely be told. Good-by, sir, and God keep you!"

Mrs. Polk stood in the doorway of Polk Place and watched the three men go down the brick walk leading to Vine Street. She heard Major Yorke call something to the guard, who answered and with a cheerful hand waved them on out. She stood there smiling a bit faintly and nodding her head as was her wont when pleased. The night was quiet and clad in black velvet. Pale blobs of thin light spread out and up from the lampposts. It was pleasantly cool and there was no hint of rain in a sky crowded with stars that sparkled coolly. For once the rumble of wagons along the outlying turnpikes was quieted, and for once the cobblestones of the streets were not ringing with the *clip-clop* of horses' hoofs. It was, Mrs. Polk thought, an unnatural stillness to attend so unnatural a war. For a few minutes she stood there creating into the unity the factors of a strange and surprising situation. Then she went inside and closed the door.

19

MAJOR YORKE in silence led the two men along Vine Street. At Broad he turned east, walking toward the river.

"Where are we going?" asked Crockett, speaking very softly.

"The safest way is by the river. It's thick with craft about the wharf and there's some risk but less than by the streets. They're guarded with really great zeal. I imagine that it's firmly in their minds that when you Southerners try to get away you'll hardly think of the river. That being the case, I have a boat waiting."

Nichol and Crockett shrugged their shoulders. So it would be by the river. That hadn't occurred to them, but Nichol was no stranger to water and the Cumberland River in various periods of time past had been Hume Crockett's playground. With a boat and under cover of darkness they would exploit their chances to the utmost.

They were challenged by guards twice on Broad Street but each time Major Philip Yorke with a touch of easy arrogance said, "Old Abe Lincoln," and the guard waved them by. At the wharf they were challenged again. Yorke gave the password.

"We're going on a mission up the river, soldier," he explained.

But the guard shifted his rifle to the alert and holding his lantern in the other hand advanced on them.

"Would you like to see my credentials, soldier? I have them here." His hand explored his pocket, the soldier standing up close and looking with curious eyes at Nichol and Crockett. Suddenly with a movement so fast as to challenge vision Yorke's hand came out of his pocket, with a pistol gripped by the barrel. This descended dully upon the sentinel's head. It was done so quickly that no cry escaped his lips and he slumped to the ground.

"We've got to hurry," said Major Yorke. "That was good for perhaps one hour."

The major knew exactly where the boat was and led them directly to it. The two men climbed in. Yorke, speaking in a low voice, directed Nichol to the front of the boat and Crockett to the stern. He untethered the boat and climbed past Nichol to the rower's seat. He lifted the oars from the bottom of the boat, adjusted himself, and they heard the oars dip gently into the dark water. Then they were moving.

"That was an error," they heard Yorke say quietly, "an inexcusable error. I shouldn't have given him our direction. He'll remember that when next he remembers anything."

"He won't remember in time to do any damage."

"He might. It was an error to tell him."

There was the assurance of an expert boatman in the manner of his rowing and in the way he sent the boat swiftly ahead. The oars bit into the current with a smooth surge of power whose reflex the two men sensed in the forward glide of the boat. The oars inscribed their arcs and made no sound except that of the gurgle of water closing in behind them, and the tinkling drop of water spilling from them in their movement through the air. The prow sliced the muddy Cumberland with a restrained hiss. The boat was not built for speed, but they were making the most of it.

To their right loomed the bulk of a steamboat, with one or two lights showing dimly, and with sleeping engines panting slowly and lazily. The gaslights of the city converged into an area less dark in the general gloom. Across the river, dark and soundless, lay Edgefield. Far down the river the blast of a steamboat echoed and re-echoed musically among the river hills. Another carrier of those mountainous supplies that were accumulating in bulk on the cobblestones of the wharf was blowing for the landing.

"I think that we should be challenged again about here," said Major Yorke.

As if in answer a lantern suddenly unmasked swung across their course.

"Stop for identification," called a sharp voice. "Immediately, please, or we will fire."

"Three officers assigned on a mission of search to the mouth of Mill Creek."

"The password, please."

"Old Abe Lincoln."

"Correct. But remain where you are for identification. Do not move, please."

Something had slipped. There was nothing to do but wait. The boat, a small one, moved alongside. Three soldiers were in it. Two of them held rifles at the ready.

"What's the trouble?" asked Yorke crisply. "We have no time to waste here. We're in a hurry."

"Two Rebel spies have escaped. Precisely who are you? Where are you going?"

"I told you on a mission to Mill Creek."

"Upon what mission and under whose orders? We're in a hurry too."

There was a second of silence. "Listen," said Nichol. "There's a boat coming up the river. Don't you hear it?"

Their interrogators were also listening now. The one holding the lantern mechanically set it in the bottom of the boat. Nichol and Crockett acted then as a team. Crockett seized the other boat and pulled it violently and at the same moment Nichol's powerful hands grasped the side of the boat and shoved down. That threw the occupants into a scramble and a rifle dropped into the water. The next instant the boat capsized and the occupants were thrown into the river. There were cries for help in the darkness.

"Try swimming," counseled Yorke. "You're not two hundred feet from shore. We're in a hurry."

Major Yorke resumed his rowing. "I was correct as to

Mill Creek," he said. "That is where I shall, with regrets of course, permit you gentlemen to withdraw from my company. I must be back comfortably before daylight. I have some other assignments of importance, and I cannot afford the suspicion of Fisheye. The fellow's cunning is uncanny, and his methods vile. I have recently been warned against him by no less than President Jefferson Davis himself."

Nichol and Crockett's exclamations fitted together in time and statement. *"President Davis!"*

"Consider it unsaid, please. I spoke hastily. Anyhow, should you ever encounter Fisheye in a safe territory shoot him first and advise President Davis second. It would guarantee a prompt promotion."

"It would take a bullet," said Nichol. "I saw Goforth hit him on the head with a pistol butt hard enough to kill a horse, and yet by night——"

"And yet by night he was after you again."

Nichol explored his middle with reminiscent fingers. "He got me."

"So he did. I think I'll have to shoot him the day I leave here—though that would involve danger curiously out of proportion to the good accomplished."

"Where is General Forrest now?" asked Crockett.

"According to my latest word up Lebanon way, perhaps out toward Watertown. One can't afford an exact answer about the whereabouts of General Forrest. Anywhere out in that general section if you'll stand still long enough at some back-country crossroads he's sure to gallop by."

"I hope we find Sergeant Goforth back with General Forrest," said Nichol.

"Very likely you will. A very doughty chap, I fancy. I daresay you will."

"Aren't you tired, sir? Let me relieve you. I can row a boat," said Crockett.

"Naturally, Captain, you can row a boat, but I know where I'm going."

"Will you carry the boat back?"

"Oh, no. I'll have a horse waiting for me. Much quicker, and I'll be a bit rushed later."

"Later! This leisure must be appalling."

"We will land just beyond the mouth of Mill Creek. That isn't far from the Lebanon Pike, but I'd try the fields till morning. Ten miles out of town you ought to be clear of the worst of them. But remember, you've been too much trouble to yourselves and others to take any risks unduly." The oars paused, held in mid-air. "Listen."

They heard it. The boat was behind them again, the sound enlarging with each passing moment, growing clearer and more ominous, a boat paddled furiously and powerfully.

"Fisheye, I fancy!" said Major Yorke in low savage tones. "That soldier came to and gave him directions. I knew it was an error to tell him we were coming upstream. I thought maybe those fellows in the water would hold them long enough for us to get to Mill Creek."

"Let me help pull," said Crockett. "We can outrun them."

"No. We'd also make enough noise for them to hear us, and we'd be in for it then, sooner or later. They've had ample report of us from that sentry and those fellows in the river. We'll try an old Indian game."

"We don't even know they're after us."

"Oh, yes, we do," said Yorke in a half-whisper. "They are after us, and coming fast. This boat is sluggish. I knew it was an error the moment I said it."

He dragged heavily but silently upon his left oar and the boat veered sharply toward the shore. A minute later they were close enough in to grasp the overhanging boughs from the shore.

"Let's wait here till they pass," he whispered.

They had not long to wait. The course of the pursuing boat lay close inshore and it passed not a hundred feet from where their boat lay becalmed in the sluggish waters.

From the beat of the oars it was clear that two men were pulling the boat.

"Hold it a minute," said a voice from the darkness. "Let's see if we can hear them."

Then the hearts of the three men in the other boat missed a beat in unison. For it was the voice of Fisheye.

"They musta landed already." The voice was evidently that of one of the oarsmen.

"Suits me," said Fisheye. "We're watching every path along that bank like it was solid gold. They didn't fool me. I thought they'd try for the place where the road runs down to the river just beyond the mouth of Mill Creek. We got men there waitin' for them."

"Well, what you want us to do?"

"Row on up the river. I think they're still ahead. I still look for 'em to land where I said."

"How far?"

"About a mile. Good thing them fellers could swim, but they slowed us down."

"Who's the other man in the boat besides them spies?"

"I wish I knowed who that feller is. He's got me buffaloed. But I'll find out."

Their voices by then had faded out. One minute passed, two minutes, and nothing was said. It was Cousin Philip who spoke first.

"I considered having him killed ten days ago and got chicken-hearted. Well, that changes things. I am going to take you men across the river and land you there. I've got to get back to Nashville."

He deftly swung the prow of the boat about and began to row for the other shore, while he counseled them in low tones.

"Don't move upstream by the river bottoms. Too muddy. I hate mud. Always did. You'll find better going a little piece inland. Go three or four miles up the river, then get back across the best way you can. You can make it. You're in less danger now than I am. I've got to get back to Nashville in a hurry. I wish I knew where the sergeant is."

"How'll you get there, sir? Won't they be watching the wharf?"

"Oh, indeed they will, and most eagerly. I'm glad Fisheye is up the river." He was silent a moment. "*Up* the river! *In* the river would suit me better. Well, I've always got back. I will this time, somehow. What worries me most, I'm losing a perfectly good horse up there by Mill Creek. I went to a lot of trouble to get it there, too."

The prow of the boat cut into the bank. "Mud!" exclaimed Major Yorke. "I hate it. Man was never made from mud, not even the Yankees . . . well, since I think of it, maybe Fisheye was."

Beasley Nichol said, "I'd go a long distance out of my way, Cousin Philip, to bespeak my gratitude."

"I'd go as far," said the less articulate Crockett.

"Thank you, gentlemen. Who knows but that in the strange unfolding of time's plan such may not be required of you? A most interesting episode, in fact, a lovely episode. I think that even President Jefferson Davis may hear of it. Good-by. Keep your wits ten paces ahead of you. My regards to General Forrest."

"From whom, shall we say, sir?"

"Why, cousin, just say from the man who hates mud."

III.

IN WHICH INFORMATION IS
DELIVERED TO THE GENERAL

1

AGAIN the Ladies were in session at Polk Place. This time it was neither shirts nor pants that consumed their attention. It was food. The idea was born of Mrs. Joseph Elliston's fertile mind, for she was unusually food-conscious. She presented the idea to the Ladies and with one accord they accepted it gladly, for they were food-conscious, too. The idea, in short, was for the Ladies to prepare a dinner and send it by Berrien Lindsley to the prisoners at the Maxwell House. It was to celebrate the anniversary of the great victory at Bull Run, though that was more of an excuse than a reason. A committee of the Ladies had met the day before and assigned to each member her part in providing and preparing the dinner.

Mrs. Polk sent word to Berrien that she wished to see him on a matter of some importance. He reported at Polk Place promptly. She told him of Mrs. Elliston's scheme. He pronounced it pure inspiration.

"It means trouble for you, Berrien. You'll have to make the arrangements."

"I need some trouble for my soul's sake. I've been gaining weight lately and that won't do."

So Berrien made a trip to the Maxwell House and requested of the officer in charge the privilege of giving the men the dinner.

"I wonder, Dr. Lindsley, if you would let us give our men such a dinner if conditions were reversed."

"The South has no prisons in the North, so I don't quite know how to answer that. But I will say this, sir. If there were Northern prisoners confined here—and there have been a few—and if Russell Houston, or W. T. Berry, or Francis Fogg, or Jonathan Meigs, who sympathize with your cause, sir, and who are among our leading citizens, should make the request it would be granted freely."

"You taught in the University. Do any of your graduates as you say sympathize with our cause?"

"I know of only a few, three or four perhaps."

The officer sat in silence, tapping with his pencil on the desk. Then he said, "Certainly, Dr. Lindsley, go ahead with the arrangements. I have the feeling I can trust you. I shall have to urge some restrictions, however. Only you may bring the food, and I cannot permit you to talk with the men. In case some communication between you and them becomes necessary you may talk with their chosen spokesman, and in my presence. Is that agreeable?"

"Perfectly, sir. We are grateful for this privilege."

"We have to be extremely careful. We have been plagued with an epidemic of spies lately."

"I am no spy, and I doubt if I know anyone who is. I pledge you that nothing in our dinner for the men will violate your generosity, sir."

So at nine o'clock in the morning on the appointed day the Ladies began gathering. The war was not old enough for the famed larders of Nashville to have shrunk seriously. Mrs. Elliston came early, bringing two fine baked hams. Then Adelicia Acklen came from Belmont with two large roasts of beef. With her she brought Clay, whose ability in carving had been a part of Nashville's prewar artistry. He fell quickly to work slicing the hams and roasts, and the Ladies, not yet engaged themselves, looked on in wonder and admiration. Mrs. Francis Fogg brought a dozen loaves of her finest bread. Mrs. Ewing came in from Mansfield with a large stone crock filled with delicious pickles. Mrs. Harding at Belle Meade could not come but she sent a whole pit-roasted sheep. At ten o'clock the Ladies descended en masse upon Polk Place, and soon the kitchen and the pantry overflowed with food. They came bringing more bread, and more pickles. Mrs. Byrd Douglas brought a dozen damson pies.

"It's the best I could do," she said. "We have five trees full of damsons but there isn't another grain of sugar left in the house, and I have no idea when I can get any more. You can't make a damson pie without sugar."

The food kept pouring into the kitchen and pantry at Polk Place, and the Ladies kept placing the boxes and bundles of food into proper assortments for packing.

"It will take Berrien four or five trips the best we can do, and if we don't organize it pretty well he'll never get it all there. He has to do all the hauling. They won't even let anyone accompany him. Who made these beaten biscuits?"

"I did," said Mrs. Demoville. "I know they may be a bit fancy for prisoners of war. But if my husband were one of those in the Maxwell House—and but for God's mercy he could be—there is nothing he'd like so well with Mrs. Elliston's hams. I got to thinking about him and I made these extra. I brought the deviled eggs you asked for."

"I've never seen lovelier biscuits. I'll see that your husband knows of this gesture."

"I do wish I could see them eat their dinner," said Mrs. Demoville wistfully.

"I doubt if anyone but Berrien could have got permission for this dinner. He went directly to the commanding officer and he gave his consent without any quibbling. Berrien has a convincing way with the Yankees. They're going to serve it on the second floor where Mr. Overton was to have his dining room. Berrien was careful not to call the Yankees' attention to why we are having it today. He got word to the men about it, but cautioned them to be very careful when the Yankees were within hearing."

"I wouldn't be quite that tactful with them," said Mrs. Morgan.

"In which case the men wouldn't get the dinner."

"We're short of fried chicken," said Mrs. Fogg as she raised her head from packing. "There isn't enough here for half a piece around. Wasn't Clara Baker assigned fried chicken? Where on earth can she be?"

"Why, Mary," said Mrs. Polk smiling, "if she had got here by now I'd feel like sending for Felix Robertson. Did you ever know her to be prompt?"

"I wonder what she'll be excited about this time? Do you suppose she will have seen another spy?"

"I wonder what *they*'re saying today."

"Be patient, ladies," said Mrs. Polk. "You'll find out when she does get here. Nothing, I promise you, will be kept hidden. You'll also see the handsomest lot of fried chicken you've seen lately."

Just then Mrs. Baker knocked at the kitchen door, and when it was opened she came in carrying with ease a tub which no woman there could more than lift. She bore the tub to a table in the pantry. The Ladies watched her with surprise since ten fried chickens did not require the use of a tub.

"Well, ladies," she said cheerily, "here's the chicken, and if it isn't fried right you can blame me. It was good chicken to start with."

Mrs. Polk lifted the cloth and peered beneath. "Goodness,

my dear, what sort of chickens do you have? They don't happen to be quadrupeds, do they?"

"Regular chickens, Mrs. Polk, and I get seven pieces to a chicken. You told me ten chickens. That's seventy pieces. You said Mrs. Wheless was to bring ten. That's one hundred and forty pieces and that's not enough to go around. I figured it out and decided something had to be done. So I drove out to Mrs. Moore's at Brentwood. I asked her if she were willing for any Confederate hero to go without a piece of chicken on the anniversary. And she said mercy no, and how many did I want and what was it the anniversary of? And I said Mrs. Wheless and I had given ten each and if she could spare that many and would have one of her servants pick hers I'd fry them. And isn't it funny—I couldn't think to save me what the anniversary was of but I had to tell her something. So I said it was Jeff Davis' birthday. . . ."

"You missed it only about six weeks," said Mrs. Polk, smiling.

"She said fine, and if it was his birthday she'd make it a dozen. And she did."

"Then you have two hundred and twenty-four pieces."

"More than that. Good gracious, the way I fried chicken last night! I didn't get a wink of sleep till two o'clock. Good thing I always did believe in frying in shallow fat or I wouldn't have a speck of lard left. Well, as I was coming back I thought of Mr. Overton at Traveller's Rest, so I stopped there. They say he's rolling in chickens. He must be. I saw hundreds with my own eyes. They were everywhere. Mr. Overton, I said, I want ten frying-size chickens. I'll fry them and see that they are served to guests in your own house. Wasn't that clever?

"He didn't seem to catch on so I had to explain to him about the Maxwell House being his own house. He looked a little dazed but he gave me the chickens. There are two

hundred and ninety-four pieces—no, two hundred and
ninety-three. I forgot and ate one piece myself. I'm sorry,
but I ate it while I wasn't thinking. Anyhow, the biggest
heroes will get two pieces. I'll go get the gravy. Must be
more than a gallon of it and I never made better. Of course,
we'll warm it up before we send it to Mr. Overton's guests.
I still think that was clever.

"They say there's a lot of excitement in town among the
Yankees. They catch spies and can't hold them any more
than you could an eel. They say they had three lately and
every one of them got loose. They say it has got so the
Yankees go about arresting each other. You remember the
day of the storm when we met here and I saw that boy from
Franklin riding down High Street with two other men all in
Yankee uniforms? I'll bet they were the three spies. You
know a boy from Franklin with a Yankee uniform on would
be a spy. He'd have to be. My gracious, I'd love to know a
real spy. It'd thrill me all over if I was certain they were the
ones. They say they had the scaffolds already built out in the
jailhouse yard to hang them on. But they couldn't keep our
men in jail, let alone hang them. They say——"

"Certainly, my dear, but that dinner has to be down there
and unloaded by noon. Sallie Lindsley, I think I'll frame one
of those chess pies and put it in my parlor."

"Is it time to start the coffee?" asked Mrs. Demoville.
"We ought to wait as long as we can."

"I guess it's time to start it. There's a lot of it to be made.
The plan," explained Mrs. Polk, "is to make it in the pots we
have, put it in that stone jar and wrap a quilt about it to
keep it hot. We'll heat the jar with hot water before we put
the coffee in."

"You ladies finish your packing. I'll make that coffee,"
said Mrs. Baker.

"That range is all yours," said Mrs. Polk, "and there's the

coffee." She pointed to a heap of small packages on the table. Then she added a bit wistfully, "And if there aren't homes in Nashville that will be without coffee from now on I'm a poor judge of supply. From that package of yours, Elizabeth Meness, I daresay you haven't a grain left."

"I'll not miss it, Mrs. Polk."

"Oh, yes, you will. You'll miss it terribly, my dear, and that makes the gift all the more lovely. Well, there's Berrien. I didn't know it was that late. We'd better hurry."

Berrien came into the house and stood in the door between the kitchen and pantry and watched admiringly the deftness with which the Ladies assorted and packaged the food with little interruption of running commentary. Mrs. Elliston asked Berrien whether there was any news of interest. Yes, there was some. He had, not an hour before, in the home of a friend of Northern sympathies read a Philadelphia newspaper of recent issue. If he could interpret directly what the paper had said circuitously it was clear that the campaign against Richmond had failed. General McClellan was attacking no more. The outlook for the Confederacy was much brighter.

"I told you," said Mrs. Baker. "It's what I've said a dozen times. The war will be over by Christmas. They say General Lee'll be in Washington by——"

"I hope he doesn't go till he can take his army. Any more news, Berrien?"

"Yes, three Southern spies got away from the city last night, and confusion reigns among the Yankees."

"Three!"

"Why, Mrs. Polk, one might think there were some you didn't count," said Adelicia Acklen.

"There were," answered Mrs. Polk serenely. "How did they escape, Berrien?"

"By the river. I gathered that the Cumberland is simply

cluttered up with those they dumped into the river, not to mention the dead and dying they left on the wharf. But the Yankees haven't entirely lost hope. They are scouring the country on both sides of the river upstream. I'm a man of peace and I hope they won't catch up with the spies. That would mean that the Yankees would lose a lot more men. If there had been ten of the spies I suppose they would have captured the city."

"That's just what I say. I tell you this war isn't going to last much longer."

Such unbridled optimism irked Mrs. Polk, so she changed the subject by making some reference to the quality of food before her.

"I did my best." Mrs. Baker's eyes were shining. "Every time I dropped a piece into the skillet, specially the drumsticks, I'd think how much I wished Dudley could have it. He likes it all, but the drumstick best."

"I can't imagine a better recipe for anything than to prepare it while thinking of one's only son. Berrien, suppose you take the cakes and pies the first load. They're ready to go and I suppose you are."

"I'm ready. Did you know it's drizzling rain? I wouldn't want anything to get damp."

"Nothing will. Everything is pretty well covered now and you can use this strip of oilcloth to cover the entire load after you've placed it in the wagon."

Berrien, assisted by several of the Ladies, carried bundles of carefully packed cakes and pies out to his spring wagon and he set out to the Maxwell House with his first load. Twenty minutes later he was back. The Ladies stopped their work for a brief while and gathered about Berrien, for they were eager to hear his report.

"The officer in charge there is a pretty decent sort of fellow. He has really entered into the spirit of the dinner and has things in far better order than you might expect. He told the guards that he'd make a prisoner out of any one of them that so much as touched a piece of the dinner. Two of the prisoners, by a happy chance, have their birthdays today. So the word is out that it is in their honor—which, of course, it is—well, one way to look at it. What goes next?"

"The pickles and preserves and things like that. There are four gallons of slaw alone."

"The officer in charge said jokingly he'd have to have proof that I was who I claimed to be and not a spy. They have spies on their minds. By the way, I saw Russell Houston— he's in their good graces, you know—so I asked him if the three spies had been recaptured. He said he supposed not since they had had no word of it."

"They won't catch them," vigorously affirmed Mrs. Baker. "I'll bet they caught them the other time when they were sound asleep. They're awake now. Why, they say a real good Confederate spy can just wave his hand before his face and it makes him look like somebody else entirely different."

"If I thought I could learn this hand-waving business I'd surely go in for spying," said Adelicia Acklen. "I could use a change in faces just now."

Berrien drove away down Union Street. The rain was no longer falling.

"He can do it in four trips," said Mrs. Polk. "We'll send the meat and chicken the next one, and then biscuits, corn bread, gravy and coffee. We must get them there hot. That's going to take some expert wrapping."

"Where is Lucy? Isn't she coming?" inquired Mrs. Elliston.

"No," said Mrs. Polk. "She has been under a considerable strain lately and didn't feel like it. She sent the Boston brown bread, though."

Someone knocked at the side door and one of the Ladies

answered. It was Ned Baker asking to see his wife, and the
look on his face frightened the woman who stood there. Mrs.
Baker hurried to the door and when she saw her husband she
knew at once that he bore news of their son.

"It's Dudley," she said, her face drained white.

"Yes, dear, it's Dudley," he answered gently.

"Is he . . . dead?"

"No, not dead. He's wounded."

"Is it bad?"

"The message didn't say. He is in a Northern hospital
near Washington. I don't think they would have carried him
that far if it had been very serious. I thought I should come
and tell you, dear. I don't suppose you want to go back with
me, do you?"

"No, if Dudley is a prisoner that's all the more reason for
me to do what I can for the prisoners here. If I failed the
men here now it would be like failing Dudley, wouldn't it?"

"That's what I thought you would say, Clara. Well, I'll
be waiting for you when you get through here. I think Dudley
will be all right."

He bowed courteously and went down the steps. Mrs.
Baker rejoined the Ladies in the pantry.

"What is it, Clara?" Mrs. Polk asked quietly.

"It's Dudley. He was wounded."

"Oh, my dear. Seriously?"

"Mr. Baker doesn't think so. No, of course he isn't."

"Don't you want to go home with Mr. Baker? We can
manage here."

"No," said Mrs. Baker determinedly. "You don't understand. They captured Dudley. They put him in a hospital
but it's a part of a prison. I have to do my share for the prisoners here now, don't I?"

"You always have."

"Thank you, Mrs. Polk. I'll be working for Dudley, too, now. Let's see, it takes eggs three weeks to hatch and a chicken ten weeks to be just right for frying. That'll be about right. Dudley will be home just about then. I've two hens that haven't a thing on their minds but setting—and that's just what they will be doing by sundown. They say this is a fine time to set hens. Let's see; that will make it late in October. That's just about the time Dudley'll be here."

Berrien came back for his third load. He drew Mrs. Polk aside and told her that a Northern officer had been at the Maxwell House and watched him unload. A very interesting man he was, too. He had told Berrien to get word to Mrs. Polk that everything went off all right, but that he was leaving Nashville presently and wished to convey to her his high regards. That was about all the officer had said. Berrien presumed that Mrs. Polk knew what was meant. His name? Oh, yes, it was Major Philip Yorke.

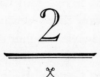

COUSIN PHILIP was right about mud in the bottoms. It was deep and slimy and all but impassable. Nichol and Crockett floundered through to higher ground where the going was relatively easy. They turned up the river, keeping it a half-mile distant, sometimes a little more, sometimes a little less. Their way led through muddy cornfields, through meadows and orchards and sometimes woodlands, and then back into muddy cornfields. They slipped and stumbled along in the dark and their progress was slow. Even the uplands were soft and slippery from the prolonged rains, and time and again they stepped into soft places above their shoes, time and again they slipped and fell sprawling to the ground. Gradually the traces of these mishaps accumulated.

"Did you ever see mud walking?" asked Nichol. "I think that's what I am."

They came to a muddy road that turned toward the river.

"This won't do," said Crockett. "It's time for us to get back across the river. We're getting farther away from General Forrest all the time."

They slogged their way through the dark down the road to the riverbank, but they could find no boat and from its sound the river was high and rapid. They could hear distant roosters trumpeting the advent of dawn. A faint mist hung above the river. A thin moon was well above the eastern horizon but an overcast of clouds blotted out most of its light. A dim glow touched the eastern rim of the sky with a promise of pearl.

"We can't get across here," said Crockett. "But we have to get across somewhere, that's certain."

They retraced their way to higher ground and again they turned up the river.

"When I get back to General Bedford Forrest's army I'm going to sleep two weeks," said Nichol. *"Ah, how our little life is rounded with a sleep!"*

"Rounded or not, two hours are Bed Forrest's limit. Don't count on more than that."

"All right then, two hours. That'll round it. I'm not one to be contentious."

"Anyhow, not with Bed."

The shadows were fast dissolving and the outlines of the world about them grew clearer. The pink and rose deepened into gold, and the unseen but advancing sun threw ahead of

it fanlike streamers that touched with glory the clouds that
shadowed the eastern sky. Then the sun came up almost
with suddenness, leaping from the gulfs of night across the
horizon into a new day. Almost as suddenly the world which
had been sleeping in silence awoke into the articulacy which
dawn brings. Dogs began to bark and calves to bawl. Somewhere a turkey gobbled furiously, and two miles behind them
a railroad train wailed for a crossing.

"Look," said Nichol. *"There's husbandry in heaven. Their
candles are all out."*

The soft, plaintive voice of a woman called, *"So-o-o-o-k!"*
and in response a cow moved patiently along a muddy lane.
The grunting of feeding hogs, and the rasping cackle of
geese, and the movements around houses became parts of
the symphony of sunrise. Blue streamers of wood smoke
began to lift in twisting random curls above kitchen chimneys.
And then the air became heavy with breakfast smells, of meat
and eggs frying and coffee boiling, with that curious and delicate pungency of fresh apples simmering in a skillet, with that
uplifting sensation, half odor, half promise, of biscuits baking
in an oven.

"I've changed my mind," said Nichol. "I'll eat two weeks."

"Twenty minutes, I think, would be ample. Would there
be too much risk for us to try to get some breakfast?"

"The way I feel the risk's the other way."

They were moving along a seamed and rutted lane, part
rocks, part mud. An old and decrepit barn bordered the road
on one side. Beyond it four or five hundred feet a farmhouse
that stood gray in the early morning light topped a little rise.
Smoke was pouring from the chimney.

"Look, brother, and regard that house with approval, for
that's where I intend to eat breakfast," said Beasley Nichol.
"If you wish to learn fast, study my approach."

But just then his approach was interrupted. There stepped

out from behind the barn an old man, who obviously had already lived beyond his allotted years. There was no hint of
weakness about him, but indeed a time-hardened austerity.
He towered well above six feet. He stood there erect and
lean and plainly of great strength. A broad-brimmed hat
stood stiffly away from his heavily bearded face. In his hands
he held menacingly an ancient but threatening gun. When
he spoke it was not in the weak and quavering voice of an
old man but in a quiet hard drawl that added eloquence to
the menace of the gun.

"I was a-expectin' to git a ground hawg, but I ain't seen
one and I do see you. Reckon a Yank would do as well."

"A Yankee!" they exclaimed in unison, forgetting the
uniforms they wore, whose blueness still showed at spots
through the accretions of mud. "You put that gun down.
We're not Yankees," said Crockett.

"Stand where you be. This ain't no stampin' ground for
Yankees, not live Yankees nohow."

"Do we stamp like Yankees?" asked Beasley Nichol.

"Anybody'd know you're Yankees."

"Since you make such a point of it, General, we'll change
our stamp. We're not Yankees."

The man's grasp upon his gun tightened and he answered
Beasley Nichol sternly. "Now, you Yanks git offn this place
quick. I got four boys a-fightin' for the South and they ain't
respectin' me if I let Yanks traipse aroun' here. Now git!"

"Wouldn't you feel better about us, General, if you knew
we were officers in General Forrest's army?"

"You mean Bed Forrest? Then what you doin' a-wearin'
Yankee clothes? I said git out."

"We are wearing them on General Forrest's orders. He
sent us to Nashville on an errand and we are trying to get
back to him. Do you know where he is?"

"What you doin' here?"

"We got across the river and we've been walking all night to find a place to get back to the other side. General Forrest is on the other side. We must get back to him."

"One o' my boys is a-fightin' with Ol' Bed right this minute. Been with him sence March."

"Who is he?" asked Nichol excitedly. "What's his name? Maybe we know him."

"Corporal Ed Wheeler's his name. And don't you try no shenanigan on me."

"Ed Wheeler? Redheaded, freckle-faced fellow about six-two, and was born riding a horse?"

"That's Ed! That's him. How'd you know him?"

"Heard him pick a banjo one night and he did it so well I made his acquaintance. Don't you know him, Crockett?"

"I don't guess so," said Crockett, "but I'll meet him the day we get back!"

"I ain't a-wantin' to make a mistake. If you're Yanks and a-tryin' to fool me, get off the place and don't walk slow neither. If you're Rebs you come to breakfast."

"If I ever was a Yank," said Nichol joyfully, "I've deserted."

3

X

OLD MAN WHEELER led them to the house. His wife, after her suspicions were allayed, received them with country hospitality and gave them food featuring the best of country breakfasts in Middle Tennessee. There were ample slices of hickory-smoked ham, with a side dish of red gravy. There were golden-brown biscuits, plump and distended. There was a great platter of fried eggs, and a glass dish filled with fresh honey. And the coffee was hot and strong.

"Eat hearty," said Mrs. Wheeler, her eyes warm and bright. "That's what the boys would do if they were at home having breakfast. Do you reckon they'll ever all be at home again?"

"Why, yes," lied Nichol. "Very soon now. I think the war is just about over."

"I think you're just a-tryin' to be kind to an old woman. When Ed was home he thought it wouldn't last long but it don't look that near over to me."

"Maybe he's right, Ma," said Mr. Wheeler. "The North ain't hardly got no first-class generals at all, leastwise that's what Ed said. Now you take Bed Forrest . . ."

"You can't win a war with just one first-class general, Mr. Wheeler. Why, they're fightin' this war all over the country. General Forrest'll whip 'em here but what about them other states? General Forrest can't handle 'em all. Have another slice o' ham. Mr. Wheeler, pass the eggs. No, something tells me this war is goin' to have a lot o' misery in it before it's finished. It'd sure do me a lot o' good to see my boys again. Please fill your cups up again while the coffee is hot."

"You will see them again," Nichol assured her.

"I'm a-prayin' for it. Ed was home last month for Saturday and Sunday. He tried to eat his head off and just about did, too. Never saw one fellow eat so much in my life. We went to preachin' in Edgefield Sunday. Take some o' the honey. Ed helped us rob the hives when he was home. He's a first-rate hand with bees and he's powerful fond of honey. I've heard him say a dozen times he could eat his weight of that honey with butter and hot biscuits, and fried dried-apple pies."

"Ma, don't you have three other boys? You talk like Ed was all you got."

"He's the youngest, Mr. Wheeler, and that makes a difference. You could sink a boat with the dried-apple pies I've seen him eat, he's that fond of them. He likes 'em anyway at all and specially with honey. I made a batch of 'em yesterday. I wish he had the whole cookin' of 'em."

Beasley Nichol had an inspiration. "I'll take them to him. I expect to see him soon."

Mr. Wheeler sensed the disparity of an officer in General Forrest's army carrying on forced marches across the country dried-apple pies consigned to an obscure freckle-faced, banjo-picking corporal.

"No, Ma, it'd be a lot o' trouble for him."

"I'd wrap them up so he could carry them real easy. I got a box I been a-savin'."

"No trouble at all," vowed the gallant lieutenant.

"It's liable to start raining," said Mr. Wheeler, "and they'd git all wet and runny."

"I'll keep them dry. They'll be delivered to Ed just as fresh as from your kitchen."

"Mr. Wheeler, keep that honey dish moving. All of our boys were powerful fond of honey, specially Ed. I don't know how I can ever thank you, sir, for taking Ed them pies. I ain't been so pleased since he left. Mr. Wheeler, don't let that biscuit plate set still."

"The picture rises before me," murmured Nichol, his intent gaze upon the picture that rose before him. "When we rejoin

General Forrest, Ed—I mean Corporal Wheeler—will be sitting under a tree resting from a hard battle. It will be about an hour by sun and he will be tired and hungry, and maybe picking the banjo to keep his mind off how hungry he is. I will go up to him and say, 'Corporal Wheeler, I am the bearer of the sacred viands, of the life-giving dried-apple pies baked by your own mother in your own home.' Can't you see the picture?"

"I can," said Mrs. Wheeler. The spell of Nichol's words was on her.

"I've had a fine breakfast," said Crockett, tentatively moving his chair back an inch or two. "It's time to go. It's not going to be an easy day."

"It's had a perfect beginning."

A loud, unpleasant voice from the front yelled, "Hello, hello! Come to the door. Hurry!"

Old Mr. Wheeler pointed to a door that opened into the parlor. "Go in there and shet the door and don't make no noise. If you have to, go out the back door, take through that orchard back there, and keep goin'."

He turned away from them and went out the front door. From his growl they knew that something had gone awry. Nichol and Crockett peered through the interstices of a lace curtain, first taking care that they stood against a dark background. What they saw was alarming. Two Yankees on horseback waited at the front gate.

"Any Rebel soldiers in your house?" one of them yelled to Mr. Wheeler.

"No, and I'm a-tellin' you I don't want no Yankees here neither. You git away."

"Two Rebel spies escaped and they're around here somewhere. Anybody that harbors them will be put in jail and

his property confiscated. We know they are in this neighborhood. We've been tracking them."

The man's words were spoken as a ritual. The other soldier added his bit. "We'll get them, and if anybody gives
them assistance we'll get them, too. There's a posse back
there tracking them. We rode on ahead."

Nichol and Crockett heard Mrs. Wheeler's voice then,
from the front porch. "Mr. Wheeler, do you want me to
bring you the gun?"

"Go fetch it, Ma. I ain't goin' to abide no Yankees on
this place."

They heard Mrs. Wheeler enter the hall and fumble with
the gun in the rack. But they heard also the clatter of the
soldiers' horses as they rode back down the lane.

Nichol and Crockett joined the Wheelers in the hall.

"Listen to me," said the old man. "You go out the back-
yard gate and git into the orchard quick. You go straight
across it and that will bring you to a lane. It's got trees along
it and they'll hide you. You foller it to the river. I got a boat
tied there. You take it and cross the river in it and leave the
boat tied on the other side. I'll get it late this evening. The
boat's painted red. It's right little but it'll hold the two of
you. I reckon you better hurry."

Mrs. Wheeler, bright-eyed, came bustling out of the
kitchen. She held in her hand a shoe box which she handed
to Nichol.

"That's the pies for Ed," she said.

"You shoulda forgot it, Ma," said Mr. Wheeler, looking
at Nichol.

"You ain't accusin' the man of being a liar, are you,
Mr. Wheeler? He said he wouldn't mind taking it to
Ed."

"If it'd start rainin' that box wouldn't last ten minutes," said Mr. Wheeler.

Ma was resourceful. "I've got a piece of oilcloth, Mr. Wheeler. I can tie that around it."

4

X

FIVE minutes later they were going through the orchard, Nichol carrying the pies for Corporal Ed Wheeler wrapped neatly and securely in the piece of oilcloth.

They came to the lane. Crockett uttered a low exclamation of disgust, for the rain was striking him in his face. It was not rain so much as enlarged drizzle. Even that was bad enough, with the day that lay ahead of them. And they had found in their experiences with the weather that a drizzle usually indicated ambitions to grow into a rain.

"Don't let your dried-apple pies get wet." There was the hint of mockery in Crockett's voice.

"*Give him an ounce of civet, good apothecary, to sweeten his imagination.* He has in him none of the sweetness of our common humanity. He is not touched by gratitude, nor is he warmed by sympathy. It is his conceit that breakfast for him favors the one who serves it. He——"

"Oh, shut up," said Crockett. "I can do something besides talk. I'll carry the pies if you want me to."

"So you are hungry again!"

"Well, one breakfast isn't permanent. I know a man at Mount Juliet that will give us some dinner—if we can get there." Crockett's mind was concerned with reality again. "If we can get across the river, we ought to be there by noon."

They could see through the trees the current of the reddish-brown river flowing swiftly. The lane ran out and the road lifted over a little rise and then dipped sharply to the river. Crockett, who was a few steps ahead, caught the first glimpse of the riverbank, saw something he had not counted on, and ducked quickly out of sight. "Yankees!" he said.

"Waiting for us?"

"It looks like it."

"I understand. They're after Ed Wheeler's pies. By my troth, they shall not have them. It is imperative, Crockett, for us to save the pies."

He turned into the thick undergrowth and started pushing his way through it up the river. Crockett followed him. They broke past the heavy growth of wet cane into a place studded with giant beech trees. There they stopped to shake the water from their clothes.

"Come here," Crockett said in a low voice. He was pointing down toward the river. Nichol could see the two soldiers sitting motionless on their horses where the road ran into the river. The drizzle had stopped and the solid cloud had broken into rifts through which the sun peeped momentarily, and then fell again into concealment.

"No use staying here any longer," they heard one of the soldiers call to the other. "They ain't coming this way."

"We got to stay. Orders to wait till ten o'clock."

Ten o'clock! Almost three hours yet. They turned up the river and resumed their plodding way. A half-mile up the river they heard the splash of oars and their beat against the oarlocks. The trees hung so heavy a curtain of leaves against the river that they had to maneuver awhile before the boatman became visible. It was a young boy twelve or thirteen years

old and he was running a trotline. The oars were laid in
the bottom of the boat then and the boy was pulling the boat
toward land hand over hand upon the line. He wasn't having
much luck with his hooks. Then they heard him give an excited shout. They watched while he expertly disengaged the
hook from the fish's mouth and lifted it into the boat.
Crockett gave a low whistle of appreciation. "A twenty-
pound catfish and good eating," he said. It was the only fish
the boy caught. He drew into land a hundred feet from
them, threw the chain of the boat around a stump, took a
tow sack from the boat, and put the idly flopping fish into
it, swung it on his shoulder and started for home.

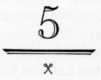

BEASLEY NICHOL and Hume Crockett looked at each other
and in that meeting of their glances each felt the other's
thought. *A boat!* They waited ten minutes to make sure the
boy would not return. Then they slipped and skidded
obliquely down the bank to where the boat was tied. Their
eyes swept the river below, then above, then met in satisfaction. They had been favored in the spot. The river turned
sharply away from them in both directions and one could
cross it there with the minimum of visibility. It was not very
wide, which meant of course that it was deep. The bend of the
river downstream was so sharp that they doubted whether
the soldiers watching below could see them even as they
neared the farther shore directly across.

"I never steal a boat except under compulsion," said Nichol. "It's a principle with me, but this is compulsion. We'll tie it for the lad when we get across."

They climbed into the boat very carefully and Crockett rowed with a minimum of sound. They spoke no word, for voices carry more clearly on the river than well-handled oars. Fish leaped in the stream and waves lapped ceaselessly against the shore, but there were no human sounds. It was a quiet and primeval world, whose major element was muddy water flowing ceaselessly toward the sea. They landed and tied the chain firmly around a young sycamore. Nichol held up his box of dried-apple pies.

"Still safe," he said. "It's an omen." But his heart was beating like a hammer.

It was difficult climbing away from the river. The bank was rocky and steep. For a little while they climbed straight ahead, pulling themselves up by the tough young growth. They came to a narrow shelf in the cliff. Beyond it the bank became sheer. They stood on the shelf and knew that they would have to follow it up or down the river. Crockett looked downstream and stood weighing the chances. Then he pointed and Nichol nodded his head in agreement. They turned upstream and moved along the narrow ledge. That way normally would have less danger, since it was away from the enemy. Four or five hundred yards farther on, the cliff flattened out to spread into a moderately level area. They emerged into an open meadow. They stood at the edge of the clearing and scanned with care the terrain opening out before them.

A small lad was driving some hogs toward a crude barn back in the meadow. No one else was in sight. The sun was shining at intervals, but the rain which had fallen lay heavy on the grass of the meadow, the drops catching and turning back brightness from the sun. For a minute they stood at the edge of the meadow, then they moved forward. It was as if every step plowed through liquid grass whose degree of wetness it seemed to them mere water could never attain. They were not at all unaware that from the margins of that meadow their movements might be perfectly visible to unfriendly eyes. By hugging the river they could have deferred the danger but sooner or later they would have to strike across an open place. They said nothing as they waded across.

They heard horses evidently ridden at a gallop and their eyes quickly searched for the source of the sound—and found it. On the rim of the ridge toward which the meadow gently rose two horsemen spurred their horses eastward on a road which ran along the crest. They were plainly Union soldiers. With one movement Crockett and Nichol flattened themselves in the drenched grass and lay there. The grass was luxuriant and their bulk did not lift above it enough to draw attention at that distance. They lay there for minutes fearing that other horsemen might be following. They were too tense for speech, held too rigid by a sense of danger.

They finally arose, shook the water from their clothes and resumed walking. They passed the barn into which the boy was patiently guiding the hogs. He saw them and his look hardened.

"You wouldn't be hanging around here if my daddy was home," he said angrily.

"Where's your daddy, sonny?" asked Nichol.

"He's off killing Yankees."

"Luck to him, sonny."

The boy, a puzzled look on his face, stood watching them as they walked on.

"I'm happier when I'm wearing gray clothes," said Nichol.

"They make people like me better. I want people to like me. It's my nature."

"We're getting where it'd be safer to change. Gray is likely in better style around here."

"Goforth hangs heavy on my mind. Where would you guess he is now?"

"It's Bed Forrest that hangs on mine. Where would you guess he is?"

"I'm more worried about the sergeant than I am about Bed. He hasn't so much help."

"Come to think of it, they both have nine lives. We haven't that many. I'm more worried about us."

"It's talk like that that makes me think of Fisheye. I wish my memory of him were poorer. It irritates me to remember him. Your girl glad to see you, Crockett?"

"She didn't complain."

"If you didn't wear your welcome out in all that time the whole family must like you."

"I suppose they felt all right about me. If they didn't, they didn't mention it. They baked a ham."

"Exeunt ham and mourners. Your girl pleasing to the naked eye, Crockett?"

"Are a million dollars money?"

"I suspected it. Your true nature crops out. It's her money you're after. How base!"

"Now you," said Crockett, "I don't wonder you're so unpopular with the girls—Shakespeare for breakfast, Shakespeare for dinner, Shakespeare for supper, Shakespeare by day and Shakespeare by night! Nothing but Shakespeare! If you couldn't find a quotation from Shakespeare telling her you loved her dearly, she'd never find it out."

"Good heavens, I never suspected you of such culture. You now not only remember the name Shakespeare, but you can pronounce it. What an inspiration I must have been to you! Where does your girl live?"

They had reached a fence and Crockett climbed it instead of answering. Nichol followed and then they stood in a narrow lane connecting cow pastures. They turned to the left and presently entered another pasture. They saw that walking was better near the fence, so they skirted the field. On the other side of the fence was a path paralleling their course for some distance, then turning away at a right angle. They climbed over and followed the path. A quarter of a mile ahead it crossed another road.

"I don't exactly know where we are," said Crockett, "but I have a good guess. Sooner or later that road would get us to Stone's River."

"Which fork would get us there?"

"The left."

"All right. One of my life's ambitions is to get to Stone's River. In fact, if I don't get there I'll likely not keep my life."

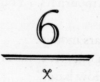

THEY stopped for a moment at the crossing. The sun moved out from under a narrow finger of cloud and lighted the world with a sudden brilliance. Long tendrils of fog traced the twisting route of the river and there was everywhere that deep lush greenness which summer rain gives to Middle Tennessee. Across the river the country stretched back until lost in the distant haze. The countryside was gentle with peace

and endowed with the aspects of a people living and working in fraternity.

There was a sudden noise made by a man straightening
from a clump of shrubbery behind which he had lain crouched.
In each hand he held a pistol. Nichol and Crockett stood
stock-still while the man advanced upon them and the cold
hand of fear laid its fingers upon their hearts.

"I got you buffaloed this time, and there ain't nobody hidin'
in a closet," said Fisheye. "I don't know how you got across
the river but I saw you the minute you got out in the clear.
They ain't goin' to put you in no jail this time. There's a
court that's waitin' to set when we get back and there's a
carpenter gettin' the scaffold ready."

They said nothing, merely stood there staring at the man's
evil face.

"Maybe you're thinkin' about rushing me. It'd be risky. I
can shoot as good with one hand as the other. I had a lot o'
practice. Don't you move a peg."

Crockett turned to look deliberately and intently at Nichol,
and Nichol knew that the look meant, *Keep him talking.*

"I thought we had dodged you for once," said Nichol.
There was a rich sadness in his voice as he continued, "You
are better than we thought. Well, I suppose this is the end of
everything. At least we tried."

"Once or twice you had me guessing," said Fisheye modestly. "There's some things I still don't understand."

"How did you ever guess that evening we'd go out by
Thompson's Lane?" asked Beasley Nichol.

"Or how did you guess that we'd come back by the Buena
Vista Pike?" asked Hume Crockett.

"It was no guess. Thompson's Lane was the quickest way
you could get back to General Forrest from where you was
seen last. Then when we'd got you—" he pointed to Nichol—

"I figured you—" he pointed to Crockett—"and that other feller would come back and make another try. You Rebels don't seem to mind getting hung, so I figured you'd be coming back. I figured you'd try something fancy. So we kept watch on all the ways we figured you'd figure we wouldn't be watching. Two suspicious fellers got by the guard on the Davidson Road just after midnight. I figured some more. That meant the Buena Vista Pike and there we were. But you just missed having some good luck there. You got there just as we was ready to give it up and leave."

"We'd have made it if it hadn't been for you."

"Well, you didn't make it. One thing I want to know is how you got out of jail that morning. That's got me buffaloed. The guard said he thought we had put the wrong man in. But that sounded funny to me. Then he got mixed up and didn't know what he was sayin'. How'd you buffalo him?"

It was an opportunity for a dramatic gesture that Nichol could not resist. "I marched around the cell seven times and blew on a ram's-horn. So the walls fell away."

He knew he shouldn't have said it. Something within him held up warning signals even before he had finished his foolish speech. And there was desperation in the look Crockett flashed him. *Keep him talking. It's our only chance. Something might happen.* Nichol resumed in even tones.

"The way it happened was I convinced the guard that I was a Northern officer put in by mistake. You see, I had on one of your uniforms. I imagine you had nothing to do with selecting that guard. He didn't seem up to your standard. I got the notion that you would never have picked him."

"He won't guard no more Rebels."

I'm glad you called us Rebels, thought Nichol. It annuls

your Southern birth. It makes me feel better. Crockett was looking at him. *Keep him talking.*

"Of course I don't want to die. I'm too young for that. But I guess we've lost the war. I'll have to go sooner or later. If not now then in a day, or a month, or a year. What difference does a little time make?"

"Watch out what you're doin'. Stand right where you are. Don't you take another step." The muzzles of the pistols had steadied ominously.

Keep him talking, Crockett's eyes said. *You can do it better than I can.*

"You're a smart man. I fancy you understand the value of money. I fancy you know some good uses to make of money. Isn't it possible that a satisfactory sum of money would be worth more to you than we are?"

"Money! Where'd you get money?"

"Naturally we don't have it with us, but we could very quickly lead you to it."

"Oh, no, you don't. You don't come that one on me. You don't lead me nowhere."

"You could send one of us to get it and hold the other as a hostage."

"I got more sense than that, to let one of you get away when I already got you both!"

"I suppose that's the only offer we could make."

Fisheye's eyes were restless. They noticed that he kept looking eastward and that there was anxiety in his searching eyes. In one common flash of inspiration they understood the man's concern. He was waiting for help. Some of the searching party had gone farther on up the river and he was waiting for them to return. Perhaps it was the two whom they had glimpsed from the meadow.

They saw then a horse hitched in the rear of the little thicket in which Fisheye had lain hidden. One horse didn't amount to an adequate technique for the transfer of two dangerous prisoners to the authorities seven or eight miles away. Fisheye was waiting for help and he was as willing as they to engage in beguiling the time. So that was it!

"Well, let's go and get this thing over with," said Nichol in an overtone of superb resignation. "If you want to start back to town we're ready."

"No hurry. It's a long time till sundown. That's when they generally hang spies." He seemed to become conscious of the package that Nichol held under his arm, the pies for Corporal Ed Wheeler. "Hey, what's that you got?"

"Something to eat."

"Throw it here."

"Come and get it." Crockett looked at him again and there was a quick shift in the language of his glance. *That's the talk. If more Yankees are coming let's bring this to an issue before they get here.*

"Drop it," ordered Fisheye.

"I drop very poorly under compulsion. Sometimes I don't even drop."

The man's eyes flicked along the road to the east. They knew from the look on his face that he had not seen what he wished. Then his brow puckered in thought but relaxed in quick decision. Nichol's and Crockett's eyes met. The issue was formed.

"If you don't drop that package right now, I'll save our hangman that much trouble." The man's tones were hard and brassy. "Drop it, I say."

The pistol in his left hand rose a little and stopped at an unwavering level. The man's protruding eyes had become fixed in a malevolent brassiness. Nichol's and Crockett's glance met for a split second in sharp focused agreement. *Watch him and at the moment his finger twitches against the trigger spring to one side and before he can recover charge him from two directions.* It was dangerous, for the man would know their plan and adjust himself to it. But they were in a hurry. If at all, it had to be then. If Fisheye's comrades returned, they were doomed. This way there was a minute fractional chance that both would escape, a much larger chance that one would. It was worth taking.

The pistol found its aim and held it. There was the assurance of expertness in Fisheye's grasp of the weapon, and his bulging eyes seemed to encompass both men completely in their field of vision. Nichol's legs grew tense. It was time to jump but he never relaxed hold on his oilcloth-covered package. What was Fisheye saying?

"I will not do you the honor to count three this time."

Nichol in the clarity of slow motion could see the finger hardening against the trigger. His muscles in quick release gave a powerful thrust sidewise.

But even then Fisheye was crumpling toward the ground. Mid-air in his leap Nichol heard the sound of the gun. By the time he had reached the ground he saw Sergeant Goforth rise from a squatting position in a fence corner fifty yards away and come running toward them, calling as he came. He could see, too, a thin wisp of blue smoke curling from the muzzle of the rifle in his hand. And then he saw Fisheye after a few convulsive sprawling movements grow quiet.

Goforth reached them. It was Crockett who first recaptured command of the situation.

"Quick, drag him into those bushes." He ran to loosen the tied horse and struck it a sharp blow upon its hindquarters. The frightened horse turned with a lunge and galloped back toward Nashville. By then they had placed Fisheye in the thicket so that the body could not be easily seen from the road. Fisheye's horse, with accumulating fright and speed, was disappearing along the road toward Nashville.

"We've got to get away from here," said Crockett urgently.

7

NICHOL and Goforth knew they had to get away from there. It was the one thing they knew best. But by which way? They couldn't take the road that led back to Nashville. That wasn't the way they had to go. If they took the other end of the road somewhere along the way they would pretty surely encounter Fisheye's comrades. If they climbed the fence and cut across the field they would be plainly visible for a half-mile.

Crockett was famed throughout General Forrest's army for his accuracy of perception and promptness of resolution. He said, "We'll try the field. Even if they see us we'll have the start of them."

He walked across the road and grasped the top of the fence and placed one foot upon the bottom rail. Then he said, "My God, look yonder!"

They looked. Three hundred yards down the road which Fisheye had watched so anxiously four soldiers came galloping noisily toward them. Crockett's alert eyes measured the distance quickly. They were too close to make any effort of escape.

"We've got a message for them," he said. "We're waiting to give it to them. We've been waiting here for some time. Don't you make any false moves. You follow my lead. Whatever I start you two keep it going."

They didn't have to wait long. The three soldiers galloped up, their horses lathered and panting. Hume Crockett with perfect composure walked toward them, holding up a restraining hand. The horsemen slowed to a stop.

"They caught them across the river," he told them. "About eleven o'clock. He's gone on back to Nashville. He said tell you to come on to town."

"Who caught 'em?"

"We weren't told."

The men clucked to their horses and started away.

"Hanging's at sundown!" yelled Nichol. The soldiers dug their spurs into their horses. It was plain that they wished to be on time for the hanging. Crockett spared a moment to give Nichol one brief glance of reproach but no word was spoken. Then he quickly climbed the fence, and Nichol and Goforth followed him into the field.

They ran through it for the cover of the strip of woodland a half-mile away. And as they ran they prayed fervently that those horsemen's interest in Nashville would not abate, that they would not look back. There would be plenty of activity by the Yankees a little later. The longer deferred the better for them.

They reached the fence and climbed over it into the protecting shadows of the trees. All of the men were panting but it was no season to take their ease. They must for a while keep going. Beasley Nichol did between gasps render something not from Shakespeare but an improvisation from the Scriptures, something that was a song of gratitude for deliverance. "Out of the wiles of the wicked, out of the fiery furnace, out of the mouth of the lion, free from the snare of the fowler."

"Let's wait and see," said Crockett. "Maybe we're not out yet. Things can happen."

They came to the end of the strip of woodland and entered a cornfield. The rows led in the direction they were going and they walked between them, at times in low places through mud of almost unbearable depth. The corn was tall and luxuriant, and up the stalks circled green vines from which beans hung suspended in thick clusters.

"Beans!" said Nichol. "Green beans! Mementos of my lost youth! I shudder to think of the amount I could eat if cooked just right—which can be done only by those of pure heart. I like them best cooked with ham hock."

"Don't shudder now," said Crockett. "If shuddering is necessary please do it later. We haven't the time just now."

In some places their way was clogged by pumpkin vines, rich and luxuriant as the beans, and young pumpkins lay thick upon the ground. Again Nichol was moved to misquote with great eloquence, "If pumpkins come, can Thanksgiving be far behind? Thanksgiving! Why, that's an omen! It's as good as a play. Let the trumpet sound and the cannon bray the prelude to the end."

"I don't want to hear any cannon bray or make any other kind of noise."

They left the cornfield and entered a rocky glade thickly set with cedar trees. At first the terrain was flat, the ground covered with a heavy quilt of cedar twigs. Sometimes they walked upon bare rock of tablelike flatness, then the ground became covered with a carpet of thick green moss. The contour of the cedar land turned upward and they climbed a little knob. Toward its top the cedars grew even thicker.

Crockett, who was ahead, threw himself on a bed of moss.

But before he closed his eyes he asked a question. "Sergeant, how in God's name did you happen to be in that fence corner at exactly the right moment?"

"I follered him," answered the sergeant, gesturing in the general direction of Fisheye.

"Sergeant," said Nichol fervently, "you shall be made a general. I pledge it. But continue with your story. You followed him. Pray reveal how you found him in order to follow him."

"It was just a plain accident. I followed the river out o' town. I was afraid of it but not as bad as the other ways out. I didn't get too clost to the water on account o' boats there, and I almost run into some Yankees anyhow, but I dodged 'em. This side o' Fairfield the river flattened out and I had to get into the open. I'd watch and go ahead when they wasn't anybody in sight and hide when they was. I heard a racket and I just did get hid in time. It was him with a bunch o' fellers. Right then I figgered they was after you and I better keep track of 'em. I tried to find a hoss to steal but ever' time they was one they was about two men in sight. Then here come a Yankee ridin' purty fast down the road. 'Now's my time,' I said, 'to git a hoss,' and I felt kind o' sorry for him. 'Where you goin'?' says I, talkin' like a colonel or sumpin'.

" 'Goin' to help ketch the spies,' says he.

" 'I'm a-paterollin' this road. I've got to borry your hoss,' said I. 'I got to get some word to the boss. You can do your paterollin' on foot for a while. I'm in a hurry. Clim' down. You'll get your hoss back.' I looked at him jest like I was a colonel or sumpin'. 'Clim' down,' I says again jest like a gin'ral or sumpin', 'and gimme that rifle you got. It's liable to be dangerous where I'm a-goin'.'

"Drekly he climbed down, and I climbed up. Well, that was a right good hoss and I burnt the wind for a while. I rode around a bend and there they were not a quarter of a mile ahead. Two of 'em had been down to the river, I reckon, to scout aroun' some and they was walkin' back acrost the fiel'. The others was settin' on the hosses a-waitin' for 'em. Then they loped off ag'in and I rode purty keerful-like after 'em. The next time I saw 'em was right where I plugged him. He sent the others on up the road, and he set there on his hoss a-waitin'. I rode back a piece and hitched my hoss and then snaked myself up to that fence corner. Drekly he took his hoss back in the thicket and hitched it, and it wasn't long till here you come a-traipsin' acrost that fiel'."

"You shall be made a general—a major general, Goforth. You are a hero."

"Well," said Crockett, "Yankees or no Yankees I'm going to rest a little. I'm not made out of iron."

Goforth too stretched himself out on the moss, but he said nothing. Nichol placed the package of dried-apple pies carefully on a flat stone. Then he sat down on a mossy place near it.

"So you are not made of iron. How you disappoint me! I was thinking of melting you down and using you for some useful purpose—a skillet, say, to fry apple pies in. How life is filled with disillusion!"

But by that time Crockett was sound asleep.

"Look at him," said Nichol pointing. *"This were a bed but cold to sleep so soundly.* He'll start snoring any minute now. You'd expect a trusted member of Bed Forrest's staff to be more alert. See, I told you he'd be snoring. It's something he learned from the Yankees. By the way, Sergeant, where have you been since last we met?"

"When I left you in the alley that night I went to see my girl."

Nichol stood bolt upright and looked at the sergeant with wonder in his eyes.

"Good God!" he said. "Did I hear you aright? You went to see your girl! You went to see your girl with your country at war, with your comrades in danger! You went to see your girl and it raining pitchforks! Sergeant Goforth, I must tell you that you leave me unnerved!"

"I thought maybe you was, sir."

"You went to see your girl! You withdrew, leaving my southern flank exposed and unprotected. You went to see your girl and the fate of the South wavering in the balance. What is your excuse, Sergeant Goforth?"

"None, sir, unless you've seen my girl. I couldn't leave Nashville without seeing her. I think you'd understand that, sir."

"Frankly, I do not, Sergeant. Now, what do you suppose I was doing while you went to see your girl, leaving me alone and without assistance?"

"Maybe you was standing on a street corner and sayin' poetry, sir."

"Ah, yes, and thus uplifting in spirit and culture all who heard me. Would that . . . but let it go unsaid. Where, Sergeant Goforth, do you suppose he went when he left us?" He pointed to the sleeping captain.

"I reckon he went to see his girl, too, sir."

"He did indeed, and left my western flank exposed and un-protected. What led you to assume that he went to see his girl, Sergeant?"

"I knowed he had one, sir. He wouldn't 'a' wanted to leave Nashville without seeing her. They caught him before he got to see her when he first went to Nashville."

"Do most Southern soldiers have girls, Sergeant?"

"Yes sir, or maybe wives."

"Then with our hearts and minds and time so divided, with our attention so distracted, how, Sergeant, can we ever win this war?"

"Meaning no disrespect, sir, I think women is worth more for winnin' the war than poetry."

"You may have a point there, Sergeant. I shall not argue with you. You fail so utterly to grasp the finer points of my logic. I think I shall relax for a season."

But before he lay down on the moss Nichol recited with great feeling an appropriate Shakespearean passage:

> *"How many thousand of my poorest subjects*
> *Are at this hour asleep! O sleep, O gentle sleep!*
> *Nature's soft nurse . . ."*

The sergeant looked at him but said nothing. There was nothing to say. Then he shrugged his shoulders, lay down upon the moss-covered rock and closed his eyes.

AN HOUR later they were on their way again. They skirted the crest of the cedar knob, and emerged into a clear view of the country ahead. In the long July day the sun was still more than an hour distant from the western horizon.

"How well do you have your bearings, Sergeant? Exactly where do you think we are?" asked Crockett.

"I don't know exactly but right close, sir. That's Stone's River yonder." He pointed to a distant twisting line of timber. He lifted his pointing finger. "And right about yonder is the Hermitage where General Jackson lived." His finger swung to the right. "There's the Lebanon Pike yonder, but I think it'd be dangerous for us."

"So do I. Sergeant, do you have any idea where we can get across Stone's River?"

"There'd be a lot of places where we could wade it if it wasn't so high."

"But it is high."

"That's what bothers me, sir."

"Wouldn't there be boats somewhere that we could use?"

"I don't reckon so. Most of the boats been stole lately. We could swim if it wasn't for these clothes." He pointed particularly to their heavy boots.

"All right," said Crockett with decision. "Boats or no boats we've got to get across Stone's River and we can't cross it standing here."

They moved on in a slanting line down the eastern slope of the cedar-covered knob. They came almost suddenly on a house at the base of the knob but they turned into an orchard to avoid it. The orchard opened out upon a country road, muddy but passable. They climbed the fence and walked eastward along the road, picking out the drier and firmer places as best they could. Chickens from the farmhouse were ranging along the margins.

"Chickens!" said Nichol. "Fried chicken! What a boon is memory! How it enriches life! Do you remember fried chicken, Captain Crockett?"

"If you'd go back there and introduce yourself, and recite some good poetry," said Crockett very crisply, "I imagine they'd wrap some fried chicken up in a box and let you take it to their son in Bed Forrest's army."

"You are equipped only with a stomach, nothing else at all—no mind, no heart, nothing. I have a heart, a very large and warm heart. Where do you think the sergeant was all that time we were in such trouble?"

"Don't tell me he was off somewhere eating. Where was he?"

"Gone to see his girl. Did you, Captain Crockett, ever hear of anything like it?"

"Never! Positively never! . . . Well, at least not often."

"That's what he did. What's that new rule, Captain, that they just got out about a soldier who goes to see his girl and leaves his officers all unprotected?"

"Death, the second time it happens."

"Stone's River is what's worrying me," said Goforth glumly. "We can't go by the bridge. That's out of the question. They'll have a regiment o' Yankees there. There's somebody coming. Looka there. By that side road."

They saw then that just ahead of them a lane crossed the road along which they were traveling. Approaching them was a man driving a bay horse harnessed to a light spring wagon. Their first thought was to hide but by then it was too late. The man had already seen them. On their second look it was clear to them that he had nothing to do with the army. Doubtless a farmer of the community on an errand. There was nothing to do but to go ahead naturally. But they slowed their gait to give him time to cross the road before they arrived.

Instead he stopped squarely in the road ahead, blocking it off. The three men in surprise looked warily at one another but did not stop.

"Wait a minute, wait a minute," said Nichol almost gaily. "That's the man who——"

"Well, I'll be stomped on by a doodleflicker and et by a catawampus," exclaimed the man in the spring wagon, "effn it ain't the man I rid with in the Yankee waggin!" His whip cut sharply through the sunlit air and destroyed a horsefly feasting on his horse's flank.

Beasley Nichol ran ahead and clasped the man's hand. "How delightful, how magnificently appropriate! Crossroads are the very means of destiny!" He turned to his comrades. "My friends, I should like to present the gentleman who rescued me from the jaws of the lion, who comforted me when I was distressed, and who in the hour of my shadow brought me a note, a letter, a missive that was balm to my soul and a sweet savor to my spirit."

"That'd sound right purty sung in a song," said the driver, bowing to Crockett and Goforth. "I reckon it don't make you fellers no difference which side o' Stone's River you on. That ain't the way I feel a-tall. Now me, I jest natchelly hone for the other side. Yes sir, I'm bound fo' Frank Cheatham's army, an' he's been a-waitin' till I jines him so he can win the wah."

"How are you going to get across the river?" asked Nichol. "General Forrest would like to win the war, too."

"They's a whole Yankee army settin' at the bridge. And they ack jest like they waitin' fo' somebody—Gin'ral Lee and Bed Forrest and President Jeff Davis and mebbe three other fellers. I got my suspicions up, and a fever in my curiosity, so I hitched my hoss in a thicket this side o' Donelson and I snook on ahead and took me a look. What I saw ain't very hope-givin', or peace-arousin'. And I ain't a-goin' to cross at the bridge, nosirree!"

"The last word I had General Cheatham was on the other

side o' Stone's River. I suppose you'll cross somewhere, though you could stay on this side and holler across to him." Crockett's voice was dry and casual.

"Yes sir, he's across. Somewheres down toward Chattanoogy, though from what I hear 'twon't be long till he'll be a-headin' for old Kentucky, and when he does I aim for to be a-headin' with him."

"You show us how to get across Stone's River and we'll make you a general instead of Cheatham."

"Climb in and set easy. This is a Yankee waggin and it's sort o' run down in strength and places to set but we'll risk it. It ain't fur to where we goin' and mostly downhill. Yes sir, I'm a powerful lucky man. Jest as I was a-settlin' into the depths o' despair, as the feller said, I happened to hear about it accidental. Effn it works it's the same as the Hebrew children and the Red Sea."

"If it works you're the same as Moses," said Nichol. "What is it?"

"It's saw logs, that's what it is, and it worked enough for Ol' Man Priestley to get his hay crop across." A horsefly lighted and died at the same moment. "Last winter some fellers up toward Murfreesboro saw-logged a lot o' timber and rafted it down the river. They got here jest about the time the Yankees got to Nashville. Well, the Yankees wouldn't let 'em bring the rafts out into the Cumberland. They had steamboats thick as ducks in the big river and didn't want to be bothered. So they chained the rafts up at Ol' Man Priestley's place to wait till Gin'ral Cheatham and me gits the Yankees whupped."

"You and General Cheatham go ahead and whip the Yankees. From what I've seen of them they deserve it. Go ahead and whip them. It wouldn't make me jealous at all. I still think I'd like to get across Stone's River."

"You must be a-gettin' a little deaf. Didn't I tell you that's prezactly what we a-goin' to do? Goin' to cross on that raft at Ol' Man Priestley's. He fixed it up to get his hay he raised on the other side back on this side to his barn. He used to have a ferryboat but the Yanks stole it. It's four miles up the river to the bridge and four back so the old man got busy and fixed him up a bridge out of that raft. He went to a right smart trouble doing it, but it worked. He kind of swung it across the river and chained it to trees at both ends. Then he planked up the cracks between the logs so the horses' feet wouldn't get caught. Then he went to hauling hay. He used a one-horse waggin and made lots o' trips but he got his first field hauled. Effn it don't rain he's goin' to cut another field tomorrer. Yes sir, this Ol' Man Priestley's a hum-dinger. When he starts to do a thing, it's done been finished. Effn the Yanks want to bust up his bridge after he gets that field in, it don't make him no difference."

"Don't they know about his bridge now?"

"I reckon it's a secret yet. They ain't been no travelin' up Stone's River this summer. But they liable to find out any time now. I expect that's the reason Ol' Frank Cheatham's gettin' anxious about me."

"I know who you are now," said the sergeant. "I've heard about you clear down to Manchester. You're the man who went off with that crazy feller that got killed in some furrin country. Why, I've heard plenty about you."

"Well," said the driver modestly, "I ain't admittin' that none of what you heard was lies."

"I know you, too," said Crockett. "Six years ago I saw you do some mighty fancy driving at the State Fair. They put two silver dollars close together on the ground and you drove at a run so that both wheels on the right side passed between the dollars. You're the one, aren't you?"

"Well, it might 'a' been. I understands hoss langwidge. It wasn't hardly no trouble a-tall. I jest told the hosses whereat to go."

"I been watchin' you drive," said Sergeant Goforth. "You haven't hit a rock yet."

"I could drive a team o' hosses up the Capitol steeple." The driver's modesty remained uninterrupted. "To tell the truth, I did oncet. Somethin' got wrong with the steeple up toward the top. They couldn't get nobody to fix it so they ast me. Yes sir, jest to save time gettin' up stuff for the *re*-pairs I took it up in a two-hoss waggin."

"On the outside, of course."

"How'd you think I'd get in that Capitol with a two-hoss waggin and team? 'Twasn't no trouble a-tall to drive that waggin up on the outside. Only trouble was turnin' around. It's purty slick up there and the hosses slipped some but I got 'em turned aroun' all right. That wasn't hardly no trouble a-tall, when you think o' some o' the drivin' I've done. Why, oncet——"

"You're the man I heard about," said Crockett.

THEY came to a gate and the driver stopped the team. Goforth pulled the gate open and they drove into a field. Then they went through another gate into a horse lot. In it was a barn and farther up on the hill a house. The driver pointed to the barn.

"That's where he hauled the hay. Why, there's Ol' Man Priestley hisself."

A heavily bearded farmer came to the door of the barn and looked at them intently.

"Howdy, Brother Priestley. Your entitlements doin' purty good? Ain't set eyes on you sence the basket-meetin' at Mill Creek Baptis' Church. Wouldn't mind us usin' your special patented bridge, would you?"

"What you doin' with them Yankee soldiers?"

"Them ain't Yankee soldiers any more'n you are, Brother Priestley. Their appearance is mighty deceivin' to the eye. Them three fellers is called and ordained Rebel spies."

"You certain o' that?"

"I done watched 'em spy. They do it fust-rate. I don't expect in a coon's age you'd see better spyin' than they do. I'm on my way now to jine up with Frank Cheatham, and I got to git acrost Stone's River."

"Shake hands with Ol' Frank for me. How'd you find out about that bridge?"

"A little Reb bird done whispered to me. Yes sir, and that bridge was as plumb welcome as a cold spell at hawg-killin' time. Yes sir, Frank Cheatham's got to pay me more money than he's a-figurin' on. Effn I wasn't a val'ble man they wouldn't have half the Nawthern army and mebbe Gin'ral U. S. Grant too a-guardin' that bridge up at Clover Bottom. They sure got a passel o' blue coats up there. As soon as I seen 'em my price to Ol' Frank riz."

"Go on across. When you see him tell Ol' Frank Cheatham to hurry back. It makes me feel sort o' lonesome not to git to cheat him in a hoss trade ever now and then. I remember one County Co't day I shore pulled the wool over his eyes. Kept me from gittin' old. Where'd you git that plug hoss you drivin'?"

"Borrid it offn the Yankees. Took it right from under their nose, you might say. That's not a bad hoss neither. For a Yankee hoss he catches on right quick."

"He ain't so bad for a plug. See that iron-gray there in the corner of the lot. Now that's a real hoss. Pullingest critter that ever stretched a trace chain. Pull a plow all day and never pant a lick. How about a trade?"

"Brother Priestley, I'd ruther trade hosses than eat fried chicken at a Methodis' meeting. But I wouldn't trade a Yankee hoss to nobody but a blood enemy. You turn that hoss o' mine loose in your barn lot and it'll spread devilment among every head you got. Yessirree, if a feller had plenty o' feed to pour to that iron-gray o' yours he might stand a chancet o' rescuin' him from the soapworks. I'd like to have him all right, but for twenty hosses I wouldn't have you turn ag'in me. And you shore would after this Yankee hoss got in his devilment. I reckon we'd better be a-gettin' on to your bridge, Brother Priestley."

"I need me a Yankee hoss. It'd set my hosses a good example in savin' and mebbe stop 'em from bein' so wasteful with their feed. They tell me Yankee hosses don't spill hardly none o' their feed on the ground. Now, that sorrel hoss o' mine yonder. That's the steadiest hoss that ever pulled a spring waggin acrost a bridge. Why, with that hoss you wouldn't stand a bit o' risk a-tall gittin' acrost my bridge. But with that Yankee hoss——"

One gathered from Mr. Priestley's tones and gestures that any prospect associated with a Yankee hoss was very depressing.

"Why, Brother Priestley, effn these fellers wasn't with me it wouldn't be no trouble a-tall for me to git across that river without a sign of a bridge. Well, anyhow, it used to wouldn't."

"I always did love a liar, but you jest natchelly suit me too well. How'd you git acrost without a bridge and the river up?"

"I'd use faith and plenty of it. One time I was a-drivin' the stagecoach, and the river was riz and had done washed the bridge out at Bowling Green. I had six passengers and they had to git to Nashville. So they ain't no way out o' it but for me to git acrost Barren River. I asts the passengers is they willin' to trust me and they said go ahead. So, I drew them hosses right down to the water. Then, I started sayin' right convincin'-like, 'You lead hoss, see that bridge? Don't you see it? Right there befo' you. You off hoss, don't you see it, too? You jest put your foot out and you'll step right on it. Don't you see that fine bridge? Ain't it steady?' I kept on talkin' to them hosses and inside o' five minutes they saw it too. And there it was. Well, sir, I druv 'em right acrost without a bobble. I jest kept talkin' to 'em and they kept seein' the bridge and goin' right ahead. Why, you could hear the hosses' hoofs goin' *plunk-plunk* again' the bottom o' the bridge, and the wheels a-grindin'. Well, we got into Nashville on time. Them passengers wanted to give me a solid gold watch but it didn't look right to me."

Brother Priestley made some gurgling noises. Then he said, "All right, you don't need my bridge. Drive right on acrost Stone's River. Le's see you use that faith."

"Can't do it. I reckon my faith's done weakened. I must be gittin' old."

"Go ahead. Bridge is at the foot of that lane. I'd ruther hear you lie than trade hosses any day."

"So long, Brother Priestley. See you the next time they have a basket-meetin' at Mill Creek Baptis' Church."

They drove down to the raft that stretched across the river in a solid phalanx of fine saw logs, whose surface was

smoothed out with planks. The driver considered it critically.

"Jest as safe as Noah's Ark. You fellers git out and walk.
You can't never tell. We might meet a railroad train or
somethin', and Yankee hosses skeer easy."

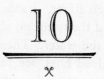

THEY got across Stone's River and climbed the bank to the
level meadow above.

"I guess the Yankees done thinned out a lot over here.
When they git real skeered they run clear back to Nashville
and this is too fur. It tires 'em out. It'd be safe to git back
to the big road purty soon now. I'm a-stoppin' this-here
chariot and a-lettin' you out at Mount Juliet. I got a secret
road from there to Frank Cheatham's army. You'll fin' Bed
Forrest somewhere the other side of Lebanon." His whip
sliced the golden rays of the setting sun and a horsefly suddenly and permanently desisted from feeding. The driver
then engaged in song.

> "I come to a river and I couldn't get across
> And I give five dollars for an old gray hoss.
> I pushed him in and he couldn't swim
> And I give five dollars to get rid o' him."

There wasn't a cloud in the sky. The drenched air was
crystalline-clear. Primroses lined the country road along

which they traveled and at intervals clumps of wild roses burst into bloom. Back a bit from the road bobwhites sounded their sad clear call. The sun touched with mellow light the rich green of the cedars standing on the crests of the knobs. Then almost suddenly the light went out and the shadows thickened. The air above was alive with swallows that glided ceaselessly through the air or swooped downward on their swift and graceful thrusts. As the twilight deepened there came from the woods the melancholy cry of that strange bird, the whippoorwill.

Said Beasley Nichol, *"This air nimbly and sweetly recommends itself unto our gentle senses."*

It was suppertime and smoke was curling from the chimneys of the few houses they passed, and the vesper air was filled with the fragrance of food. In one of the houses a woman bustled about at work. She was singing in a sweet and poignant voice, the notes turning with a little country quaver.

"...Oh, be not dismayed
For I am thy God and will still give thee aid."

A man at the milking gate moved in and out among the feeding cows, and, near by, hogs grunted with the satisfaction of the well fed. How lovely was the evening! The purple shadows deepened, and heaven's lamplighter touched the stars one by one with pale flame.

Beasley Nichol was thinking of Hunter Cragwall. The blaze of her hair and the blueness of her eyes filled his inner vision. And he heard again her voice, tender and hushed, telling him the words he wished to hear. And out of the spell which was upon him arose a voice. It was the voice of Romeo that sounded fittingly on the summer twilight.

"The brightness of her cheek would shame those stars
As daylight doth a lamp; her eyes in heaven
Would through the airy region stream so bright
That birds would sing and think it were not night."

"Did you know, Captain, that he used to be one of them actors that plays in shows and circuses?" asked Goforth.

"I always thought he was a tightrope-walker."

"Crockett, what does your girl look like? Give us her features, her lineaments, the details of her eyes, her cheeks, her lips. Does her voice sound like the tinkling of a waterfall, does——"

"Think up the very best you can and say it yourself."

"It could be that she bears a name. It's an old and honored custom. What's hers?"

"Lucy Stratton."

"Lucy Stratton! Wait a minute while I steady myself against the sergeant. Did you say Lucy Stratton?"

"I did. I suppose you remember her. What do you need steadying for? She knows you. She met you at Beersheba Springs two summers ago. She thinks you are cute. Anyhow, that's what she said."

"Bear witness, heaven, that I know not whether I'm praised or blasphemed. So Lucy Stratton is your girl? Why didn't you ever tell me?"

"I haven't had a chance. That's something one doesn't stop a fellow from spouting poetry to tell. But it's no secret. Why didn't you ever ask me?"

Nichol said nothing. There was no sound except the commingling of the songs of the little creatures of the summer dusk with the grind of the wheels and the steady *clump-clump* of the horses' hoofs. A mile, perhaps, they traveled and no

speech intruded on the awe of the evening. Then Beasley
Nichol matched his voice to the night's music and started to
render the renunciation speech of King Richard II, but it didn't
seem to fit. His first thought had been wrong. It wasn't the
speech for the moment.

The glow of Hunter Cragwall's hair was still about him.
He said:

> "... Look how the floor of heaven
> Is thick inlaid with patens of bright gold."

The driver's whip cracked in the thickening shadows. "Yes,
it's a right purty night," he said. "You gents better onlimber
your laigs. It ain't fur to Mount Juliet. Over that ridge
yonder and we're there."

At Mount Juliet the driver pulled his horse off onto a
little road that bore southward. The three men arose from
their cramped positions and got out of the spring wagon
preparatory to continuing eastward toward a reunion with
General Bedford Forrest.

"Ain't a-stoppin' nowheres," the driver told them, "except
to feed this hoss, or to talk myself loose from any Yankees I
run into. Effn this Yankee hoss holds out I'll be a-jinin' up
with Frank Cheatham sometime day after tomorrer. I hated
to leave Nashville but it's done come the time."

It was too dark to see a horsefly but he thought he heard
one buzz, so his whip hissed through the air as a gesture of
enduring enmity.

"So long, gents," he called. "Up to now I'm a wayfarin'
man o' peace, but I reckon Ol' Frank Cheatham and me'll git
the Yankees whupped sometime, and when we do effn you

want to take a ride in a sho'-nuff stagecoach pulled by four
milk-white hosses, why, I'll be a-drivin' it."

He drove away singing joyfully.

"Oh, who will come and go with me?
I am bound for the promised land."

11

THE three men stood there till the sounds of his singing sank
into the silence of the night.

They left the main pike. There might be ambuscades laid
along it. It would be serious to underestimate the alertness
of the enemy. They found and followed the side road by
which Nichol and Goforth had journeyed to Nashville.

Sometime before midnight they passed the roadside spring
and the maple tree standing by it. They trudged silently but
briskly ahead. Nichol and Goforth each sensed what was in
the other's mind, but Crockett didn't know that the vision of
a lonely grave among the cedars on the slope of the ridge
above was vivid in his companions' thoughts. Unconsciously
Nichol ran his hand over the blouse of his uniform. And his
fingers trembled a bit, for by rights it belonged in that grave.

Five minutes later a clatter farther down the road warned
them. Almost in one motion they swung themselves over a
fence and into a cornfield. From between the rows of corn
they watched the shadowy forms of eight horsemen ride past
at a brisk canter, clearly a Yankee scouting party on its way

back to Nashville. The three men waited a minute and then climbed back onto the road. For a moment they stood listening. They heard the horsemen stop and knew that they were at the spring, where their horses could drink.

Hume Crockett started walking toward Lebanon, and his companions fell in behind him.

A delicious coolness had come into the night and the men walked without tiring. The sky had been swept clean of clouds, and in the sky stars shone in numbers beyond the imagination of man. A war was being waged all about that lonely road by which they traveled, and not far away men were dying in the terrible routines of war. And yet it was a friendly night. A soft and tranquil wind gently kissed the trees. From somewhere, a drone whose beginning harshness changed presently into music started from the cicadas and ended in the enveloping wholeness of the night.

At two o'clock they reached Les Campbell's place. There they were given back their old uniforms and offered places to sleep, but they had no time for that. They did, however, pause long enough to eat some cold food. And then again they shaped their course toward Bed Forrest.

12

THEY were told at Les Campbell's that General Forrest was in the neighborhood of Lebanon, perhaps by then in the town itself. At any rate, he was pretty sure to be there by the time they rejoined him.

The three men didn't go directly into Lebanon. They approached the town gingerly, bearing around its northern tip. If Federal forces were about—as they likely were—the gray uniforms, as yet indistinguishable in the dark, made caution imperative. The east was lighting up, and the full light of day came almost suddenly. All at once a dozen dogs began barking, a hundred roosters crowing, and a million birds broke into their matin song.

"Halt!" sang out a Southern voice. "Stand where you are! Don't move!"

They halted and stood and didn't move while the three sentries came hurrying to them, guns held at ready.

One of the men recognized Captain Crockett, who explained their presence and requested to be carried immediately into the presence of General Forrest.

The general with no trace of sleep in his eyes, but hair tousled and uniform in some disarray, sat on a log and drank hot coffee. He was in a good humor and smiled broadly when the three men were brought into his presence.

"Well, I've failed again," he said laughing loudly. "I tried my best, short of shooting, to get you off o' my hands, and here when I don't need you most you turn up. It's got so I can't depend on the Yankees any more. What's in that package? Something for me?"

"No, General, some dried-apple pies for Corporal Ed Wheeler. His mother sent them. I'm sure she'd like to make some for you. Would you like for me to go back for them, sir?"

"Dried-apple pies! I dream about dried-apple pies. I was raised on them. Very good; I'll save you the trip. I'll confiscate these. Send for Corporal Ed Wheeler. I'll have the rascal court-martialed."

"Certainly, General——"

"Anyhow, send for him. Well, don't just stand there. Sometimes when I send soldiers out on a job they make a report when they get back. That's just plain good soldierin'. Anything happen to you besides practically gittin' hung? You look like you had been."

"Sometimes," said Crockett, "when we've practically got ourselves hanged besides having a lot of other trouble and being up two nights straight, the general gives us some coffee. We report better after that."

The general softened visibly. "Of course, of course," he said hastily. "I was just having my little joke. What good's a war if you can't get some fun out of it? Orderly, get some coffee for these gentlemen."

General Forrest listened intently while they told their story.

"You couldn't have served me better," he said explosively. "Now, we'll have some breakfast. Then you go and sleep till two o'clock. Can't let you lose your good looks. Without 'em you'd be a total loss. At three o'clock I'm sending you, Crockett, down toward Chattanooga. There are a lot of things goin' on down there that I want to find out about. Don't get hung if you can help it. A hangin' looks bad in the records. Besides, it wastes time. You come to my tent right after you wake up. I'll give you the instructions you need then."

"Very well, General."

"And you, Sergeant, go along with him."

"Very well, General," said Sergeant Goforth. "I thought that's where you'd be sendin' us."

"Well, well, a regular prophet, aren't you, Sergeant? Did you think I'd be sending you back to Nashville, Nichol? You got any prophet blood in you?"

"Back to Nashville? I can't go anywhere, General, till

I've given these pies to Corporal Ed Wheeler. I'm sure you understand that, General Forrest."

Then a soldier appeared at the tent's opening and bawled out, "Here's Corporal Ed Wheeler, sir."

"Wait a minute and then send him in. Nichol, I think the Yankees are diggin' in at Nashville for the whole war. I want a map of all the fortifications they are puttin' up, and about how many soldiers they goin' to keep there, and what the outfits are. My nigger boy is still at the Saint Cloud and he'll help you. The fiddlin' man is still there, too. But I hear that Yankee major is being sent to Louisville right away. I guess Nashville's gittin' too hot for him. That man is the best spy in the Confederate army. Personal friend of Jeff Davis. But it looks like you'll have to do without him this time. Any objections to goin' back to the Saint Cloud, Lieutenant?"

"Certainly not, sir." He remembered that Fisheye would no longer be at the desk, or anywhere. "I shouldn't want to go back to the Saint Cloud until I had been disguised most expertly. I'd be afraid the Yankees might still have some of that hanging rope. But I think a disguise can be attended to, sir."

He stopped suddenly, staring at the tent wall. "Why, it's as good as a play!" he exclaimed. "It's better than a play. . . . Why, as Shakespeare says, *hanging and wiving goes by destiny.*"

"Don't bother about him, General Forrest," said Crockett. "Sometimes he has fits. I've seen him have some mighty bad ones. He used to worry me, too."

Lieutenant Nichol's fit took a classic turn then. *"This is the third time; I hope good luck lies in odd numbers. There's a divinity in odd numbers."*

Then there was a quick shift in the classic focus of Lieutenant Nichol's interest.

*"But soft! What light through yonder window breaks?
It is the East*—I mean west—*and Juliet is the sun!"*

He considered a brief instant and added a postscript. "But that still is not right," he said. "Juliet isn't her name."

Date Due

JUL 7 '60			
09. V - AON			
NOV 1 '60			
	PRINTED	IN U. S. A.	

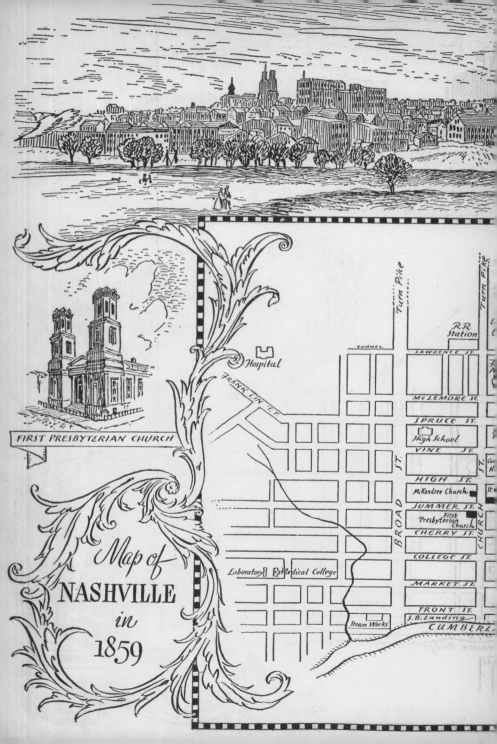

FIRST PRESBYTERIAN CHURCH

Map of
NASHVILLE
in
1859

Hospital

FRANKLIN T.P.

Turn Pike

Turn Pike

R.R. Station

TUNNEL

LAWRENCE ST.

McLEMORE ST.

SPRUCE ST.

High School

VINE ST.

BROAD ST.

HIGH ST.

McKendree Church

SUMMER ST.

First Presbyterian Church

CHERRY ST.

CHURCH ST.

COLLEGE ST.

Laboratory Medical College

MARKET ST.

FRONT ST.

S.B. Landing

Steam Works

CUMBERL